VANILLA SHEETS

A RAW NO HOLDS BARRED MEMOIR WITH A SHOT OF FICTION

Cecil Hicks

VANILLA SHEETS
A Raw No Holds Barred Memoir With A Shot of Fiction

I know there is going to be a lot of people out there that will judge me for my indiscretions. I also know what I am risking by putting my life and experiences in this book. By the way, just pick a chapter that may seem relatable, interesting, intriguing, or disgusting.

Cecil Hicks

VANILLA SHEETS

A RAW NO HOLDS BARRED MEMOIR WITH A SHOT OF FICTION

FORWARD

Cecil and I have been close friends for several years, so when he told me he had aspirations of being an author, I really wasn't all that surprised. He's done so many things in his life...he's run his own businesses, made a music video, and created an incredible documentary on police violence...just to name a few. He's always been a guy that speaks his mind on topics which others might shy away from, for fear of what the friends or family might think if they let their true selves be seen.

When I learned the topic of the book would be related to his own sexual experiences, I knew he'd put his whole heart into it and create something that would be honest and raw, not to mention a huge success. After reading several chapters as they were being written, I've found an even greater admiration for my friend and wish I were as brave as he. Unfortunately for me, I have a profession that if someone were to associate me with this type of content, it certainly wouldn't be beneficial to my career.

Am I in a chapter or two? Maybe, maybe not (see statement above about that job thing). But I can say for certain, I am incredibly proud of my friend for sharing something without fear of judgment from others.

Read the book, you'll agree.

FORWARD

This book will change lives. It will inspire millions of readers to pick up a book, start reading, and share these stories with their friends, family, neighbors. It will inspire readers who haven't picked up a book in years to develop a passion for romance and intrigue their sexual desires or fantasies. It will save marriages and start love affairs. It will inspire creative souls to begin telling their own stories. It's a one-of-a-kind memoir with explicit details daunted by singular tastes and dark secrets.

Cecil Hicks is an incurable romantic searching to satisfy his dark erotic desires. After years of living this dark, sensual lifestyle, he decided to share his experiences. I am sure that there are others who have experienced similar encounters but have never talked about it, at least never written about them. Most people have fantasized, but never acted out their fantasies.

Cecil is a perfectionist and therefore he poured his heart and soul into writing this memoir. Relive the sensuality, the romance and drama of Cecil Hicks. Come discover Cecil's dark secrets and erotic tastes. Come encounter his scorching, sexual affairs. There is no other book like it!

This book is intended for mature audiences.

Because of my profession I cannot be associated with this type of content. Unfortunately, I cannot divulge my name as it wouldn't be beneficial to my career, or anyone associated with me.

TABLE OF CONTENTS

NOTICE

ENTER
AT YOUR
OWN
RISK

Under The Cover

irst, before you read this chapter, just go ahead, and think of me as a nasty opened-minded, pimpish-looking African American, sitting on a throne. Not to mention, the wife of the man kneeling is pouring me a shot of Hennessy in his glass. I'm going to share my sexual adventures with you. In fact, this is not an entanglement as someone famous once said at a red table. All my adventurers were with, White, kinky ass muthafuckas. So, relax in your favorite chair, legs up, and be ready to salivate. All you need to do is, imagine yourself peeking through a cracked bedroom door, like your parents are fucking. Now that I slapped you in the face with a warning, buckle up muthafuckas!

Let me tell you about this White couple, Mr. and Mrs. Lucas, who lived in Miami. And they lived on the fifteenth floor of a condominium overlooking all of Miami Beach. In all honesty, when walking onto their patio at night, it was always amazing when visiting them. Being around them made me uncomfortable, all because of my own insecurities. From the moment we met face to face, they were nothing short of generous with their time, and money. Usually, you associated their lifestyle with people who would treat other's less than human like the Black people in a movie called *Mandingo* in 1975, produced by Dino De Laurentis and directed by Richard Fleischer. In other words, people who live in places like Mr. and Mrs. Lucas feel they are better than everyone else. That was not the case with this couple at all. They would call me to visit or spend the night three to five times a month. This continued over a six-month period as that was their way of getting more acquainted with me. And because of the way they originally discovered me on The Cage, a BDSM website, it made them take extra precautions to protect their identity. After three months, I was detecting energy that made me cautious. The most bizarre thing was, he always wore long sleeve shirts, no matter what the weather was like.

Also, during the first couple of months, there were moments I noticed something peculiar about their communication between one another. It was noticeable after three or four lengthy conversations in our first-time meeting face to face. From my observation, Mrs. Lucas (Eden) would make Mr. Lucas (James) stand up and directly face her, then she would slap dafuck out of his face for saying nigga. Watching Eden slap James publicly and privately helped me understand the dynamics of their relationship. Every time James said anything demeaning, Eden would apologize on his behalf, then slap the fuck outta him. After the first time

Eden slapped James, why wouldn't he stop, right? The first couple of years being around James was uncomfortable knowing he used nigga so freely.

There were no indications he and his wife were closet racist that I could tell. What's a closet racist, right? No differently than being in the closet, just racist as fuck. Keep in mind, James never directly or indirectly called me nigger, he knew that would destroy us getting acquainted.

The bizarre thing is, every time Eden slapped James, she would look directly at me deviously and wink. Certainly, their arrangement is different than most vanilla relationships. In all honesty, it turned me on when Eden wanted James' attention and would slap his face directly in front of me. There was this one time, Eden slapped the right side of James face so hard, it left an indentation of her hand on his face. Eden had her arm so far back, her arm had every time zone it crossed through to slap his ass. From my understanding and observations, every time Eden slapped James' face, he obviously deserved it.

James would look directly down at the ground after his wife slapped him. Right afterwards, he would turn around embarrassed and walk away, like a little bitch. Damn! Might as well have told him to stand in the corner, on one leg with a dunce cap on his head. Before Eden met James, I was surprised someone didn't clock him for his attitude towards other ethnic groups. When I first met them, I was cautiously watching their behavior and trying to understand their sexual arrangement thoroughly. I'd been in the BDSM lifestyle long enough to understand there will be instances when the husband has a desire to be submissive to his wife. And from my observation, I wasn't sure whether James was a switch or not just yet. Oh, pardon me, allow me to quickly explain what switch means to you vanilla muthafuckas.

Quick reference: Someone who enjoys both roles being submissive and sometimes enjoying being dominant. Google "switch" if you are interested in knowing more about it.

That's why it was unusual at first, considering James' behavior when he wasn't around Eden. They were a unique couple, the way they spoke to one another. It's not something I'm accustomed to seeing in my household. The alpha in our family was my dad, even while drunk majority of the time. He still behaved as the head of the household with mom and me. It was virtually impossible for me to wrap my head around why Eden would suggest treating James like a submissive.

She looked over at me occasionally, hinting to treat him no differently than she did. She would clue me in by secretly texting me in their living room. James was nearby while I texted Eden back. It was my way of acknowledging text received without James being aware of our conversation. There was no need to act on it right away, this was going to require time to figure out their level of trust and love they had for one another.

Eden looked over at me again and smiled, she knew to give me space and time to study their sexual arrangement. Not to mention, in the months' I'd known James and Eden, his wife and I never discussed or mentioned cuckold or sexual humiliation. At that time, I was knowledgeable of cuckold relationships and knew my assessment was precisely right. After twenty minutes of receiving Eden's text, I decided to have an intimate and private conversation with them together. By openly discussing their kinks, it would allow me to analyze their relationship. James and Eden knew I was nonjudgmental and opened-minded, which made it easier for them to express themselves. They were able to talk freely about their desires, experiences, and expectations. I've had similar cuckold encounters with other couples, prior to meeting James and Eden.

Majority of the couples I've met were on different websites affiliated to BDSM. After reading most couples' profile, after three or more conversations, they usually would try to meet with me in person, which is how I met James and Eden. The difference is, trust was already in place with James and Eden, it made our conversation interesting and unusual, to say the least. Let's break to help you understand my method of meeting cuckold couples online. While visiting couples, I evaluate their body language, eye contact, posture, demeanor, and overall comfort relating to why they chose me to be a part of their fantasy. In addition, evaluating their mentality and maturity towards other's living within their truth.

My metaphor is, we all tend to hide our sexual desires behind closed curtains. And while preparing ourselves for the curtains to open, we're clinching our fist because we are expecting rejection and humiliation from how judgmental people can be.

And it's a shame that we can't live in our truth while freely expressing ourselves. We should be the same person behind the curtains and after the curtains are open. I said all that above to say this: women and most couples stop themselves from getting acquainted with me. My insight comes from the universe when I'm evaluating a couple's mannerisms. Hopefully, this chapter, "Under the Cover" is proper.

Back to my friends James and Eden in Miami. While trying to understand their relationship, Eden would intentionally leave James and I alone together in the living room. Eden must have known, every time I was alone with him, he would become subservient to me, if that makes any sense. I could not understand why James became that way, considering we were in our late forties. It was so subtle at the beginning the way James acted when we were alone, even when watching football. I would watch him change his mentality to become subservient to me. In all honesty, we had played basketball, pool, and watched football on Sundays. It made me wonder how a man would want to submit himself to another man.

The only way to make sense of his behavior while writing this chapter is to say, he had a top-bunker prison mentality. Like clockwork, James and Eden always made sure their accommodation was second to none, especially James' catering nature. It seemed like every few minutes, he was asking me if I needed anything. This made me scratch my head because I am independent and doing for myself wasn't a problem. It wasn't noticeable right away that every time I said "no," it upset James. Or he became frustrated, and at his age, put on a pouty face. A grown ass muthafucking man, with a damn pouty face, can you believe it?

On the next visit, I knew exactly what to do to get James' attention. Just like before, Eden left us alone in the living room, and right away I told him to cook chicken wings (you know damn well us Black people like chicken wings). With no hesitation, this mofo went into his kitchen and put on Eden's apron and hair net. Then looked at me with a smile on his face, which made me a little uncomfortable, but knowing why he was smiling, it was okay. While relaxing in the living room and waiting for my chicken wings, he was looking for my favorite drink he bought earlier. Yep, you are smiling right now in disbelief, right. Let me see if I can guess why.

As an African/Black person telling a White man what to do, in his own home, is role reversing in the purest for, right? Wait! I'm trying to think of one major movie that has a White man serving an African/Black person in it. Well, I'll be damned, there isn't one, is there? On the other hand, google that shit and let me know what you find.

Eden had texted, asking me to make James my servant while I was sitting directly across from him. Otherwise, I would not have had anything to go by as a reference. At first, I was a little uncomfortable allowing James to serve me. The last time I remember a White man serving me was at a fancy restaurant. And the difference was, I didn't have to tip this muthafucka. There's an old expression used by Don King, "Only in America," catering to me made that White boy extremely happy.

Note: James was wearing a long-sleeve shirt, and I hadn't asked why yet, but I was certainly curious.

Here are my observations why James was comfortable following commands. Always wanting to pay for dinner and pay the muthafucking tip. Hanging out with him was always weird when he did that for me, he went beyond to make me happy. Close your eyes for a moment and imagine being in my shoes, you are six foot six inches tall, shaved head, and people say you look intimidating.

And here is this White man treating me like a bitch he just met on Tinder, trying to impress her on the first date. Fuck! Muthafucka might as well pull out my chair while he's at it, right? It took time to adjust to James' subtle on and off subservient behavior towards me. He was behaving like my friend but altered his persona while around me.

Quick Note: Most White men I've met personally call me Sir. I can't even remember one time in my entire adult life a Black man ever called me Sir. Which is only a sign of respect period, and nothing more. Well, unless we are in the BDSM community.

Are you thinking to yourself, this man has a nurturing personality, and what's wrong with that, right? Nope, that's not what this is about, trust me. There is a major difference between nurturing and being subservient. James and Eden had a hidden agenda I was unaware of when they first contacted me on a BDSM site.

Besides, I am not about to explain the difference to you vanilla folks. Let me put it this way, when I say vanilla folks, I am not, let me repeat, I'm not referring to White people. I'm saying vanilla folks are unexciting, normal, conventional, boring as fuck.

That's what vanilla means in my world. Now that I've broken dat shit down for ya, let's get back into "Under the Cover." I asked my closest friends about James' behavior, none of them had an answer for me. They all joked about it, but I didn't think it was funny. They made innuendos of him wanting to fuck me, and in fact, I was damn certain that wasn't the case. I gave them the middle finger and walked away. Finally, I said fuck it. When James called me to come over again to watch the football game, I set aside my independence. I allowed him to be a serving submissive to me this time. Whoever is reading this part, I want to make it clear, there's never been a sexual attraction between James and me, only between me and Eden.

Oh, that's right, I have not mentioned what James' kink is, right? Then I might as well tell ya now. It was watching me fuck Eden in the bedroom, in the bed they slept in. Of course, I never objected. There is a psychological reason for that, and it's because every time he sleeps in his bed, he reminisced about Eden fucking me in it. Hey reader! Don't you dare say to yourself, no way. It's his kink not yours, so keep your judgment to yourself. I intentionally and purposely decided not to mention this delicious piece of information earlier in this chapter for a reason. I wanted to keep you guessing about the nature of my relationship with James and Eden. Did it work?

Oh, I done fucked up your brain now, didn't I? Are you saying to yourself, does this shit really exist? Damn sure does, that's why you are still reading this chapter.

One morning, I decided to alter what I normally did with James and Eden. This time, James was subservient to both his wife and me. I told him to take off his pajamas and put on the pink apron Eden usually wears. Again, as a vanilla person, you may not be able to understand my reasoning for making him wear that pink apron. It's a form of humiliation, and he appreciated it coming from me. To be clear, I'd firmly tell him what to do, and it was simple but effective. This is another grown ass man I was speaking to, but I was aware of his kinks also, so I had to sound convincing. While James was making us breakfast in bed, Eden told me, "Don't be nice to James under no circumstances this morning." She also told me to ignore his need to dictate and feel in control of this fantasy we were experiencing.

As soon as breakfast was close to done, I yelled out, "What the fuck bitch! Where is our breakfast? And you better have everything we asked for." While James was preparing breakfast, I made him repeat aloud what we wanted like he was our waiter.

Keep in mind, I'm an African American/Black person and acting as if I owned James as my slave in his own home. Eden smiled and thanked me for knowing what he needed and how to convey it. Three minutes before James walked in, I had this big cheese-eating grin on my face. Eden asked me what I was smiling about? I told her, "During slavery, lying in the bed with a White woman, lynching would have been immediate." Mentioning that made her appreciate our arrangement even more. Right after I responded to her question, James walked in with our breakfast, one hand under the tray just above his waist like a waiter. You could see the steam coming from the food. Surprisingly, he knew protocol and served my breakfast first, until I had everything I needed. Then James served Eden. I said, "Good boy, now leave us you peasant and go into the living room, until I ring this bell on the nightstand." I seriously could not believe what the fuck I made a White boy do while his wife watched. This muthafuckn' White boy skipped out of his own bedroom like a college co-ed girl. Years of watching and listening to Eden humiliating James paid off.

Later that evening, while alone in the living room with James, I told him to get up from the couch and make me a drink; he failed the task intentionally. As a result, I made James walk towards me and stop because I wanted him within arm's distance. As he stood in front of me, I slapped the right side of his face with the back of my hand. He knew exactly why I did it, he wanted the punishment, so he consciously disobeyed me. Once I proved my presence, he knew his refusal to fulfill my desires would result in me slapping him with the back of my hand. Btw, did you know slapping a man is more degrading than hitting him with a closed fist?

This is the last time I'll mention this, I honestly feel that's why a famous rapper/actor/father/husband chose that method to express his anger rather than using his fist.

While James was soaking and throwing a tantrum, Eden texted me from the bathroom. She asked me if I would be willing to humiliate James in the living room while he was throwing his tantrum. I texted her back quickly, "Yes, not a problem."

Eden also texted her twin sister and her best friend to come over to watch her husband humiliated. Eden's sister texted back with a response saying, "Hell yea!" Her sister asked who was doing the humiliation, Eden texted back, "By a pimpish looking nigga and he is in the living room right now." Eden's sister sent laughing emojis with a thumbs up and said they were not that far away. I was really surprised James wasn't a little curious what his wife was up to. While I was sitting in the living room, near James, it was obvious Eden, and I were texting one another. You know that sound your cell phone makes once you receive a text, right? I guess it really didn't matter to James, he trusted us enough to know we must have been up to something interesting. When the doorbell sounded, Eden walked over to the door with that mischievous smile and opened the door. Scarlett, her twin sister, walked in first. She was an attractive White chick with dark blonde hair, black dress with silver shoes. Scarlett must have been at least five feet six in height, carrying a 2011 Hermès So Black Matte Alligator Birkin 30 PVD Hardware purse over her shoulder.

No sooner than three to four steps through the door, Scarlett reached down into her purse and pulled out a bottle of Macallan Anniversary 1928, single malt. And while Eden and Scarlett were talking and hugging one another, I googled the name of her Macallan Anniversary Malt and the Hermès purse. Fuck that, I wanted to know, go ahead, and call me a nosy muthafucka. You would too, those two items looked fucking expensive, especially the liquor she pulled out of her purse. Of all the liquor stores in da hood, I'd not heard or seen this kinda shit. That liquor she brought ain't even top shelf, it's an armored truck with two guards and guns drawn kinda liquor.

Let's not even compare women in da hood getting their purses. Fuck it I'll say it, the local flea market near the hood and trailer parks, and you know damn well those purses will be Chinese knockoffs. Don't get mad at me for speaking my truth, y'all know I am right. I couldn't believe it, what the fuck! It made me wonder what Scarlett did for a living, buying something that damn expensive to drink. Never mind the cost of the purse. Nevertheless, I had to play it off, like I've been around people with expensive taste before.

The only distinguishable difference between Eden and her sister, Scarlett had dark blonde hair with silver shoes and a silky short black dress, and Eden had red hair with a white blouse and shorter black skirt with white knee-high boots; she looked like a seductive high school teacher with the glasses she had on. Damn! Both had big ass titties and plenty of cleavage showing for this special evening. Scarlet's best friend walked in shortly after and was a stunning, five foot seven sista with a natural, red-tinted black afro. Royal walked in with confidence oozing through the pores of her dark chocolate skin. It was undeniable Royal had a beautiful smile and body that turned me on.

Royal also walked in with an expensive handbag from Hermès Birkin 35 Diamond Bordeaux Porous, red satin pants, above the knee red leather boots with black buckles, and black gloves. I am not sure where she bought her tight fitting BDSM styled corset, but gauging by the embroidery, I bet it was expensive. I watched every move Royal made like a dog waiting for someone to jump over the fence and come close enough, just so I can bite their ass.

Going back to when Royal walked in, I said to myself, I ain't saying she's ah gold digger, but she ain't messin' around, with a broke ass Black man. And while I was salivating over how attractive Royal was, the three of them were whispering among themselves.

I was trying to listen to their conversation, I could only assume Royal, and Scarlett were curious why there was a throne in the middle of the living room, just like I was. As I was walking over to ask what they were whispering about, they suddenly huddled up and turned their backs towards me. I can take a hint when women do that.

I'm certain the three of them were whispering about something to do with me and the throne. I walked towards the middle of the living room and stopped, then looked at Royal and pointed at the throne. I couldn't help but ask Royal, "What's your plans for this throne?" Royal raised her right hand near her juicy natural lips and put her index finger over her mouth. She was obviously not going to tell me why the throne was in the living room. Eventually, Eden, Scarlett, and Royal said it was for me. They asked if I was willing to explore whatever they had whispered about. Thoughts ran through my head, but I knew they were not going to ask me to do something I may not want to do. So, I agreed with a big ass grin on my face.

James and Eden just wanted to fulfill one of their fantasies with someone they trusted and wouldn't sell their privacy to the highest bidder. So, I sat on the throne, waiting patiently for whatever the ladies had planned for me. It was at this moment Royal walked in my direction then leaned over and whispered, "It's restitution time for this White boy, are you ready?"

I knew exactly what she meant, and it made me hotter than a man sitting across from a woman wearing a dress with no panties. I sat with my back completely against the throne and comfortable. In fact, I was ready for whatever the ladies had in mind, while James was standing in front of us with a puzzled look. The moment she whispered in my ear earlier, I was confident she knew exactly how to direct this scene.

I liked how Royal directed the twins to stand next to me while on the throne, and her directness was on point. She pointed where she wanted the twins to stand, on my left side of me. She had to verbalize it because Scarlett and Eden were about to stand on the right side, Royal wanted to be on my right side while James was waiting for the next command, like a good boy. At that moment, the twins and I were waiting for whatever Royal had in mind. I asked Eden to pour me another shot of liquor. Of course, she wasn't paying attention and spilled it. I gave Eden a certain look and she knew exactly what to do, she leaned over and licked my finger.

Royal watched Eden while she licked my finger clean, then went ahead to reach into her expensive handbag and pulled out a gold dog leash, with a leather gold spiked collar connected to it. Since you weren't there as the reader, I'll describe the collar, okay? It was a custom-made collar, exclusively for James, because it also had gold spikes on the inside of it. The spikes were customized inside the collar, to get James' immediate attention when the leash was pulled on.

I knew what was going to happen next, but Eden and Scarlett didn't. I smiled because I knew Royal had been in this situation prior to being with us. Her black book was full of powerful White boys just like James that she had dominated over the years. Fuck, Royal knew exactly what to say and do to get our attention. She stopped James from what he was doing and made him stand in front of her. Honestly, how she spoke to James in a firm voice turned me on. She almost sounded like Sade with a raspy voice and a Southern drawl. I like the tone she used to convey her demands to James. She said, "Come here you little White bitch and stand here and don't you fucking move until I say so."

James said, "Yes ma'am," with his head down.

Royal pulled up Scarlett's dress past her waist and replied, "You nasty little White bitch, now lean forward and lick Scarlett's asshole." Scarlett looked shocked that Royal was telling her sister's husband to lick her asshole. Shit! I was shocked, I didn't know they got down like that. Royal's insight was spot on because Eden didn't even try to stop it from happening.

Of course, James licked her asshole clean and then stood straight up. Royal made James turn around, and while she placed the dog collar around James' neck, she yanked on the leash just for the fuck of it, just to get his attention. Royal then told James to stand directly in front of me, like a good little White bitch.

Note: Considering Royal is an African American/ Black woman, she calls James a little White bitch consistently throughout this chapter for a reason. And that's because White folks are too comfortable calling us nigger. So, she's turning the lazy Susan turntable on his ass.

When James intentionally ignored Royal, she knew exactly what to do to get his attention. Royal grabbed that muthafucking dog leash and yanked on it, which forced James's drop to his knees. While he was on his knees, Royal had a treat in her hand for him, and told him to look down. While James was looking down, Royal reached into her purse and pulled out something that looked like a dog biscuit. It wasn't, it just looked like one, just to humiliate him. Of course, James had to eat it from the palm of her hand like a good boy. When he finished eating it, he said, "Thank you Mistress Royal."

The commanding voice Royal had made James wait for the next command. She must have been a Femdom in her momma's womb to have so much poise and confidence. Royal and I looked down at James while he was on his knees like a White begging pathetic-little cock bitch. For ten minutes, Royal stared down at him with one finger in front of her lips, expressing James not to say anything.

As James was waiting for the next command, I looked at Royal with a devious smile. I told James to pull down Eden's dress in front of me and wait for the next command. Just as James was pulling down Eden's dress, Royal suddenly asked James to stop. Royal wanted Eden to lean over and place her hands directly on the arm of the throne. In fact, Royal purposely did this to make James expect what was about to happen next for not satisfying his wife. As James was about to pull down Eden's dress, Scarlett decided she wanted to be a part of the scene. Royal and I told Scarlett to take off Eden's panties. Scarlett knew what to do next and that's exactly what she did. She lifted the dress up and over her sister's head until she was in her birthday suit. Eden and Scarlett had never been a part of anything like this, and you could tell by how they were giggling.

One of James' fantasies was to put on a chrome Titan Chastity cock cage and watch Eden have sex with me, the HNIC (google it). At that moment, I took over and pulled down my pants. I looked down at my cock, which was hard as a sixties Coca-Cola bottle and told Eden to turn around and place her hands directly on James' shoulders to balance herself. As I stood behind his wife with a hard cock ready to fuck, Royal added lubricant slowly up and down on my shaft, as if she were trying to jack me off or something. Looking down at the way Royal was lubing up on my cock almost made me cum, seriously. Once my cock was all lubed and ready, Scarlett made the kneeling White bitch use his right hand to guide my cock into Eden's pussy from the back. Damn, I almost came again because Eden turned me on. The look on my face made Royal say, it was okay if I had cum early. Royal was planning to use my cum for something else she had in mind.

No sooner than Royal saying, "Relax Sir," I blasted a load of my fresh hot cum into Eden's pussy, and sat back down on the throne, legs shaking. Royal then yanked on James' chain and told him to bend over, and in a firm commanding voice, she said, "Lick the cum off the floor that has leaked from Eden's pussy and down her leg." Fuck that sounded sexy as a muthafucka coming from Royal. Unexpectedly, Scarlett walked over and placed the palm of her hand on the back of James' head. Scarlett guided his head towards every drop of cum she was able to see from a standing position, just like a dog that shitted on the carpet.

Not realizing how late it was, just before Royal had to leave, she yelled out one more command for James. "Look you little White bitch, I want this floor clean, and there betta not be one drop of cum anywhere." Scarlett was also looking for drops of cum that may have leaked out my cock onto the seat of the throne. As disgusting as that sounded, James pre-came right in his pants. His fantasy changed the dynamics of our relationship dramatically, and especially between me and Eden. I did not understand when I first met James and Eden, but I do now, why Eden wanted to watch her husband being subservient to me. In fact, I learned more about their lifestyle than any other couple I had ever met prior to them.

Years had passed, and I decided to call them, and from the sound of Eden's voice, she was happy to hear my voice. It must have been the universe connecting us again because they were also thinking of me. While on the phone with Eden, James interrupted and said if I was doing anything this weekend, why not come over and spend the night with them. So, I didn't waste any time, got in my car, and drove over to their house. As soon as I walked in the door, I gave Eden a big hug and enthusiastic kisses on the lips.

When Eden turned around, I slapped her on the ass while James was on the right of us, he extended his hand for a handshake with a smile and said, "I am glad you called." James said they had lost my number and that's why I had not heard from them. Again, the universe works in mysterious ways. Oh, I did not mention, Eden texted me just before I arrived and mentioned he trusted me and was ready for whatever I wanted while visiting this time. I walked in and sat down in James' favorite chair as I had before, and James started cooking dinner. James wouldn't be happy unless I was happy, and his wife knew she was my servant also while visiting. In other words, he becomes my servant and no one else is as important as me. After dinner, he wanted to massage my feet while Eden watched. Just like at a nail salon, he had everything ready and sat on a little pink stool. James placed my feet in his lap and started massaging my feet. Yes, that's correct, I am degrading him once again.

James massaged my feet with a lemon revitalizing and moisturizing foot scrub, and I'll admit, I fell asleep because it felt so good. Afterwards, I told James to take off Eden's panties in front of me slowly, and he did that with a cheese-eating grin on his face. Once Eden's panties were off, I told James to put her panties inside one of my pant pockets that were hanging on the chair. Eden had an idea why I wanted to take them home and didn't ask why. Now, even though that may not seem important to you as the reader, it was for him to complete the task I gave him. That evening for his reward, I told him to put on his chastity cock cage and a diaper and walk out from the bathroom. Don't ask me why I knew he wanted to be in his favorite chastity cock cage and diaper that evening, the only thing that matters is that he put it on, right?

Of course, it's James' unique kink and I was rewarding him for putting it on. I then told him to pick up Eden's clothes from the floor, and then fold and hang them up accordingly. Yet again, he completed that task with a smile on his face. After the floor was clear and the clothes were on hangers, I walked into the bathroom. And as I was looking into the bathroom mirror, I asked James why was the throne still in the living room? He told me, it's a continuous reminder of the fun they had when I was last there. I was happy to hear that because I missed them too.

As the evening was approaching, Eden picked up her cell phone and started texting. I'll just assume it was her sister Scarlett and her best friend Royal to come over and spend the night this time. I had already been there one night, and fuck it, I might as well stay one more, right? When the doorbell rang, naturally I was happy to see them again. Royal and Scarlett dressed more laid back this time and Scarlett didn't bring that expensive liquor with her.

And of course, Royal was looking delicious as usual, and I made that clear the moment we made eye contact. Normally, I don't have an attraction for a dominatrix, but it was something about Royal that was completely different than any sista I had ever met. Anyway, we all sat down on the couch getting reacquainted and talked about what happened after the last time we were all together. Scarlett said her life changed dramatically and found herself questioning the men she met on Tinder. And Royal decided to quit her job of thirty years to become a dominatrix full time. I looked out the window and was wondering whose Bugatti Centodieci that was next to mine. Fuck! I began to realize it belonged to Royal, judging from the custom-made Bugatti Centodieci neckless she had around her neck.

Royal got up from the couch she was sitting on and sat next to me. OMG! Royal had on this dress that was about two inches below seeing her pussy lips. Just before Royal was about to say something to James, I asked Royal what the race and background was of people who contacted her for her services. Royal smiled and looked around and said, "Mostly White men and three women who are in high profile jobs and business owners." Royal trusted her instincts to tell me about this one client, and if I were to mention his name in this book, it would blow your fucking mind. I damn near didn't want to believe her, considering we all know who he is or heard the name before. Let's just say, he is so high up the food chain, that I might as well lock my own self up in jail. Hell, I've seen this man's commercials and on talk shows. I asked her if any of her clients were Black, and she nodded her head no.

In disbelief, I said, "You mean to tell me you have not had one Black client."

She responded, "NOPE! Honestly, from me to you, that's a White thang anyway, seriously."

Anyway, after ten minutes of us reminiscing, Royal suddenly stood up and told James to get up from the couch and walk towards her. When she stood up, her big juicy ass was three inches from my damn face. So, when I finally stopped staring at Royal's ass, James was standing directly in front of Royal, and the smile on his face was priceless. We all knew what the grin was also but kept our poker face. As the husband stood directly in front of Royal, she opened her purse and pulled out the gold dog leash with attached gold spiked collar again. Then she reached back into her purse one more time, pulled out a long piece of rope, and placed it in James' hand. All of us but Royal were wondering what was up with the rope, considering she didn't bring that last time we were all together.

Royal told James to turn around and spread his legs apart. WTF, right? James was barefooted with blue jeans on and a long-sleeve shirt again. Royal didn't ask Eden about James' obsession with wearing long-sleeve shirts, she knew something that I didn't without asking. I thought he must have had a serious skin condition and was scared I would judge him. When Royal told James take off his long-sleeve shirt, he became anxious and looked at Eden, then looked at me and Scarlett. Eden had a concerned look on her face and told Royal that James wasn't taking off his long-sleeve shirt. Now, I'm concerned, and I asked, "Is there something y'all wanna fucking tell me?" At this point, I raised my voice and asked Eden, "Why in dafuck is James reluctant to take off his shirt?"

James looked at Eden one last time, and she nodded her head in approval to James finally taking off his shirt. Well, I'll be damned, it wasn't because of any skin condition as assumed by me and Scarlett. While his back was towards us, I finally was able to see why James never removed his shirts. It was because there were Nazi symbols tattooed on the inside of both arms near his elbow. No fucking wonder why this muthafucka always wore long-sleeve shirts. You are wondering if I had known about this earlier, would it have made any difference, right? Well, it's too late in the game now to be asking me that question, and honestly, those tattoos looked fresh.

It made since why Royal had brought the rope earlier, she remembered James got off on bondage and feeling helpless. Royal went into full dominatrix mode and told James to kneel in front of her. As I mentioned, Royal had a way of getting a man's attention by the tone in her voice. While James was on his knees, she took the rope I was still holding and carefully and strategically tied him up with it. Eden found out quick that James still came in his pants the moment the rope touched his skin. It took Royal about an hour to tie James up with her bondage rope she had in her purse. I was wondering why she required James to fold his arms and now I understood. It would make his Nazi tattoos more visible when she decided to punish him for whatever reason. Royal knew all along that James had those tattoos on his arms. Because Royal remembered her partner Vivien talking about James' tattoos when he made an appointment to see her, who was also a dominatrix. Vivien described her session with James in detail and mentioned his tattoos and cumming in his pants the last session they had together.

Vivien also mentioned James booked one session a week, for months, before he met Eden. Once James married Eden, the sessions stopped because he feared she would find out and wouldn't marry him.

Back to the story:

Royal told James stand up and turn around. Eden, Scarlett, and I laughed at James because there was a big ass wet spot in front of his pants again. I stopped laughing because I knew Royal wanted to continue dominating James. Therefore,

I stood in front of James, and I told him to kneel before me and respect the HNIC that I am. And just before his knees touched the floor, I asked him to return to his feet. That's when we all applauded him for overcoming his fear that niggas were taking over the planet and allowing himself to fulfill his desire for humiliation by someone he trusted.

James genuinely believed Black people were taking over this country that he called the United States of America. Never mind the fact, when he sings the National Anthem that clearly says: "The land of the free and the home of the brave." Free does not necessarily apply for slaves according to his behavior. James must have forgotten; we were all forced to sing that song growing up. Those were the lies he heard as a child by his family and especially from his father, from as far back as he could remember. That same day, James drove to his favorite tattoo artist and had that Nazi symbol removed from his left arm. Eden and Scarlett had known all along he had a dark and buried desire for humiliation.

Eden also knew, humiliation had to be by someone that understood his desires. In fact, trust played a major part of why they chose me initially. And being an African American was just a bonus. For years in James' business, they would not advance Black people within his company. For high turnover positions, James hired Black people, so that he could call them lazy. He knew how to avoid lawsuits for discrimination with his review practices. Majority of the promotions were White employees.

Never mind the fact, his ex-president ass kissing family encouraged and agreed with his hiring practices with racial bias. James would smile all in his African American employees faces and yet humiliate them behind their back. African American women who worked for him advanced faster and differently than the men. I knew of this because he decided to sit down with me and go over his hiring, firing, and promoting practices. It was obvious what his intent was by promoting the African American women at a higher rate than Black men that had more experience. His reason was to create jealousy and division among the Black employees. Here it is 2022, and that shit still works to this day. Nevertheless, under the current circumstances, he's always in charge of himself, family, and his employees. He knew he needed to abandon that mentality and his wife figured that out easily.

Before they met me, they didn't know of a way to heal him from his racist past. After that scene was over, we did a group hug, and I will remember that moment for the rest of my life. Peace!

UPDATE: Since January 2022, James' company has promoted one of his long-term Black employees named Mellick to management. Immediately after that announcement was made, there were more than a few White employees that expressed their concerns, even though they had only been with the company three to five years. Mellick's work ethic spoke for itself. In fact, Mellick should have been promoted back in 2017. James could not understand why a few of his White employees had a problem with it. It was then he had a revaluation, how he was accustomed to working with other's who looked like him. He wasn't aware how widespread discrimination was until he reflected on himself. One day while visiting him at his office, there was obvious tension you could cut with a butter knife. Before walking into his office, we decided to go into the break room for some water. We noticed immediately a few employees whispering among themselves and looking over their shoulder at us.

We both thought that was suspicious behavior considering they remained quiet. In fact, those employees did not realize there were microphones throughout the building and especially in the break room. Just as we walked into his office, he asked me to shut the door, and he closed the blinds. My first thought was fucked up. I ain't saying what that thought was either and you are just going to have to assume that one. Anyway, James wanted to show me some video footage of employees in the breakroom. James said, "Listen to what those employees were saying in the breakroom."

I was shocked to hear they were plotting against Mellick, and James held his head down in disbelief. Once James realized they were planning to set up Mellick to fail, he separated them into different departments. Eventually, he was able to fire two of them for misconduct that secretly had everything to do with the plot they wanted to carry out. My woke friend never realized how damaging his racist mentality was affecting his health and those who loved him unconditionally. He told me something that was profound but truthful.

James said, he never thought about how indirectly his decisions could affect a generation. This is something he has never had to endure or deal with personally. Before he started business, his bosses, nurses, doctors, teachers, and principals were all White. In fact, James' friends were also White. As I mentioned earlier his parents were racist as fuck, and I am glad he didn't teach any of his children that behavior. But, as you know from reading "My Gay Ass Cousin," you don't need to be taught to hate when you are indirectly exposed to it subconsciously. No matter if it's subtle or blatant. You can tell by what's going on in our country now. White and Asian people are feeling comfortable expressing their ignorance and racial insensitivity.

Make This Make Sense:

The interesting thing is a mass majority of African Americans are okay with being treated like third-class citizens here in the United States of America. I can find a shit load of videos on YouTube, which backs up my assertion. Every fucking time I turn around, there is another damn Karen on the loose in a video, and of course she is not minding her own fucking business. These are some of the fucked-up questions Black people are asked while minding their business: Do you live around here? What's your name? Do you have business in this area? Why are you parked here? Are you waiting for someone? What's your apartment number? Which house do you live in? Do you have a key to this apartment? Is this your car? For whom do your work? Where are you headed?

It's like Black people must show their freedom papers walking amongst White folks. I can say confidently, some White folks want to take America back to 1831, when teaching Black people how to read and write was against the law. What's even more fucked up, intelligent Black people intimidates White people. Honestly, Black people don't give a fuck where ya'll are going, coming from and been, and you know why? It's none of our damn business, and additionally we don't give a fuck. If you are a White person and have read this far into this chapter, I have a question for you. Why do y'all White folks change your appearance to look like Black people? So, in other words you want your cake and eat it too, right? You want our complexion without the history that comes with it, does that sound about right? Anyway, if you have a problem with what I just said challenge my opinions. I am always ready for a good debate. Otherwise STFU!! Peace!

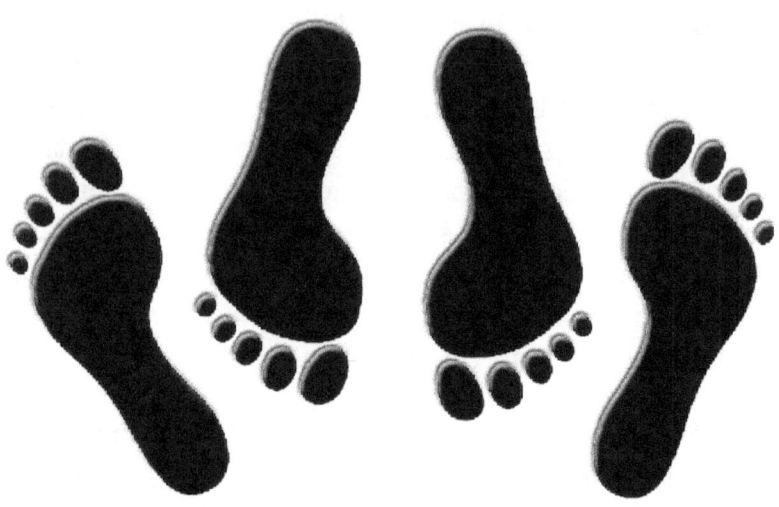

2 B Or Not 2 B Vanilla

s I've said before, it bothers me that a lot of single men don't take the opportunity to get to know the woman before fucking, and I realized even more while in the swinging lifestyle. In a vanilla setting, you find yourself guessing what a woman is or is not into when it comes to a sexual encounter. I'm a grown ass man, and I have no intention of playing games. Also, I don't want to wait for months trying to get to know someone only to find out we're not into the same things sexually. With swinging, there's none of that, which is why it's perfect if you're a very sexual person, like me. You can't tell me that at a nightclub or private party you can't find someone you can vibe with within the lifestyle, especially if you are a single male.

I've always been a person who wants to know the woman I may fuck later; I would never walk into a party assuming just because I am the only Black male my vibe is right for any of the wives there. I like getting to know the husband first by asking him about his family, work, etc. and his marriage to his wife, because he's the gate keeper. So, while I am talking to the couple at a private party, I stand more so on the husband's side and try to have a genuine conversation in efforts to understand his mindset. Keep in mind, I already know his wife is interested in getting to know me. Body language and eye contact tell me everything I need to know to proceed or walk away. Usually, the wife has already made it known to the husband she wants to play with me or as we say in the lifestyle, party with me. She's seeking her husband's approval which I completely understand. Sometimes, the husband will have an intuition and knows his wife may become uncomfortable. If this happens, I will not be partying with the wife soon. It's happened a few times to me, and I don't have a problem with his decision.

I repeat, nothing happens between the wife and me if the husband does not approve. Here is a real scenario on how I approach couples, I survey the room and wait to see if I receive eye contact from one of the wives at the party. If I receive eye contact and a smile from more than one of the wives, then I walk over eventually and introduce myself, one at a time. In some cases, the woman is aggressive, and I shy away from that personality. Being straight up, aggressive women remind me of two out of my three ex-wives and one in particular. Besides, aggressive women only care about themselves or have a dominant personality and I'm not down with either one of those two personalities. Don't get it twisted, in a couple of minutes with watching the body language and some conversation I can detect if a woman has an aggressive personality. Besides, I ain't down with being pushed down onto the bed while trying to ride my cock. Shit, I may not even be hard yet and now must explain why I'm not hard. As you can tell, I've been in this situation before, right? Trust me, it's uncomfortable having to explain a soft cock. One last thing I am going to say about aggressive women is, they tend to want to slap my ass and that's another thing I'm not down for. Just saying.

By getting to know the couple, I'm making sure we are on the same page. It's one of the reasons I love the swinging lifestyle, it takes away all the barriers and we, at least, have one thing in common and that's fucking. And when both partners are sexual and open-minded, it's phenomenal. Vanilla folks don't understand that about the lifestyle. It is just fucking. Yes, some people separate or get a divorce from participation, but that's likely because their relationship wasn't strong enough from the beginning, or TRUST was an issue before they started. To me, it's all about enhancing the relationship between two people. Couples can still have sex with other people, but when it's over, it's over, and you two come back together again. There are other alternative lifestyles that work for some people, and those people get it.

I'm comfortable with sitting around having a conversation about whatever, it doesn't necessarily have to lead to sex. If I've made a good connection with even just one woman, then I'm likely to get together with her at the next party. I should have said this at the beginning of the chapter, so I'll say it now. If you are a Black male at an event, nightclub, or private party, and most of the women there are White, please reframe from asking them if they have ever been with a Black man. Take it from me, they hate that shit because they tell me after a Black male has walked away while I am having a conversation with her. Introduce yourself and let your mannerisms speak for itself. Flirt a little but not too much, because that makes you creepy in her eyes. Also, don't be all touchy feely when you first meet the wife, and keep a safe distance, just in case she may have had a horrific experience with a Black man, or a man in general. Give her space and watch for the clues and always be respectful. Peace!!

2 P Or Not 2 Pee

omeone just came to mind, and I might as well share it with you. There was this lady I met who I am only going to use the first initial of her name, J, and she will know who she is if she happens to read this book. I met J and her boyfriend at a swinger party at my friend's home in Tampa Florida. I immediately had a good connection with J from the moment I laid eyes on her, she just had a freaky look about her. I said to myself, I may not be fucking her tonight, but hopefully, at some point I will soon.

Sometimes, I can attend a party and not have the right connection for me to play/party/fuck with any of the women at the party. When that happens, occasionally, I would just chill for a little and converse with a few of my friends. Anyway, back to J, we didn't fuck the few times we saw each other at different parties, but while at that party we kept talking when we had the chance. After a few months of seeing each other at my friend's home in Tampa, we finally had sex, and it was fun. She made it clear when we first met that she loves to suck and fuck, but no anal sex. J and her boyfriend made an agreement prior to attending the party. I was okay with that because I completely understood the dynamics of their relationship. Some couples do not believe in kissing, it all depends on the couples' arrangement with one another. And just in case you were wondering what those are, I will address this at the end of this chapter. It must have been around the fifth party that J acted extremely comfortable around me. Her boyfriend kept on hinting to me to fuck her every chance he got since that's the only time I was able to meet J, were at the parties we both were attending.

Eventually, J asked me to do something unimaginable.

As I passed by the bedroom, J whispered my name and asked me to walk into the bedroom with her. First, why was she whispering and what was she up to, I thought. J kept looking around, and it made me paranoid.

If you are a White woman reading this, you must understand my mindset. White women have and are still making false accusations against innocent Black men, so, of course, I was hesitant taking another step towards the bedroom.

I was not prepared for what J ended up asking me, she said, "I do not want to say it right here, so follow me to the bathroom." I followed her cautiously into the bathroom, and I became uncomfortable. She whispered again, "I am going to wait till everybody is out of the bathroom." It was at that point I was wondering if she wanted to take a shower with me. When the last woman walked out of the bathroom from douching, we walked in.

She hurried in first, then I walked in behind her, as I walked past her, she locked the door behind us. I was hesitant, but not scared, it was just odd she wanted to lock the door. Well, I understood why she wanted to lock the door. She said, "Look, I need you to pee in my mouth."

Like a parakeet, I repeated her exact words, "You want me to pee in your mouth."

She said, "Yes, and I have been wanting you to do that for some time."

I can't believe I'm telling you this. With a confused look on my face, I said, "Well, alright then."

She took off her clothes, stepped into the shower, and kneeled submissively inside the bathtub with her arms behind her, her mouth wide open. In porn the men are at least semi hard while peeing in the woman's mouth. There was an assumption I had to be semi hard too. I was wrong because, J didn't care if I was semi hard or not, she assumed I was freaky as she was.

Here is a nigga looking down at a White woman kneeling, ready for me to pee in her mouth. Here's the thing; I watched it in pornos, had it done to me unexpectedly, and did it on one of my ex-girlfriend's stomach while in the closet. With an opportunity of a lifetime, I could not pee in her mouth to save her life. *I'm pissed off as I am writing this part of the chapter (no pun intended).*

I tried, and she kept waiting and waiting, and I kept pushing and pushing. Nothing came out of my cock, and I was so fucking disappointed. She said, "That's okay, it happens to most people who have never tried it before." She was right, I had never pissed in a woman's mouth before. She was disappointed because I was unable to pee in her mouth. Well, I thought I was freaky as hell to even try it. But it was not enough. And, what's so fucked up, the moment she stepped out of the bathroom, I had to pee.

By then I was pissed off (no pun intended) that I couldn't pee earlier. There is nothing sexier than a woman on her knees, with her mouth open waiting for me to cum in it, not urinate. I am sure her boyfriend must have done that with her a few times. I have seen it in videos, but it doesn't turn me on. I had an opportunity to pee in a woman's mouth that wanted it, and I could not do it. Oh, well, life goes on and I'm okay with not being asked to try that again. So that's my "To Pee, or not to Pee" story.

Now it's time to address the diverse ways of participating in the swinging lifestyle that two people can agree on:

WHO IS GOING TO GRIN AND BEAR IT:

The title says it all, right? Simple, if I am not attracted to another person's wife or girlfriend and my partner is attracted to her husband or boyfriend, then I ain't taking one for the team just so my partner can fuck him. It is not fair under no circumstances to play/party/fuck unless it's equally satisfying. It would be a great idea to establish a code word to convey to your partner your level of interest to continue or run for the hills. Honestly, I should be able to have an idea immediately if my partner would be interested or not and vice versa.

DISCUSSING DRINKING LIMITS:

There has not been one party I/we have gone to where there wasn't alcohol. I have only dated one alcoholic that I would have to worry about.

Other than her, I would not have to be concerned how much my partner drinks. But, if you partner does, then both of you need to discuss the drinking limit rule to avoid embarrassment. Having one drink usually helps women to overcome nervousness. Especially, if she isn't confident in her own appearance. I could easily make a chapter on this subject alone, but I have said enough to get a general idea.

CONDOM OR RAW:

This is one rule that needs to be discussed before even considering the lifestyle. There is nothing else to say related to this topic. Just be aware there are always risk without condoms, but if someone is cheating without using condoms, then, again, that's a whole new chapter I could discuss, just not now.

ANAL:

Self-explanatory; men come in all thickness, shapes, and sizes. Depending on the girth of some men, this may be uncomfortable but when you are at a party, anal could be enjoyable if it weren't before with your partner. Something else to discuss before fucking others, period.

TO KISS OR NOT TO KISS:

Up to you when it comes to kissing because in the heat of passion, I would think it would be weird not to. Anyway, also discuss this prior to fucking anyone else.

SAME ROOM VS. SEPARATE ROOM:

The level of trust and comfortability makes this a simple choice. In fact, if both trust and comfortability are in question, please seek help in general and do not proceed until this has been taken seriously.

Same Room: It just means all parties involved are in the same room fucking or whatever feels comfortable between adults.

Separate Rooms: Two couples fuck/play with one another's partner privately which can be fun also. Sometimes being around your partner will make you nervous, and it allows you to relax without concerns of what you may or may not do differently.

I am going to be brief with both subjects because I could easily elaborate on more.

NO FULL SWAP WITHOUT PENETRATION:

Usually, this is reserved for new couples just trying to find out what they are comfortable with exploring together. Me personally, this is also called soft swap, and I might as well just sit in the room fully dressed and have a conversation if we ain't fucking, LOL. That's just me though because no matter what, do what makes you happy. Especially, if one or the other has performance issues.

Trust is important, no matter
which one you choose above,
you should be comfortable.

First Situation

In this light chapter, I'm going to give you a shot of liquor with no chaser. In other words, some situations I regret being in without a storyline or build up. If what I just said didn't make any sense to you, let me say this another way you may comprehend. If you like watching porn, do you watch the entire fake ass, dull acting, or do you scroll through that just to get to the fucking and sucking part. Well, this chapter passes by all the fluff and gets straight to the fucking and sucking, feel me?

I remember this one chick I used to go to high school with, we stayed connected for a couple of years after we graduated. After years of talking shit on our cell phones, she finally invited me over to her house. Shit, we may have only talked for a few minutes before I told her to remove her pants and panties.

Before I continue, I just want y'all to know I'm lucky to be alive writing this memoir. I wasn't cautious about where I placed my cock or tongue back in the day. Keep in mind that this woman I am writing about right now, I didn't even ask if she washed her pussy before I arrived. So, now I am going to continue. Reflecting back in the day, I was nasty ass teenager, Sometimes I pinch myself, because I'm surprised

I must have been eating that bitch's pussy so good, that suddenly, I felt something wet squirt into my mouth, and I wasn't sure what the fuck it was. I immediately took my mouth from her pussy and asked, "What dafuck was that?"

She didn't look embarrassed and said, "Oh, I'm sorry" and got up from the couch. After a few seconds I realized this fucking bitch peed in my mouth. When she got up from the couch after peeing in my mouth, she went into her bathroom and locked the door. I was cussing that bitch out and was banging on the door.

I kept on repeating, "Why in dafuck would you think it was okay to pee in my fucking mouth."

Seriously, think about it. She had to know that was about to happen and didn't warn me. I'm going to be straight up wit ya, I've never asked or wanted this bitch to pee in my mouth. Remember me saying I'm lucky to be alive? It also applies to what I am about to say next: the universe had her back that evening, because that could have easily turned ugly, read between the lines. If I had been a gun

carrying thug, do I need to say anything more?
Now, have I peed on a woman? Sure, once, it was
my girlfriend at the time, and she wanted me to do
it, that's it. I could have fucking slapped da shit out
of that bitch for peeing in my mouth. Not wanting
to end up in prison to be another man's bitch kept
me from caring out my anger.

Second Situation

There was another girl I wanted to fuck from
junior high school. Like the girl above, she also
finally invited me over to her house, sounds
familiar, right? Wait ... Here it goes again, like the
girl above, we talked for a few minutes, and she
pulled off her panties. Our conversations were about
what she wanted to do to me, and what I wanted to
do to her. There was a clear understanding before
I rang her doorbell what to expect, so I thought.
I ate that bitch's pussy till she came all over my
face. I had her juices all around the top of my lips.
In fact, I tried to be silly by grabbing my top lip
and pulling it up to my nose acting as if I could
taste and smell her pussy. While she was laughing,
I sat down on the bed and started pulling down my
pants because it's time for her to suck my cock or
something, right?

She tells me, "I'm not going to suck
your cock or let you fuck me."

I stood up and looked her dead in the eyes and said, "You know what, you're lucky as hell my momma taught me to never do anything that could send me to prison. Honestly, if you ever do this again to another guy after he's eaten your pussy, and suddenly you play innocent, you could be murdered, or he beats the fuck out of you. So, I'm going to put my clothes on and leave, please take my advice, and don't do that shit again." I hurried and walked out the door, and I whispered to myself and thanked my mom in for the wisdom she gave me.

Third and Final Situation

When I turned twenty-one, there was a nightclub I used to like going to called Rasputin's Night Club in Point Loma, California. Imagine finally turning twenty- one, going to your first nightclub, and some older woman sees a young boy toy and offers her number to him. Of course, I said yes and called her shortly afterwards. This woman didn't waste any time on my first visit to her place. No sooner than walking through her front door, she guided me towards her bedroom. I was a pup, and this older woman told me to take of my clothes. Here I am, standing in her home butt ass naked, while she checked me out like I was some kinda fresh meat. She started taking off her clothes, and I wasn't impressed whatsoever. Remember, I am twenty-one and she's fifty-two years old, and I am used to looking at naked girls around my age. Anyway,

I was game to continue, and she started sucking my cock, back then I was not into eating pussy. I guess her sucking my cock made her cum a few times. She immediately got up and turned around doggy style and placed her tits against the bed. I said that so you could have a visual, in other words, she was bent completely over, ass up. Damn right I did, I got behind her and stuck my cock in her pussy. I was so into it and wasn't paying attention to anything else. She loved what I was doing behind her, but suddenly, there was a foul odor coming from somewhere. It's hard to concentrate when something stank like a muthafucka, especially when you don't know where it's coming from. Now don't get me twisted, I still got my cock in her, fuck dat shit. As she's cumming, I ain't ready yet because the smell became stronger. I'm glad she couldn't see my face behind her. If she had turned around and saw my face, I'm damn certain she would have asked why the face?

When I eventually looked down between my hands on her ass, I saw this cave where her asshole was supposed to be. Her damn booty hole was wide open, and my cock had not been in there yet. Gauging by the size of her open asshole, my cock would not have touched the sides going in anyway. I ain't got enough girth for that cave and was determined to keep fucking her. But, between the cave for an asshole and the stank, I couldn't cum. Let me give you another visual, I was looking everywhere else but down, trying to keep her stanky ass from penetrating my nose. Sometimes, a man should know when to fold his cards. To this very day, which was the stankiest open asshole I have fucked and that was thirty plus years ago. Obviously, it was a moment in time I'll never forget. I know there is no such word as stankiest, but I am using it anyway.

Against The Wall in Pine Hills

 **here** was this blonde lady I was seeing for a while; she lived in Clearwater, and at the time, I lived in Pine Hills, Florida. Sometimes I would get in my car and drive halfway to meet her. The drive for her to see me was far, so she would pay for the hotel room halfway between us, so we could fuck. Considering she had young children living with her at the time, I always made sure she did not drive the full distance to see me.

One afternoon, she decided to drive the entire distance not knowing all of what I had planned for her. When she arrived, I was like a dog waiting in the window wagging its tail. I'm glad she didn't see me opening my drapes with my nose as I wondered what took her so long to get out of her car. I must have opened the shades enough times, I thought I better calm the fuck down. I watched her walk towards my front door through my window, if I could have barked and wagged my tail like a dog, I would have.

She was not expecting what I had in mind as soon as she walked in the door. Once I closed the door and locked it, I immediately frisked her like a police officer and passionately slammed her back against the wall. After being with her three times, I could tell she was not expecting what I did to her. I used one of my hands to hold her arms above her head against the wall. Then used the other arm to pull down her pants and panties. She acted as if I was supposed to stop, but the wet spot I saw in her panties told me something entirely different. I told her to kick off her shoes, her arms still in the air. While she was taking off her shoes, I kissed her passionately. She loved every fucking second of it; no one had ever done that to her but me.

Still pinned up against the wall, I started playing with her pussy before I fucked or ate her. At that point, she was so fucking hot and ready, you could blow in her ear, and she would cum.

On a different morning, I remember driving to see her at her home instead of her visiting me. She lived in a beautiful spacious home, and I was extremely impressed.

I am saying all this because, hopefully, she'll read this book and remember me.

Just as she planned it, the door was unlocked and without waking her up, I walked in while she was sleeping.

That always scared me because the way I am wired, I thought, what if someone else walked in while she was sleeping and harmed her or worse. In fact, me being a Black man walking into another White woman's home in a nice neighborhood would have not been a positive experience.

While standing directly above her, I observed her sleeping. I gently pulled the covers off her like a prowler in the night. There is nothing better than watching a woman sleeping naked with her legs slightly open and you still see her pussy.

Normally, I would jack off just watching her sleep naked; this time instead of cumming, I held off busting a nut on her sheets. I crawled into bed and started kissing her on the back of her neck.

She went from snoring to grunting which meant she was awake. I slipped my cock in her pussy, and after a couple of strokes, I came because I was so excited. To not leave her hanging, I went down on her. She came so hard on my face that if she could squirt, she would have. That is how sex was between her and me, a little short woman with blonde hair. That is all I am going to say on that because as I have said before, I am not dropping names in this book, but I am saying enough for the person to know who I am talking about. Anyway, that is my experience with the White woman in Clearwater.

All Pussies Are Not The Same

sually, when I meet a woman for the first time, we must meet halfway, just in case we're not attracted to one another. Never mind the fact muthafuckas out here catfishing.

In this case, there was this Black woman named Shay I knew that lived in Riverdale, Florida. I drove to her city making it convenient for her to meet me. I asked Shay to choose the place and she gave me the directions. It was easy making the decision to drive two hours to meet her because of our conversation on the phone, plus the photos of her, and we connected. We met at this bar she knew. I watched Shay as she got out of her car, she was in her early fifties and dressed so fucking sexy, just the way I like a woman. Prior to our meeting, we had talked about sex, and based on our conversation, sex should have been phenomenal between us. She was slim with some ass and small tits but made up for it with a cute face, legs, and a great personality.

We had fun at the bar, and what I really liked about her also, is that she bought a round of Jell-O shots after I bought one. Some women will take advantage of a thirsty-minded man and hint they want a couple of drinks and never offer to buy the man one. I always sit back and watch a woman's behavior because, "I don't play dat shit."

Off the subject*: I've never felt the need to take advantage of a woman while intoxicated. These days, that's not necessary, as it's damn easy to get pussy. Besides, why would I risk being prosecuted, just to end up being passed around like a blunt in prison by the Black and White prisoners. That sure in dafuck don't sound like anything I wanna be a part of.*

Back to Riverdale. Shay felt comfortable with me, so she invited me to her home when we left the bar. As the evening wore on, she felt it was too late for me to drive home so she asked me to spend the night. That sentiment was kind of her, and no, I wasn't expecting it. Thirsty muthafucka's behave childishly on the first date, either being too touchy or expecting the pussy. A real playa takes his time and gets rewarded for it.

There was absolutely no reason for me to ask for the pussy right away, I liked her enough to wait until the right time to pursue her. Shay went into her bathroom and came out with something sexy on. I knew the time was right when she was in her bed with me. While conversing, I made sure she was thinking what I was thinking, so I proceeded cautiously.

I started playing with her pussy with my fingers, then out of nowhere, she closed her legs and stopped me. She may not have had muscular thighs, but she was able to close her legs in such a way that if my head had been a coconut, it would have cracked, and all over the walls and ceiling would have been coconut juice. I thought to myself, "Huh, what the fuck was that all about?" When I asked her why she stopped me, she said she had cum, so I didn't need to continue. She straight up stopped me, dead in my tracks. After that, I was completely turned off.

Thinking back, it could have ended badly for her if I had been someone with little or no self-control. My momma didn't raise me like that anyway.

Off the subject: When a woman rejects me sexually or while I'm trying to please her, I stop immediately, and I don't want to fuck with her anymore. The one thing I know (and every man SHOULD know) is ... no means no. And sometimes, a woman won't verbalize it, and it may be in the form of closing their legs tightly. Once I hear the word no, I stop immediately and don't start over or try again another day. When a woman stops me from pleasing her, there is always the possibility she will do it again under the same circumstances. There are many reasons why a woman might stop a man from pleasuring her. In my opinion, some of it is attributed to mental or physical abuse (abusive parents, rape, molestation, etc.), or past experiences with men. Some men don't like women squirting, and they'll try to make her feel bad about it. From that point on, the woman will tense up and become afraid of it happening again. In other words, she can't fully enjoy herself because she's worried about something some other motherfucker said to her.

I never had someone stop me from licking their pussy before, but in the exact same way as the woman in Riverdale, Florida, it happened again several months later. Another Black woman named Dian I met who drives a red Mercedes, yes, and you know who you are. I'm still wondering why you drove two hours to see me. Then asked for one of my shirts to put on with nothing else under it, then suggest I follow you to my bedroom, and as soon as I start playing with your damn pussy, you did exactly what Shay did in Riverdale, you closed your damn legs. Honestly, in all my fucking days, not one White woman has ever done that to me. However, two Black women in a row did. What the fuck is up with that?

Back to Shay in Riverdale, Florida. When she stopped me from playing with her pussy, my dick quickly became soft as ah muthafucka. Trying to continue was not going to happen, at least not as far as I was concerned. She and I had discussed anal sex, and I was really looking forward to fucking her in the ass.

Hell, I even tried licking her clit again, she took the palm of her hand, and placed it on top of my head and pushed me off her pussy.

I was confused, and for the first time, wasn't sure what to do next. We had talked about sex before I drove to Riverdale, I assumed all I had to do was hang in there, no matter how hard she pushed my tongue away from her pussy. Initially, I thought that was her kink, pushing her man off and I was supposed to pin her down and lick her pussy anyway. It was hard for me mentally after that happened, especially while trying my best to not be selfish.

Besides, I don't want to be conservatively eating her pussy while thinking to myself, will she push my head away again, just before or after cuming? I wasn't about to try again, for the fear of being rejected a second time. So, I was done, and now we do not talk much at all.

We never got together after that. I tried to remain friends with her on the phone. I was willing to see her one more time, but she told me that driving on freeways made her uncomfortable. And we just faded apart. I think we would have been a good couple together. But it just did not work out, unfortunately.

Off the subject: I realize every woman is different, so when I'm eating pussy, I'm doing whatever I can to see what turns them on. Some just like the pussy lips sucked on, some like the clit licked softly, and some like it bit. It's easy to tell when a woman likes what I'm doing down there. I watch their body language, listen to their breathing, and heart rate. Some women are vocal, and will say, "oh right there" or "a little softer" or "a little harder." I've never had a problem being told what to do in this situation. Some men's egos get in the way of pleasing their partner when she's trying to tell him how to eat her pussy. These dumb bastards have the nerve to say some shit like: "I know how to eat pussy" or "I've been eating pussy for years." As a man, if you give a fuck about this woman, you're getting ready to stick your dick in, you really should listen and take directions. Besides, if you KNEW what you were doing, she wouldn't be giving directions in the first fucking place.

Some women may not say anything when you're not pleasuring them the way they want, but I can promise you they aren't going to cum. She'll lay there pretending to enjoy it, but she's really rolling her eyes in the back of her fucking head at your stupidity. I'm not even sure why she would continue to date that selfish motherfucker after that. And if she does continue to date a motherfucker with this mentality, hopefully she'll come to her senses and drop the fool. She should have walked away immediately when the asshole said, "I know how to eat pussy." That's why I called this chapter: "All Pussies Are Not the Same."

All Wrapped Up

here is the creativity between two people that love sex and each other. With many of you the spark is missing, all because of long work hours, kids, health issues, weight gain, menopause, ED, drinking too much, lack of energy, sleepless nights, arguing all the time, being harassed, the war, racial tension, gas prices, food shortages, baby formula shortages, baby momma drama, pregnant again, vasectomy failed, being laid off. Then beyond any doubt, it's not easy being sexually creative anymore, right?

While reading this chapter, I need you to do me a favor, imagine yourself walking around in your favorite local hardware store and sexual fantasies pop into your head, like in an X-rated cartoon. You look up into the sky or ceiling as if you can visualize the way to utilize something you just had in your hands. I am always thinking of ways to surprise my partner so that it's not predictable. Even as old as I am right now, you can call me a dirty old man. As I mentioned earlier, where is the creativity these days? An example of an inventive mind is by using shrink-wrap, you know, the stuff that you can buy at any industrial supply chain. If you don't know what shrink-wrap is, Google it. I have used it more than a hundred times where I worked, not even considering other sexual purposes.

Just before the weekend on a Friday afternoon, I clocked out early from work, got in my car and headed across the street to the local industrial supply chain to buy one role of shrink-wrap. I've shopped there before, and knew exactly what aisle it was in. I didn't waste any time looking for anything else. As soon as I picked it up and had it in my hands, I had a big ass smile on my face. In fact, my cock was getting hard as I thought about my plan on what to do with it. Anyone watching me on the monitor, while walking with it in my hands wouldn't know my plans for the shrink-wrap. Now, if you see me walking in an aisle with it and you smile at me, I will know you read this book.

Back to wrapping up this White woman named Jackie, I never called her or mentioned the shrink-wrap fantasy, I just showed up with it, and she had a confused look on her face. Jackie asked me what my plans were for using it, and I said, "It's a surprise." I went into her bedroom and sat down on the edge of the bed. And of course, the shrink-wrap was already next to me. I told Jackie to come into the bedroom where I was waiting for her. When she walked into her own bedroom, I asked her to stand in front of me and not say a word. Even though she's an alpha female, it was in her best interest to stand there, shut up, trust me, and be vulnerable for a little while. I told her to turn around so that I was looking at her back. Then asked her to remove her blouse and big ass bra. To be so small, she had big ass titties, seriously! She felt more vulnerable with her clothes on the floor. Trust means everything in this situation. I asked her to take off her pants and remove her panties. She kept on asking me questions, and I had to say in a firm voice, "Stop asking questions."

She needs to always be in control, so I am certain this was making her uncomfortable and excited at the same time. I asked her to turn around, and at this point, she was naked in front of me. That is when I reached for the shrink- wrap and asked her to put her arms straight down by her side. I pulled on the shrink-wrap and tucked it under one of her arms. As she stood there in front of me naked, I began to walk around her, wrapping her up like a Christmas gift.

While I was walking around her with the shrink-wrap, Jackie had an idea, and a damn good one at that. She said, "Why don't you stay still on the bed, and I'll spin myself around while you place the shrink-wrap where you need it." I'll be damned, that was a great idea and that's exactly what I did. Are you paying attention, she was excited enough to make it easier for me to shrink-wrap her. I was smiling the whole time when she suggested the idea. To me, trust is better than sex because she offered me a solution.

My cock was hard the whole time as she spun around in front of me. While all wrapped up like a Christmas gift, Jackie asked, "What's next?" I smiled and stood up and walked around to the front of her and helped her onto the bed, all wrapped up. I am not about to say that this was easy, depending on the weight and size of your partner, shrink-wrapping could be difficult. With her helping me it was easier. While she was lying there naked, I looked like a kid in a candy store. Imagine if the cashier said on the PA system everything in the store was free, for one day only, and you may take whatever and how much you wanted; that's how it felt. So, of course, I poked one hole in the shrink-wrap. Wait! I know what you are thinking, one of those holes was for her anal, right? Even though I had full access to whatever hole I wanted, she trusted me and knew I wouldn't stick my cock in a hole that we already discussed was off limits. If I were Satan, that would have been the best moment to take advantage of all her holes, right? I was thankful she was open-minded.

Anyway, while Jackie had her arms by her side, I made sure her arms were not shrink-wrapped behind her back, which would have been extremely uncomfortable. If I had shrink-wrapped her that way, I would have to unwrap her immediately and rewrap her again with her arms to her side. And that would have taken us out of the mood. So, I made sure her hands and arms were down by her sides. With her arms and hands by her side, it didn't matter if she was face down on her stomach or lying on her back. All I cared about was her hands and arms being out of the way. I also made sure I did not shrink-wrap her above the neck. While Jackie was standing shrink-wrapped, I had full access to her pussy. Since she had a bad habit of scratching me while eating her pussy, I had to produce something to prevent that from happening. I could have tied her up, shrink- wrapped her, or used handcuffs.

I decided to use shrink-wrap, and I made sure to shrink-wrap her just enough that she could unwrap herself, just in case something happened to me, and I was unable to get her out of that situation. Shrink-wrap her enough to make it fun, but not too much, in case there is an emergency. You must try it at least once, and I would only suggest shrink-wrapping your partner if you have known each other a while. Imagine, if you have not told your roommate or family member and they walked in on you all shrink-wrapped? How do you think they would respond? I would call 9-1-1, personally. This is not a first date thing if you know what I mean. I also would not try shrink-wrapping if someone else is in the home.

There is nothing sexier than a vulnerable woman. And if she is into anal sex, you poke two holes into the shrink-wrap. Oh, man. And if you are into rough sex and trust one another, it could be fun for both of you. Can you imagine that your partner is shrink-wrapped, and you can fuck whatever hole you want, and toss in the fact, they can't do anything to stop you. You can tease her clit until she is ready to cum, then you stop and leave her hanging, begging you to continue. As I already stated in this chapter four times now, trusting your partner must be clear for rough sex which could be fun for both parties. A role-play fantasy could be shrink- wrapping and slapping your cock against her face. I'll say this one more time, trust is everything. Anyway, that is my shrink-wrapping story.

Anal Fetish

⬧FETISH⬧

(noun) a charm superstitiously believed to embody magical powers;
(noun) excessive or irrational devotion to some activity; (noun) a form of
exual desire in which gratification depends to an abnormal degree on son

hen a woman tells me she hasn't tried something before and already made up her mind that she's not willing to try (or even consider) it, I'm turned off. A good example would be anal sex. Some women feel anal sex is forbidden because of how they were raised, or something they learned in school or worse. Or, they just had a horrific experience with some bitch ass muthafucka who's cock was too thick and didn't use lubricant or prepare her.

And being straight up, if a guy goes ahead and pursues fucking her anally, after she's given him a firm, NO, no mean no, that's rape. That motherfucker doesn't deserve to be with a woman ever again. In fact, send that fucker to prison, so he can get his ass repeatedly raped. Just so he can feel what it's like when he says no to Bubba and gets fucked anyway. Yeah, I said it.

Even if she's in the doggy-style position, and her asshole is staring at me, I better not attempt to sneak my pinky finger in her ass either. Let's say I tried to anyway, from that point on, she'll be uncomfortable and tense up. Plus, I've lost her trust and the opportunity of changing her mind, and believe me, you don't want to blow your chance over lack of patience.

The best response a woman can give me when discussing anal sex is, she's never tried it. Depending on her age, I am certain she was asked at least once in her life. Trust is important when it comes down to getting to know someone. Unfortunately, for most men it's a numbers game, how many they can fuck? I'm no saint, I used to be one of those guys years ago, but after I realized how comfortable a woman becomes by taking my time, I earned their trust.

Listen up men, if you don't care about who you're fucking, then don't fuck at all. Not once have I put my cock in a woman's ass, pussy, or mouth I didn't have chemistry with. Men who choose to rush and not prepare the woman for anal sex, fucks it up for any man who follows behind that shit. Now, I will try to convince the woman I know what the fuck I'm doing, and I'm not like the last asshole they were with. Again, that's why it's important for me to get to know the woman first, make her relax and hopefully TRUST me. I don't usually care how long it takes to fuck, as I want the person comfortable enough to want to fuck me. Let me just put this out there, I don't like dating a woman who doesn't like anal sex. For me, I become bored without that being a possibility. Now, if you dated me without having anal sex, I'm sure you just had an aha moment, right?

Anal Technician

inally, here's my technique. After you've had a mature conversation –about anal sex, make sure your nails are cleaned and trimmed. Don't you fucking dare go from ass to pussy and that includes your fingers, cock, toes, or butt plug. Fuck it, let's just say, whatever you pulled out of her ass doesn't go into the pussy, unless it has been thoroughly cleaned. And, if she tenses up, don't let that be the deciding factor to stop having fun. The rest of this chapter is based on trust. Otherwise, don't even think about it.

Back to Anal Technician: While eating her pussy, gradually play with her ass with only one finger, very slowly at the beginning (without penetrating). Eating the pussy and playing with her ass with your fingers should be a pleasurable distraction, with lubrication on your fingers.

As she relaxes (you'll notice) the phobia she had about anal sex will start to fade. Keep licking her pussy and slowly insert one finger inside her ass slowly. You'll know if you are doing this correctly because you will have her cumming or squirting all over your face or as I said before, she'll tense up.

Keep listening and watching for cues from the way she's responding to what you are doing, and if she's enjoying it, you'll know. Continue eating her pussy and eventually insert two fingers into her ass slowly. While your two fingers are inside her ass up to the second joint, start moving in a circular motion as before. Continue licking dat clit until you're able to get three fingers into her ass up to the second knuckle. I am certain you are asking yourself, why three fingers up to the second knuckle right? Because three fingers should be equivalent to the width of your cock. And if you're using my secret handy dandy circular motion, it's stretching the opening of her ass, and now she's ready for anal penetration. Lubricating her ass is the key; I can't stress that enough. If you are as nasty as I am, then shit on your cock won't faze you. Just clean it up with soap and water and stick it back in. But if fresh hot shit grosses you out, then I suggest you wear a condom.

This technique works best if your cock is under five inches in girth, if you're thicker, you will have to stretch the asshole more, some women are okay with that, others aren't. I've even known women who preferred girth over length of the cock because they like their ass stretched out. They even use their own hand deep into their asses. For me, I've never gone more than four fingers, knuckles deep, into a woman's ass. You might even run across a woman that enjoys fisting. I've never personally met one, but I'm sure they're out there with the other mythical creatures of the world. Four fingers up their ass seems insane to me, but who am I to say what's insane? That's my technique for having anal sex with someone that hasn't given you an absolute hell no.

If she is willing to try anal then take your time, go slow, use lubrication, and keep building TRUST. One finger, then two, and three in a circular motion inside, preparing and stretching the asshole. I've found success with this method, who knows what else she's willing to do.

Authoritative Vs Demeaning

If you are a married couple and still have sex, I would like to offer one of my favorite things to do in a car. When a woman is wearing pants with no panties in my car, it won't take long before I give her that look. Kinda like "The Rock." If we are going somewhere together and the trip is going to take a couple of hours, I'll make her pull down her pants slowly and take them off. The last person I told to do this was shy, and you could tell by how red her face became. I know what you are thinking, do I only date White women? I'm not responding to that question in this chapter. Anyway, her being shy was turning me on, so I said it in an authoritative voice. I said authoritative, not demeaning, there is a substantial difference. If you are a male reading this and you don't know the difference, let me give you just two fucking examples.

Demeaning: Dumb ass bitch, just pull down your fucking pants will ya, can't you just do what the fuck I tell you, without repeating myself! Damn, you are slow as fuck!

Authoritative: Baby, take your pants off slowly, lean back and play with your pussy, and you better not cum until I tell you. Now, which one is better? Wait! This all depends on how she likes being addressed. Only you would know, so choose wisely.

I had to reassure her that no one can see through my tinted windows from the passenger side, that's how shy she was. As the reader of this chapter, if this is something you want to try, I have one major suggestion, make sure that the fucking doors are locked, especially the passenger door. Click the button that locks the doors and can't reopened under any circumstances. I will not be accountable for anyone falling out of your vehicle. I just don't want you to unlock the door accidently. There's nothing better than a woman with her back against the passenger door and facing me with her legs wide open. Close your eyes and just imagine this scene, while you are in the emergency lane briefly, just so you can look over at her pussy and even reach over there and play with her clit just a little bit. Hell. I am certain she's wet as fuck right about now, depending on her age, LOL. Ladies, if you are in my car half naked, and in the emergency lane briefly, I may lick my fingers a little bit and stick it inside your pussy. I'm certainly not doing this while the car is in motion, that's dangerous as fuck and may cause an accident. I know what you're thinking, I'm doing all that while parked? Yes, that was back in the day.

I don't do that shit anymore because I don't drive as much as I used to. I've had enough women in my car back in the day who took off their panties from under their dress so from the waist down, they are naked. I really don't need an energy drink, if I have my baby girl playing with her clit while I'm driving. Listening to her playing with herself and not looking over is a nice tease also. The entire time she is over their playing with her pussy, you may want to pull over, I guarantee it.

To all you married couples that've been together so fucking long you've forgotten how to be all sexy, then it's time to spice it up. I can't tell ya how many times I met a woman that has not had these experiences. I know it's the fucking car, but damn! As a couple, if you both become used to fucking in the bed and that's it, that's a damn shame, what a waste. How do two freaky ass people end up just having sex in the bedroom? If you both come to that conclusion of keeping sex to the bedroom, then that's fine, I guess. But if both of you still have freak in ya, then talk about it. I would not want to be in a relationship where every time I thought of sex and initiated it, all I heard was, we need to wait till we get home. I'll tell you right now, the person that keeps hearing wait till we get home will eventually find somebody that will say yes. This does not apply to men that already have a freaky ass woman at home and still think they gotta fuck around and lie.

Those motherfuckers need help. Swinging is different because that's a mutual decision to fuck other people. But, as a man, if you already got a freaky attractive wife or girlfriend at home and you still feel the need to fuck around, then you just don't love yourself. You mean to tell me, your freaky significant other will suck your dick and swallow your cum. She likes gagging on your cock, because she likes it; you can slap your cock against her face, because she likes it; you can pull her hair while you fuck her in the ass, because she likes it, and she squirts on command? Damn brah! The fact she'll let you do all of that because she trusts you, and yet, you're gonna fuck around on her still? Man to man, if you are becoming bored with your partner, try role-playing. Spend some time at a strip club clothing place in your city somewhere.

Google or Bing sexy clothes or garments for her to wear, if needed. Hopefully, the time you put into this idea will not go unrewarded. If she happens to notice your effort, who knows, right? If she's game, imagine her as a stranger and produce a name that suits the look you have chosen for her. Peace.

Bad Boys and Good Girls

 **I**t amazes me how women tend to want someone who has that bad boy mentality, because with that mentality, you also get a player. These bad boys typically have a don't give a fuck attitude and at least two other women at the minimum, but for sure, one other bitch out there somewhere who they're fucking occasionally.

Ladies, if a good-looking guy has his shit together, he's fucking someone somewhere, trust me. And, when I say has his shit together, I mean he has charisma and takes care of himself emotionally and physically. He can keep your attention without mentioning sex and, at the same time, have you laughing your ass off. In addition, he has a nice car, a roof over his head, and great taste in clothing. Granted, some women's bar is set so fucking low and considers a guy with his shit together having on saggy ass pants, a fake ass gold grill in his mouth and driving a car with gold thirty-inch rims on it. How about those muthafuckas that have on wife beater T-shirts and don't have a toilet to shit in, while living with their mommas. Some girls like that, and that's okay but most don't. I consider those types of girl's hood rats. Again, I say there's nothing wrong with it, it's a personal preference, I get it.

I repeat, whatever preference turns you on, keep in mind, he has at least one bitch nearby he's fucking occasionally. Please, don't try to have a relationship with this muthafucka either, thinking you're going to be the only woman in his life. I'm certain he knows of some decent pussy within a ten-to-fifteen-mile radius of his residence. The chances of him not seeing someone is rare. It could also be a warning, or should I say, a sign of behavioral problems. I've never been able to understand how women could consider a long-lasting relationship with a bad boy. Before even getting involved, her instincts should be screaming, he's going to fuck around on me at some point or another. And when your instincts tell you that he is fucking someone else, ask. We all know he may just lie about it. In that case, if you have facts to back it up, then pack up and leave that muthafucka.

As an alpha male, you should be brutally honest from the very beginning. If a woman asks if you are seeing anyone else, then your answer needs to be, "Yes, I am fucking someone occasionally," and especially, if you are. Just keep dat shit. Don't say whatever you think she wants to hear. When you're not being truthful, you fuck it up for every man that comes into her life afterwards. There is only one question a woman should ask if she's considering getting involved with a single male: When was the last time you had sex? If he says it's been within a month, I'll say that's an honest man. You, as the woman, must figure out if you still want to be involved with him, or decide just to hook up with him occasionally, as a booty call.

If a monogamous relationship is your preference, there is no way in hell you're going to change him until he's ready to change for himself. You have a couple of choices, you can either shut the fuck up and keep seeing him or move on. Here's my thoughts, if early into the relationship you have a gut feeling that makes you uncomfortable, then why stress about something you have absolutely no control over; is that one man worth all that? Ladies let's keep it real, if a guy looks good to you, other women are looking at him too. And more than likely saying to themselves, he's fuckable. He may not be married, but he's fucking another woman somewhere.

Thank him for being honest with you. It gives you an opportunity to make a choice on what's going to work best for your current situation. When women don't ask the question, usually, they don't want to hear the truth. Men appreciate directness, if it's important to you, ask. He's entitled to ask the same question of you, and to receive an honest answer. I've come to the realization that women can turn off their sexual desires for months, and in some cases, years. That all depends on how the previous relationship ended. Hey ladies, take your time before being involved with a man and keep it simple, and only be involved with someone who is being honest from the very beginning. More than likely not everything will be ideal, just evaluate what's important to you and your journey going forward.

Earlier on in my life, I've juggled five or six women at a time. The one thing I never did was lie about it. Fortunately for me, I was never asked specifically how many women I was seeing at the same time. If someone would have asked, I would have been honest. I always told the truth, and sometimes it pissed off the woman that asked. I always thought to myself, well fuck, you asked me. My opinion, the type of man that can be trusted is a nerdy, big, fat, unhealthy eating motherfucker. A below average earner, with four inches erect cock, and very seldom wipes his own ass. That's right, I guarantee, he's not out there fucking anybody, except prostitutes. So, if you want to get involved with that motherfucker, rest assured he's not going to be out there slinging his cock around like the married man I mentioned in another chapter. He will worship the ground you walk on.

I've had my fair share of dealing with attractive women, and when I do, I already have in my head that they might be fucking someone else. I've always said, if she's giving me some of her attention, that's all I need to proceed. I do not give a damn who else she's fucking, I am okay with being among the men she likes fucking. I don't want or need to be all up in her business either if she's giving me the pussy, or better yet, the ass. And what about these jealous bitch ass motherfuckers with attractive girlfriends. You know the ones, when another man is walking towards them, he reaches out for her hand, then pulls her closer to kiss her. I've seen it happen so many fucking times when I approach a couple.

To me, that shows he's not confident within his relationship. How in the fuck can you have an attractive partner and think nobody should look at her? I know I'm wired differently because I'm always confident, and I don't pretend to be anyone other than who I am. The way I look at it, if I'm not the one for this woman, that's fine, I'll find somebody else. I don't think I'm all that for every woman, in fact, I know I'm not. I absolutely don't understand men lacking confidence in their relationships. Fellas, when you met the woman that you're with now, did you think she was attractive when you initially met her? If the answer is yes, are you expecting other men to not look at her now that you are fucking her? As far back as I can remember, I'm not out intentionally looking for someone to whom I am not attracted. Here is another thing I can't understand, if you are the man fucking, you're attractive significant other, why does it matter if she wants to wear something sexy? If either one of you have jealous tendencies, please seek a therapist as soon as possible.

Two times in my life I have felt jealousy creep into my head. As soon as I realized it, I put myself in check and have not felt like this since. I have one more thought that I'd like to share with you. I knew this one White woman who had the ass of a Black woman, and that's only assuming most Black women have big asses. We were at a movie theater, and she was buying popcorn because I bought the tickets. While she was walking away, I watched two women looking at her ass while talking among themselves. Do you think I became jealous? The answer is hell no. In fact, I looked at the two women and I smiled. My white woman's ass was PHAT. I never told her why I bought tight fitting jeans for her. Sometimes I would intentionally let her walk ahead of me, and I'm sure you know the reason. And if you don't, I'll tell you why, because she had this big juicy PHAT ass. I even saw a man get slapped by the woman he was walking with. No, I don't have jealousy issues obviously.

Big Clit & the Black Freak

ne White chick named Lexie, I met here in Florida, was married to a truck driver. He was okay with his wife occasionally finding Black men on the Internet to come to their apartment and fuck her. We only had a few conversations before she invited me to her place. The moment I walked in the door, she warned me, before she even closed the door, about her big clit and pussy lips right up front. I thought it was weird and not necessary. Before meeting me, she had warned every man she met online about her pussy. It soon made sense why Lexie felt the need to warn me as I entered her apartment.

Every one of those assholes she told, laughed, or freaked out, turned around immediately, and walked back out the front door. I am certain that had a lot to do with her trying to prepare me. I walked in and sat down on her couch, she was hesitant, so we talked for a little while to make her more comfortable. In fact, face to face is entirely different from talking on the phone. Lexie's body language told me everything I needed to know. I asked her to stand up in front of me, there was still some hesitancy. I was OKAY with that because I knew where it was coming from. She finally stood up and took off her dress, her face was red as a firetruck.

I'll admit, when Lexie lifted her dress and showed me her pussy ... OH MY GOD ... it turned me on like you would not believe! She had the biggest pussy lips and clit I had ever seen on a woman. Her pussy hole was big enough to look up inside her; it didn't close. Even though it looked beat up and sloppy, it still turned me on; it was something I had never seen before. I told you, something is fucked up about me. When she realized I was turned on looking at her big, thick, sloppy- looking pussy, it turned her on even more. She was game for anything at that point, once she realized how open-minded I was.

While there, I took my cell phone back out of my front pocket, and called another freaky ass Black chick named Natasha, who I also met online. I asked her to come over and join me at Lexie's house. When Natasha walked in, I did not waste any time and told Lexie to take off Natasha's clothes. It was quick, because Natasha only had on a sun dress with no panties and no bra. I told Natasha to face Lexie so that Lexie could lift her dress up and over her head while her arms were in the air. As soon as Natasha's dress was past her nipples, both Lexie and I was excited immediately.

I told Natasha and Lexie to start eating each other's pussy, which they did with no hesitation. While they were on the floor, an idea popped into my head. I told them both to lay down on their backs, while I grabbed the double-headed dildo. I brought one just in case. I inserted one end into Natasha and the other end into Lexie, the palm of my hand in the middle of the dildo going back and forth, fucking both their pussies at the same time.

I knew the neighbors heard everything, she lived in a hallway and her apartment was right in the middle. They both wanted to suck my cock, and I wasn't ready for that at the time. Unbelievably, I was suddenly shy, what dafuck! Afterwards, I knew Lexie enjoyed herself, she called her husband while he was still on the road and gave him the details of our evening together. I am certain he was jacking off while she was telling him what happened. That was the first and only time I had ever done that. I never saw either woman again, but what amazing memories I have. We all had a blast. I'm sure there are women who fuck themselves with double-headed dildos. If any of you ladies out there reading this need help with holding the dildo, you know how to find me.

Saving the best for last, while there with these two ladies, I bent Lexie and Natasha over doggy style and had them turn the opposite direction with the bottom of their feet touching. Then I told these two freaky girls to arch their backs until their elbows were on the floor. That's when I brought out a different double- headed dildo. I inserted one end inside Lexie's ass and the other end in Natasha's. I proceeded to use both hands to fuck them both with the dildo. Fuck it, I'll say it, there was cum and shit all over the place. Sometimes, I wish I knew where all these ideas came from. Back then, I wasn't watching any porn to get these ideas, and I certainly shown any of this freaky shit by my parents or my gay ass cousin. I am certain whoever is reading this right now may have done far more than I. One day I hope to have a convention of nothing but the freakiest people on the planet all under one roof, one love.

Bitch Got Me Fucked Up

 **remember** this one bitch named Mya, on the first date, I took her to listen to a house band together. When we arrived, she was impressed with the place I chose. From as far back as I can remember, I've always had a ballplayer mentality while living on a Top-Ramen budget. Of course, it's the kind of place where you must tip $10 to the parking attendant. The walk in was always very impressive because it made you feel as if you were walking the red carpet. Once you walked through the door, you would see lit candles on roundtables, the host would walk up with a smile on her face, and you would follow her to the table she had chosen for you. You take a seat and enjoy the surroundings while waiting for the band to start playing contemporary jazz. The kind of place where you better wear name brand clothing. No more than two minutes after sitting down, a waiter came over to our table and asked if she and I wanted anything to drink.

Before I could look up at the waiter to tell her not now, this bitch, wait sorry, I meant Mya, ordered a double iced tea with lemon. You know I had to order one just to fit in. The server came back to my table and said, "That will be forty-three dollars."

I said, "What?" I asked my date in these exact words, "What the fuck did you order?"

She looked down while laughing and said, "Oh! I ordered a double iced tea with lemon."

I said to myself, *Bitch, you got me fucked up.* After paying for the drinks, I told Mya, I'll be back in a few minutes. I had to act fast, so I walked over to the waiter who served us those expensive fucking drinks. I leaned over and whispered, "Do not come back to our table," and I tipped her ten dollars. The way I looked at it, tipping the waiter $10 was better than my date ordering another round of double iced teas with lemon, right? I must have been around twenty-three years old when this happened to me. Even at twenty-six, I had enough wisdom to not be played by a female. I did not see Mya after that; she had my wallet confused with motherfucking Shaquille O'Neal's.

I did not give ah fuck how fine that bitch was either, she ain't going to use me again after this last and final date. I can't blame Mya for assuming I had ballplayer money, ballplayers spoil the fuck out of bitches like her, just for pussy.

That's never been my attitude; I had to work for everything I wanted. I know what you're thinking, pimping that was different. If I do not get sixty-forty in a fucking relationship with me being sixty and her forty, though depending on how fine she is I might do seventy-thirty, fuck that shit I'm out. Bitches can easily find men who are stupid enough to pay 100 percent of everything and haven't fucked. I am going to say these three words again, fuck that shit. I like dating bitches where if I buy the tickets to the movies, they get the snacks, or vice versa. I ain't got a problem with that.

Choking the Snow Bunny

NY man who has fucked an of abundance women should know they are like unicorns. There is no reason to think, what pleases one woman will please another. Every woman on this planet is uniquely different sexually, and that's something that takes time and patience to discover. Speaking of being uniquely different, not all women like to be choked while fucking them. Before choking the fuck out of a bitch, I make no assumption all women like rough sex. Here are twelve questions I have asked and so should you, before having vanilla sex:

- ✓ What was sex like with your past partner?
- ✓ Do you like to experiment with toys?
- ✓ Do you play with yourself?
- ✓ Can you cum vaginally?
- ✓ Can you cum from anal?
- ✓ Does your clitoris need to be stimulated to have an orgasm?
- ✓ How do you feel about rough sex?
- ✓ Have you ever been slapped in general and where? Did you like it?
- ✓ Have you ever been choked? Who did it and why?

✓ What kind of relationship do you have with your father and mother?
✓ When, and with who, did you realize you liked to be choked?
✓ Can you cum without being choked?

These are extremely important questions to ask before fucking a unicorn. That is if you plan to have sex again. The reason for asking questions is to disguise the choke question. Imagine asking, do you like being choked as the first question. She will assume that's all you like and want from her, or him to be politically correct. Besides, attempting to do something so fucked up as choking, you betta make damn sure she or he is into it.

Some women like being choked while fucking, especially Lara. While fucking her, something came over me to grab her by the throat and choke her while having rough sex. She trusted me enough to know I was aware of what the fuck I was doing, for her safety and mine. While choking her, I carefully watched her face turn slightly red, and I knew she was okay. At any time, if her face became a dark reddish color, I'd loosen up my grip and listen to her breathing. After a couple of minutes, I watched her face become dark and reddish in color as I was prepared for. I held her throat long for her to feel helpless, but Lara knew what I was doing. While Lara was masturbating and using a vibrator on her clit, she was being choked. The combination must have sent her through the roof. The next thing I knew, her eyes rolled into the back of her head, and she froze for three seconds. I was inches from her face and witnessed the transformation as it was happening like in part one of *The Exorcist*.

It scared the hell out of me when her hand released the vibrator, and she dropped it between her legs. She was staring at the ceiling like she was possessed by the devil. Like the priest in *The Exorcist* throwing holy water, she just snapped out of it right before my eyes and asked me what happened. I explained what happened in complete detail and all she said was, do it again. Lara got me fucked up. Oh, hell naw! Imagine if I had made a mistake and the police had showed up? As an older Black man and Lara in her early thirties, trying to describe what happened while choking a White girl would not have gone well for me. The only thing that would have saved my Black ass would have been a Black jury, judge, and prosecuting attorney. In fact, the officers would have to believe my story and lied on the report saying, it was an accident. I damn sure would not have been convicted, in their minds, they would say she had it coming, deliberated for two hours, and acquitted me of all charges.

If a juror had been asked about the case and why deliberation only took two minutes, the juror would have said, she got what she deserved for fucking a Black man, case dismissed. Btw, it was a unanimous decision. To this very day, I haven't done that again. I'm not going to jail or prison over a kinky ass White girl. Fuck dat shit, no one is worth that.

DIFFERENT SCENE WITH LARA

Another time between Lara and me, she was sleeping at my apartment while I was at work. While driving home, I wondered if she would be awake or asleep. Honestly, there is nothing better than walking in, and your girl is sleeping in your bed. As I walked up to the door, I quietly put the key in and opened the door. In fact, Lara must have heard the front door open and close. All I heard walking down the hallway, was her getting back into my bed pretending she was snoring. So, I stood in the doorway looking at her half-naked, ass up and face down. Obviously, by her hurrying up and getting back into my bed the covers were on the floor.

She knew I was staring at her in the doorway, because she arched her back and slightly opened her legs, just enough to see her nicely shaved pussy. I was thinking of all sorts of nasty thoughts I could do to that bitch while she was lying in my bed sleeping. I took off my shoes, socks, and everything else. Once I was done taking off my clothes, I snatched the covers off her and firmly placed the palm of my hand in the middle of her back. I told her in a firm commanding voice, "Don't you dare move until I cum." Then I grabbed her blonde hair, and I pinned her down in one of my favorite positions, spit on my cock, and I shoved it in her ass.

I came in five minutes, while she slept face down, ass up. I would not have tried that with a one-night stand but knowing what somebody likes and what you can get away with is more exciting. She liked rough sex sometimes, and I didn't mind providing it occasionally. If you are wondering what ended our relationship, she felt the need to lie unnecessarily. You have read enough about me to know, I am non-judgmental, right? There was nothing she could have done or said that would have made me feel differently about her. Lying to me will not be tolerated and I don't give a fuck who you are. Peace!!

Crazy Ass Latina Chick

hile working in the Altamonte Springs area, there was this five-foot tall Puerto Rican girl named Lisa who flirted with me. Every time we saw each other, there was a lot of flirtation with eye contact. She was so damn cute, and we looked forward to seeing each other every morning while she was delivering and stocking the floral cooler. At the time, I worked as a forklift driver in the foods department and her flower stand was near one of my aisles. Every time I saw her, I intentionally made sure I was in the general area. Our conversations were genuine, and I always looked forward to watching her walk down the main aisle, with her big juicy ass, and a shopping basket full of fresh flowers. Occasionally, her husband came in with her, depending on how many flowers were sold the day before. Obviously, while her husband was around, our behavior was different.

It was always strange for both of us when Lisa's husband, Joe, was with her. Every time his back was turned, we smiled as if we had a secret. I didn't have to flirt to get her attention like most guys I worked with. I've always been confident and realized by coming on too strong, it makes a man look thirsty and weak. At some point, my back was hurting so badly, that I had to miss a few months from work. When I was home recovering, I'll admit, I missed flirting with her. I didn't have her cell number so there was no way to text or call her. Never mind the fact she's married, which reminds me of a song by Billy Paul, "Me and Mrs. Jones." That will forever be our song.

I wasn't aware Lisa was missing me; after a few weeks, she knew something was wrong. She kept asking everyone where I was, and someone from work gave her my phone number. She reached out to me and told me that she missed me and asked if I was okay. Eventually, she asked if she could stop by and see me. I seriously did not have a problem with that, considering I had not seen her for a while. In her first visit alone with me, I knew something special was about to happen. One thing led to another, and before you knew it, we were kissing. Oh man, she was a fun little thang to kiss!

If I had known the things I know now, licking Lisa's pussy would have been on the menu. My skills today would have fucked her head up for sure. Back then, I had a shy conservative personality. I guess without licking her pussy, I must have been doing something she liked. I'll explain why "she must have liked it" below.

Besides the fact we used to fuck in Lisa's bed while her husband was away, she started to get fucking weird crazy on me. She'd show up at my fucking door, no call, no text, nothing. This bitch (notice I'm calling her a bitch now) is married and shows up at my motherfucking door? I absolutely hated that shit then and even today. One time she was at my home (unannounced) again, while I was making some deliveries for a business I owned. Pay attention to what I am about to say next: One afternoon, Lisa knocked on my door and there was no answer, then she rang the doorbell, yes, no answer. Then she decided to call me and said, "I'm at your door, let me in." Are you reading this part and scratching your head? Because, if you are not, then you should be.

I asked Lisa if she saw my fucking truck around the side of my house, she replied, "Well, no."

"Then it's a good chance I'm not home," I said sarcastically.

She told me, she'll wait for me in her car, and then had the audacity to tell me to hurry up. What the fuck! I explained it was going to be a while, and I didn't have any idea what time I'd be back. Dear reader, while writing this, there is something I am saying to myself: I was acting like a little bitch back then. I say this because I should have told that bitch to take her married ass home. Additionally, I should have not been explaining myself either.

Lisa didn't seem to care and said she'd wait anyway. That bitch waited two fucking hours at my front door before she finally left. She was acting like that all without licking her pussy, I must have been doing something she wasn't getting at home. Can you believe she was mad at me because I didn't stop my deliveries, I thought to myself, *Bitch, you're fucking married and you're acting like you're single and shit.*

I should have started with this: she was adventurous and liked to try different things. One time she wanted to fuck in the backyard, without a tall fence or wall. We could have easily been seen if anyone had been walking by, as there were some lazy ass muthafuckas that lived in the same neighborhood. And those same lazy ass muthafuckas would climb over my wall, instead of walking around the corner into the neighborhood.

Anyways, we laid a blanket out in the backyard, her idea, and fucked. It was fun, but I was concerned about the ants I knew were in my yard. I knew if we laid a blanket on an anthill, red ants could get on my dick or crawl up into her pussy. I nutted quick, and we rushed our asses back into the house. Never mind the fact someone could easily see us from the other side of the brick wall.

Another time Lisa called and told me she brought a friend with her and was waiting for me to come home. Of course, it was the one day I had a full load of furniture on my trailer, and a long day ahead of me. I really wanted to stop my deliveries and come home so fucking bad, but just couldn't. I couldn't fucking believe my luck; I was so fucking mad. I could only imagine her friend being cute as a motherfucker, and I could have had them both. Eventually, we stopped seeing each other; she was married and the delivery business I had was more important than fucking two horny bitches. Occasionally, when I reflect, I'm extremely happy I had the common sense to know she would have been a problem. The way she was behaving could have caused a lot of problems for me.

What woman in her right mind would tell a man to stop what he's doing when he has a business to run. What woman in her right mind would wait in front of someone's home for two hours. And what woman in her right mind would eat where she shits?

Crazy Shit in San Diego

grew up at 4110 Hemlock Street in San Diego, California. Growing up, I was a loner and was always picked on because of my height, and anyone who was shorter felt they had something to prove. And they could easily prove it with me because I was never a kid that fought back. I was bullied and cried like a little bitch. One kid used to bully me, and I don't know where the courage came from, but I decided that enough was enough. I said, "Look, man, I am not backing down. I'm not crossing the fucking street anymore. Leave me alone." I said something to that effect, and what do you know? The weirdest thing, as much as he was a bully, he stopped. We became friends after that; I stood up to him and I learned something from that.

Let us get into the darker shit, for example, where my kinky nasty ass sexual desires came from. I don't even know, I have no clue, but if I were going to reflect, I'd say I was a pervert early in life. Honestly, it could have been at birth as far as I'm concerned. One day I was playing with my cock with soap, just playing with it like kids do, when suddenly this white shit came out of my cock hole.

I didn't know what it was, but it felt good. I'm like, wow, what was that? I'm shaking and carrying on, loving the feeling. I wait a while and do it again, more white stuff came out. I quickly became addicted to jacking off all the time, of course, there were no girls in my life yet.

I was always trying to figure out new ways to jack off. If I use my hand, that works. I asked myself, what else can I put my cock in so I can cum? I was at this cemetery one time and was so horny. I decided to stick my cock in a can meant for flowers, you know, with dirt in it. I was grinding in the grass with my cock in this can of dirt, but I just couldn't cum. After a while I said, *okay this don't feel right*. I needed a different kind of hole. This is a glimpse of my life that a lot of you may not understand. And those of you who do understand, I have much love for you in allowing me to express myself. Am I taking a chance? Yes, of course, I am going to be criticized, and damn near crucified, but it's okay. I am sixty-three years old, and at this point, I have seen and done some things that most people are secretive about.

Over the years, I have seen and heard about the crazy shit people do living in San Diego, things that would make you cringe when it comes to sex, and in most cases, their own families don't know about it. I'd like you to brace yourself for what am about to say next. I've had a woman privately tell me that she allowed her dog to fuck and cum in her, and another woman told me she likes when her dog licks her pussy. Now that had my attention for some fucked up reason. I just had to ask, "How are you able to make the dog lick your pussy?" You would never guess how. She used creamy peanut butter, go figure. That response made me even more curious, which led me to ask another question, "Why peanut butter?"

She looked at me with a straight face and said, "Because dogs like peanut butter and they tend to lick it as opposed to trying to bite or eat it."

Well, I'll be damned! That explanation made sense to me, and I had no more questions to ask her, oh hell naw! I'm not sure what it is about me, but people tend to tell me their darkest secrets (apart from if they've murdered someone). Once they tell me, I look at that person with a poker face, as if I already knew. I'm not easily shocked by what people are into, there are a multitude of options out there, and personally, IDGAF either. I'm aware that having sex with a fucking animal, well, it's sick enough, but there's far worse on the Internet and that's all I'm going to say. FYI, the reason I know there's some sick shit on the Internet is because most of it I've jacked off to. LOL.

So, if that is you, and you can relate to something I wrote about, you are not alone. You can act as if you have never met me or reach out and acknowledge me anonymously, it's okay. Nobody needs to know all the fucked-up shit you've gone through and experienced. Some people will not risk admitting they're closet freaks, as I've done, in fear of being misunderstood and criticized. You shouldn't give a damn because it's something that has made you who you are today. The same people that may judge you for buying or reading this book are the same muthafuckas reading it privately. I am prepared for whatever criticism that is coming my way. Matter of fact, I anticipate it.

So, I'll tell you now, do not read the rest of this book if you feel what you have read so far is disturbing, or if you have a weak stomach or if you feel I'm not going to heaven. I don't need you slinging your holy water at me unexpectedly. I'm not sure where you started in this book, so all I can say is this book is not for the weak. It is for open-minded people who understand and realize people have their kinks. If you have read this far, then good luck.

Dear Momma, Beatrice Hicks

**ear Momma**, Beatrice Hicks was cremated on June 25th, 1998, and I want to give a personal shout out to Anderson-Ragsdale Mortuary on 5050 Federal Blvd, San Diego, CA 92102. They managed my mom's burial with class and professionalism. In fact, during a crucial time in my life, they oversaw the details precisely. I was a momma's boy, I'm trying not to cry as I am drafting this book and will only mention her in this chapter. So, bear with me as I tell you a little bit about her. I know most of us, not all of us, will say this about our momma: she

was the sweetest giving mom you would want in your life. Well, she was. She would give you her last dollar and starve herself a few days if you needed it. I knew this to be true because I watched her loan money to my cousin, that no good muthafucka who never paid her back. When I close my eyes, I can see my cousin's devious smile asking my mom for $20. My mom would say to him, when are you going to pay it back, knowing damn well he was full of shit. Side note, that's why I don't borrow money from anyone because of that lying ass muthafucking cousin, always lying to my momma.

Anyway, I could see the smile on her face, even as I am writing this right now. I see her grayish hair, beautiful brown eyes, dimples, and a smile I'll never forget. To this very day, no one could cook like my momma, and a lot of women have tried but couldn't duplicate it. In my three marriages, I never made any of them feel their cooking wasn't good enough. If you are one of my three wives reading this book, you can smile knowing your cooking never measured up to my mom's and I never admitted it. My momma could make this Nilla banana pudding, and to this day, there was only one place that duplicated it, a restaurant in Georgia. In fact, I immediately thought of my momma as soon as it hit my taste buds, that's how good this banana pudding was. Do you wanna know how good it was? It was so good I was trying to figure out a way it could be mailed to me, while keeping it cold, and hopefully, it kept its texture and taste. If you're thinking what I'm thinking? It must have been some damn good banana pudding, and it was.

So back to my mom again, my mom dealt with a lot from my father. She knew he was cheating on her, but he was also an alcoholic and she dealt with it, as I've already mentioned in another chapter. I'm extremely happy with myself, that I didn't take that after my father and became an alcoholic. I am telling you a little bit about her as I'm trying to convey how close my momma and I were, watching her deal with my father. I finally made a major decision I felt was the right thing to do.

On Monday, July 17th, 2022, I finally released her ashes back into the earth. If you are using a calculator or your fingers and toes, trying to figure out how many years I've had her ashes with me. Well, it was twenty-four years and two months. As bad as I am remembering shit or destroying something, I am shocked that I've had her ashes all those years.

Seriously think about it, I've had my momma's ashes through three marriages, three divorces, a Titanic shipload of single women I fucked, licked, and sucked on, fifteen used cars, such as a Cadillac, Cutlass Supreme, Pontiac Bonneville, just to name a few. Also, one new paid off truck I had for seven years, sixteen years through my last job, two failed businesses, two successful businesses, one home bought, one home lost, three apartment moves, and three move ins. These people were born and died at twenty-two to twenty-four years old: Cooper Noriega, Lil Keed, Sad Frosty, Goonew, Lil Bo Weep. So, yes twenty-four years is an accomplishment as far as I'm concerned. Are you following along with what I am trying to tell you? Allow me to bring this all together for you before I continue this chapter. I have had my mom's ashes with me from June 25th, 1998, until July 17th, 2022. I found a place I could peacefully visit to spread her ashes. Seems to me no sooner than releasing her ashes, a week later, July 24, my revelation revealed itself.

Before my mom kick the bucket, in nineteen ninety-eight, I've known I have an angel following me, and here is an example that I do. Before transferring to another state with one of my ex-wives and still residing in San Diego, I was on Interstate 805 headed to my girlfriend's house. I am not sure where I was coming from, but I do remember where I was headed. Usually when I was on Interstate 805, there was no need to stop and say hello to my momma. During the day, I normally called her at least once, and I always asked if she needed anything from the store.

Considering my momma was unable to drive a vehicle, I always called throughout the day, no matter what, and sometimes twice a day. What was strange, while I was driving, a weird feeling came over me about five miles away from the exit

I would take to visit my momma. The closer I drove towards the exit, the stronger the weird feeling became. I knew I did not have to use the bathroom, and I was not hungry. A few miles away from the exit, I wanted to throw up. Two miles away, the feeling worsened, and I had to pull over for a few minutes. I got out of my car and walked around it during those few minutes. I thought my car was releasing poisonous unscented gas through my car's air conditioning. Not feeling any better, I decided to get back into my car, this time with all four windows completely down.

Seriously y'all, I could not comprehend why that weird feeling wouldn't go away. Whatever that feeling was made me nauseous, and I decided to take the exit towards my mom's house. In fact, a mile away from her house, I started to feel a little better. I'm still confused and don't understand why I felt that way in the first place.

That weird feeling was gone completely after I stopped questioning it. My mom lived no more than thirty minutes from the freeway. My plan was to call her once I had arrived at my girlfriend's house. Please keep in mind, there was no reason to visit my momma that day.

I pulled into the driveway and got out of my car as I usually do; I opened the door and heard momma calling my name. She sounded so distant, as if she were in the backyard, laying down by the bathroom window I used to peek through. I knew something was bizarre because momma was not sitting in her favorite chair. So now I am wondering, *why isn't she in her favorite chair? And why is she calling my name from behind the closed door to the hallway?* I said, "Momma, where are you?"

She said, "I'm in the bathroom."

My first thought was, she must have had an accident, and she didn't want me to walk into the bathroom while she was in there. I looked in her bedroom first to make sure she wasn't in there. Now, I am concerned because she kept calling my name. I walked towards the bathroom and opened the door. Sometimes when you're in shock you can't believe what you are seeing. I stood there in disbelieve, my momma had slipped and fell inside the bathtub sideways. In a panicked state of mind I asked, "What the fuck happened momma?"

Even then, my momma said, "Okay boy, don't you talk like that."

Of course, I had to apologize for my bad choice of words even in that situation. Anyway, if you're thinking why I didn't immediately pull my mom out of the bathtub, I will explain that right now. As far back as I can remember, she has always been a big woman.

Later, she became even heavier, she wasn't working out and eating properly. In other words, she was too heavy to lift out of the bathtub by myself. I had to think quickly what to do, and what came to mind was my neighbor. I left her in the tub sideways, I asked if she was feeling any pain where she had slipped, she said no, and reassured me she was okay. I immediately ran to my neighbor's house, and I thanked the universe he was home. When I told him what happened, he didn't waste any time and walked over to help me. My momma was naked so I'm sure she was embarrassed when my neighbor walked in with me.

I had to reassure her it was okay because I had no other way to lift her big ass out, at least not by myself. I'm damn certain, I hadn't saved enough cheddar (money) to hire a crane service to immediately come out and cut a hole in the roof, just to lift her big ass out of the bathtub, even though the situation called for an emergency. Another thing I am certain about, if I had tried lifting her out of that bathtub while she was sideways, I would not have been able to draft this story, if you know what I'm saying. So, when my neighbor walked in, he was also surprised to see her in that predicament. We stood there scratching our heads, trying to figure out a way to lift her out of the bathtub together. It was like, trying to collectively figure out Chinese calculus, while in China with a teacher who doesn't speak English. Did you just laugh? I did too when I thought of typing it.

My momma had been in that bathtub sideways, for a while. She had a bigger upper body and skinny legs. Therefore, I'm not trying to be funny when I say she reminded me of an ostrich. Why am I mentioning this? Because my neighbor and I knew, once we pulled her out of that bathtub, her ostrich-sized legs would be weak. Neither one of us would be able to keep her upright, without yelling out timber. Besides, we had not placed anything on the floor and walls to cushion her fall. Now it's time to lift my momma out of the bathtub. I remember my hand on her left arm and my neighbor had the right. We counted down together one, two, three, and not like in that movie *Lethal Weapon* with Mel Gibson and Danny Glover. Seriously speaking, we lifted her out gradually at the count of three.

Trust me when I say, this was not an easy task, but we did it. We were able to pull her out of the bathtub, and she was able to stand up all on her own. There she was, standing there in her birthday suit with no candles to blow out. Our neighbor left shortly afterwards. He knew while she was standing there naked, my mom was embarrassed to say the least. I'm shocked that he and I were able to do it because my neighbor, who was already in his sixties, was frail. All of that doesn't matter now, does it? He and I were able to pull her out, without the crane services I mentioned earlier. If my neighbor and I could have chosen one theme song to be played while lifting my momma out the bathtub, it would have been *Rocky* starring Sylvester Stallone and written by Bill Conti.

When he left, I asked my mom how long she had been in that position; she told me at least two hours. I cried right there in front of her as I'm doing right now. It was impossible for me to believe my momma had been in that position, in the bathtub for two plus hours, without the telephone near her to call 9-1-1. That had to have been the universe doing everything in its power to make sure that I went home that day. If I had not gone home, I would not have found out until the next day. Who knows what could have happened if I had not gone home.

That had to have been the reason I was feeling weird while on the freeway. Did I or didn't I say earlier that I have an angel following me? Since then, I have not felt the weird feeling that haunted me. What other explanations are there for the feeling I was having while driving? I told you a little bit about my mom to give you an idea of how spiritually and emotionally connected we were. Since that day, I always pay attention when I feel something within me. It's not failed me this far. It's the same feeling I have drafting this book; I feel propelled to tell this story. This is not about glorifying my sexual activities or should I say my discretions. It's about sharing and inspiring others.

My Revelation:

I typed everything above to say this. On July 24th, 2022, Sunday around four o'clock in the morning, I woke up out of a deep sleep from crying and looked up at the ceiling. My pillow was soaked, and my covers were damp. I laid there wondering what the fuck was I dreaming about because now I can't go back to sleep. Here I am wide awake, crying and trying to snap out of it. If it had been a nightmare, that's something I could have remembered easily.

Whatever that feeling was totally caught me off guard. In fact, most times, I'll figure everything out. This time I could not, which made me uncomfortable. I laid in my bed for over an hour, and the entire time, I was crying uncontrollably. At some point, I started questioning myself, as to why and where this was coming from. The only thing I can contribute it to is, just before going to sleep, I was reflecting on all the women I either fucked, dated, married, and had one-night stands with. Consequently, and disturbingly, I realized monogamy hasn't been easy throughout my entire dating and married life.

I could not figure out why I have not been faithful to the women I've met. I even cheated on my first girlfriend in San Diego. I am trying to think back at the time of writing this chapter, has there been just one damn woman with whom I've ever been monogamous. If I were my own psychiatrist, I now have a diagnosis because I woke up crying.

I attribute it to my father cheating on my mom, which I've already mentioned in one of my chapters. My uncle cheated on his wives and girlfriends.

The reason I know this to be a fact, I was with him when he was doing it. On many occasions, I have watched every woman he was involved with cry and beg me to set him straight. Like at that age I would know how to do that. Sometimes these women would pull me aside and ask me questions about his day-to-day routines. They wanted me to spy on my uncle. When my uncle found out I was reporting back to those women, I paid the price for it. It wasn't fair to me because the women asked me, he was fucking over. I didn't know the difference, to me what he was doing was perfectly normal. I was always in the middle of everyone else's lies.

My brother-in-law cheated on his wife because he told me. He would pull me aside sometimes and tell me about his affairs with other women. I was fascinated by his stories as he always made them sound interesting. He made an affair sound like something men do. Many times, he would brag about all the women he was fucking even though he was married to my aunt. It's a damn shame now that I think about it, they had no idea how confusing they were going to make my life become as an adult.

In one of my chapters, I talked about married couples who came to my home and had their affairs. My most impressionable years have been around dishonest people. When I think about it, it seemed perfectly normal at the time, not realizing the long-term effects it would have on me as an adult. I remember this one woman I was dating, everything was going well, so I thought. While at the beach, holding hands, she suddenly stopped and faced me. She then looked me straight into my eyes and asked had I slept with someone the night before. I've always been a straight up person as far back as I can remember. That's one thing I am glad I didn't take from my brother-in-law and cousin.

Well, that's a lie, I would if I felt someone would be hurt from it. In fact, that's what I watched repeatedly from the adults that were in my life as a child. Nevertheless, I responded with a yes, she cussed me out and hit my arm with her fist. Even then as angry as she was, I could not understand why she was so upset with me. I have always thought honesty is the best policy, but that wasn't the case. I was hesitant responding to her question because how did she know.

Her intuition about me must have prepared her for the answer to her question. Once I admitted the truth, she was quiet and asked me to take her home in an angry voice. That truth ended our relationship right then and there. By no means am I asking for forgiveness, just to understand, why I am the way I am. No wonder why I can relate to someone who behaves like myself. No wonder why I am relatable for people who are going through this and unaware why. So, this makes me a hypocrite because I cheated while being married (which was three times) by the way. While one of them was working, I had two different women inside our home and fucked one of them on our carpet.

I was always so damn horny while she was at work than when she was at home. I found myself jacking off a lot while watching porn and would shoot cum all over our carpet and never cleaned it up. One day she asked, "What are all those stains on the carpet?"

I just shrugged my shoulders and said, "I don't know." There was a White woman I got involved with that lived ten minutes away. That is one of the women that I fucked on our carpet while my wife was at work. This is the same White woman I was involved with for about a year of my marriage. The White woman finally got enough courage and broke it off with me.

That same woman met a nice man and they got married, and the interesting thing is, she even invited me to their wedding. I remember shaking his hand, saying how nice she was as if she was my coworker, so I'm sure he didn't have a clue who I really was.

Here I am talking about other couples who are married and cheated on their wives or should I say, their significant other. Side note, I must be politically correct these days, that's why I changed it from wives to significant other. So, ladies and gentlemen, I will end this chapter with saying this: when you meet someone for the first time, you're meeting their representative. The only way you can truly know who you're dealing with, you must go back to their childhood before you judge them. And before judging them, check your own closet, make sure you don't have any baggage you're bringing into the situation.

If nothing I have said in this chapter convinces you why people act the way they do, then maybe you need to reflect on your own childhood. When you do, I guarantee you it will emerge unexpectedly. In fact, just like me, you won't be able to comprehend why you respond or manage certain situations negatively. There is no one answer as to why we all act the way we do.

Why is the swinging lifestyle acceptable for those involved in it? Why is degrading someone acceptable to some people? Why is being lied to forgivable? Speaking of being lied to, why would you forgive someone after they have lied to you. Something in your past has made that acceptable, unfortunately.

Even what's going on in our country right now, people still want to believe the lies they have been told, and there is a reason for that. If we researched everyone who believes lies over the truth, only then could we understand and may be sympathetic to their way of thinking. Unless you're above the clouds, who are you to judge another for how they were as a baby, as a child, teenager, young adult, middle-aged adult, and last and most importantly, how can you judge me?

Update: Since my revelation, I have taken some time alone to reevaluate how to deal with the memories I discovered. It's not been easy for me whatsoever knowing what I know now. Some relationships I have had were amazing and I wish I could turn back the hands of time. And, since I am a realist, then it is time for me to challenge myself to do better.

Dirty Magazines

he Revolution Will Not Be Televised" by Gil Scott-Heron. Just so you know, I used the title of the chapter to lure you in. Therefore, I dare you to keep reading. **Warning: are you easily triggered, and disgusted with Black men fucking White women, but watch interracial porn?** Do you have a family member that's racist? Lately, have you showed hatred towards Black people? Do you say nigger among your family and peers? Have you confronted a Black family with aggression lately? Does it make sense to vandalize a Black family's home because it's nicer than yours? Have you ever said they must be drug dealers? As a bank teller, are you suspicious of all African Americans' deposits? When is a Black person driving a nice car do you immediately assume they are selling drugs? Why can't a Black family move into an all-white neighborhood? As a White person, have you ever said, "Go Back to Africa"? Does taking down are relocating the confederate statues make you angry? As a White person, would you prefer segregation and segregated schools? As a White person do you know the words to the Black National Anthem, "Lift Every Voice and Sing"? Honestly, I don't, seriously. I should know the words but, because I never had to sing it, I'm struggling with the words even as I am writing this sentence.

As a White man, have you ever called a Black woman nigger? Do you follow Black men while jogging in their own neighborhoods? Are you scared when approached by a Black man? Do your parents refer to Black people as niggers? Do you feel it's necessary to call the police on a Black child while selling lemonade? Have you intentionally promoted a White person with no qualifications over a Black person with qualifications? Have you intentionally promoted a White person with no recommendations over a Black person with recommendations? Have you asked or felt the need to ask a Black person to prove they live in your neighborhood? Do you think all Black teenagers are drug dealers and gang members?

Hey White woman, have you ever tried to touch a Black woman's hair without permission? Have you ever said this to a Black person: you are able to articulate your words very well? Have you unknowingly said to a Black person: you seem intelligent? Have you accused a Black underage child of stealing your cell phone, then tackled him while he was with his father? Which was a false claim. Black people don't deserve reparations, right? White women, are you jealous of Black women's natural beautiful dark skin? Have you asked a Black person, where were you born? The reason they ask, is because they have not adjusted their intelligence and ignorance to comprehend our ability to overcome all their obstacles and still succeed. Does a Black person manage you currently? Did you complain more because that person was Black? At your job, are there Black people in management? Have you consciously used your White privilege to your benefit? Do you say, I don't see color? Were you angrier with George Floyd protestors, than the White rioters on January 6? Do you still wear your MAGA hat proudly? As a security guard in a major department retail store, do you intentionally follow more Black people than White, and why? Do you teach your children your hatred? Do you refer to Black people as niggers in front of your children? As a teacher, do you ignore your Black students consciously or subconsciously?

Do you honestly believe "ALL LIVES MATTER"? When you hear someone say, Black Lives Matter do you feel propelled to say, ALL LIVES MATTER? Have you ripped down any signs that relates to BLM? When a White person wears a BLM shirt does it irritate you? Which irritates you more, a Black person wearing a BLM shirt or a White person? When a Black person is not allowing your ignorance to upset them, does that irritate you? Do you live in Boston? As White parents, do you discourage your kids from listening to rap music?

As White parents, how would you feel if your child drowned in a supervised pool by a Black woman? Would you demand a full investigation? Why were the charges against Amy Cooper dismissed? Even with evidence of lying to the police department on video. Have you aborted a Black fetus? If Black people were visually armed with a gun in a right to carry state, are you okay with that?

Is your daughter fucking a nigger, and you no longer talk to her? As a White woman, have you secretly fucked a Black man? As a White woman, are you afraid to tell your current racist husband you fucked a nigger? As a White woman, do you glance at Black men's crotch? As a White woman, have you masturbated while fantasizing about fucking Black men while held down? Do you refer to Black people as niggers subconsciously? As a realtor, are you consciously bias towards Black clients? As a loan officer, have you intentionally given a higher interest rate to Black clients? As a White doctor, are you a closet racist with most of your clients being Black? As a White nurse, do you intentionally ignore Black patients? As a White police officer, do you intentionally pull over Black drivers more than White drivers? As a White mother, have you slapped a Black child in broad daylight and no police were called on you? As a White parent, have your children shown compassion towards Black children and you shut dat shit down immediately? Are you disgusted when you see interracial relationships and mixed children?

You do realize, it was the White male slave owners who created interracial children with Black women during slavery. The White male slave owners should have encouraged their nigger slaves to continue breeding among themselves.

But instead, they were creeping out in the middle of the night raping their own Black female slaves. In fact, White male slave owners ignored their White wives crying for sex. Just saying. Damn! Dat Black pussy must have been good to ignore their own wives White, pink pussy? We'll never know, will we? Furthermore, tread lightly calling me a nigger, until you have researched your entire family history as far back as you can. For this reason, you might as well do it right now with Ancestry. Because no matter how European you think you are, you just may have a Black relative in your bloodlines.

The above questions are directly and indirectly related to this chapter called "Dirty Magazines." I am trying to provoke you to think from my perspective. In fact, the above questions I've wanted to ask an authentic White person. The rest are just provocative unanswered questions. Alternatively, I wanted to take a break from writing about sex. Just to shock you with one thousand volts of questions I pondered while I was a teenager, and now as an adult. It's my way of preparing you for what your about to read. Because, if one or all the above questions apply to you, do not read this chapter.

As a colored boy (that's how white folks use to refer to Black people) growing up in Southeast San Diego, White men have been strategically and psychologically brainwashing me/us to think Black women are inferior to White women.

I have a question for all you spoiled grade D milk colored looking White folks, has a Black person ever made you feel inferior in the entertainment field, in school classrooms, or in fact, period? Or have your own insecurities made you inferior?

Did you say something? Speak up. Allow me to convey my message another way to ya. White people have never portrayed Black people positively on television or in dirty magazines back in the early eighties.

All White people did then, and to this day, is bombard our visuals with stimulating stereotypical negative images of Black people on social media and news sources. So, how in the fuck does a Black baby, that eventually becomes an adult, stop preferring White women to fuck over Black women? How in dafuck is a young impressionable Black teenager supposed to think of my own Black women, besides my mom?

Why do racist White people become irate when a Black man is fucking White women. Let's go deeper down the rabbit hole, shall we? All I see in commercials, television, movies, and of course dirty magazines, are White women. Plant the seeds in Black men's head and dress it with your White imagery, you get Black men craving, fantasizing, and lusting after White women.

Search through major streaming channels looking for movies or series starring Black women in leading, strong, positive roles. Muthafucka, I can tell you right now, the pickings are slim. Movie producers and commercial makers, y'all ain't slick. You even have the audacity to have Black people only as co-stars in major roles. When Black entertainers are in starring roles, we are liars, cheaters, and wife beaters. While you are researching what I just said, be prepared to find us in demeaning roles. Last thing I'm gonna say before you read the rest of this chapter, why do White television producers always have niggas dancing at the beginning of the show?

Dirty Magazines let's get into it:

Do you remember adult magazines and bookstores, or have ever been inside one? Back then you had to be at least eighteen years old to enter. Well, I was a big ass fourteen-year-old that looked eighteen at the time. Even then, I was able to go inside of the Pussycat Theatre in downtown San Diego to watch *Deep Throat* starring Linda Lovelace. If you are a millennial, I know damn well you don't know anything about adult magazines or the movie I just mentioned because of the Internet. So, if you want a trip back to the days of adult magazines stores, sit back and keep reading. I remember a place called: The World-Famous Body Shop, a shabby strip and adult magazine club/store in San Diego, California. Probably owned by the same company and made a shit load of dinero. How did I discover adult bookstores? I often walked past an adult bookstore and saw nothing but fat men inside.

Additionally, the men smoked cigarettes, and if I planned to go inside, I might as well wait until there was no one smoking. Hell, when I walked past the bookstore there were fat men packed inside like a can of Vienna sausages. In fact, I could see the cigarette smoke coming from the adult bookstore like an early morning fog across the street from a Chinese food joint my family liked eating at. I ain't stupid! Obviously, my dad wasn't either because he hid his selection of dirty magazines from my mom under the mattresses, which I later found out.

Back then my parents called places that sold adult magazines, dirty magazines. Let me explain how I discovered dirty magazines existed. Downtown San Diego had adult bookstores on every corner, it seemed like. Back in my inquisitive teen years, the main entrance was wide open enough for curious underage muthafuckas like me to glance inside. That's what I thought anyway.

Night One:

In one of the adult bookstores, I mentioned earlier, three quarters of it was wrestling, sports, and news related magazines. However, in the back of the bookstore, there was this slightly open mysterious area blocked off with a black curtain across the front of it. In front of that black curtain were big ass bold letters that read, adults only. I made sure the sign did not specify what age to enter. That made me even more curious. Finally, an evening without parents, I was determined to walk into that adult store across from my parents favorite Chinese restaurant. At the time I did not have a car, so I caught the bus everywhere I had to go. My destination was the adult bookstore downtown San Diego. I arrived later that evening and walked in. After walking past the curtain, I glanced in and realized what was back there. When they say curiosity killed the cat, I wanted to walk through the curtain so badly, but at the last second, I chose not to enter.

I feared the cashier would have had me arrested because I was underage, even though the cashier had never asked me for ID. Instead, I looked like a homeless kid wondering around picking up magazines. I ended up buying a WWF magazine instead. I paid too much for it, especially when that was not what I had in mind. I left the bookstore frustrated and without the magazine I wanted. Let's just say I hadn't gone through the black curtain.

Night Two:

I walked back into the same bookstore, and I felt like the cashier from the night before remembered me. That was my underage guilty conscious fucking with my head. In all honesty, I acted like I had been his only customer from the night before. Anyways, hopefully with a change of clothes, he wouldn't remember me. This time I was determined to walk in front of the cashier and head towards the black curtain. The closer I got to the black curtain, the more nervous I became. And like that song by Johnny "Guitar" Watson, "Ain't That A Bitch." Guess what? I bought another WWF magazine, fuck it! I went home and decided to try the following week.

Yet again, going home with blue balls and no adult magazines. I did not want to take a chance on the cashier calling the police even though I bought something each time. With two WWF magazines, I might as well put them to good use, so I donated the magazines to my high school.

Night Three:

Next week came up, and it's time to get on the bus and head back to the bookstore again. This time I stopped and had a conversation with the cashier. My reason for doing this was to see if the cashier remembered me from the prior week. Nope, he didn't! The whole time he was talking I was thinking about the adult section.

During that boring conversation with the cashier, another customer walked up. It was time to make my move and walk towards the black curtain finally. And guess what? I did it y'all. I walked through the black curtain that had adults only.

There were six men and one underage teenager in that room with their backs turned. Guess who that was? So, I turned my back towards them too. Not one of the six guys in that room said anything.

It was so quiet you could hear a mouse walking across the carpet. It was weird and that is all I am going to say.

Now that I'm in the adult magazine room, all I see is naked White women on the front of all the magazine covers. Every damn magazine I picked up had White women showing their tits, spreading their legs while showing their shaved pink pussies or flat asses. In fact, I was a Black teenager looking at White women with their legs spread and showing their pussy; it looked good to me. Here are the adult magazines that had White naked women on the front cover: *Barely Legal, Beaver Hunt, Club, High Society, Juggs, Penthouse Forum, Playboy, Screw, Swank, Adam Film World, Chic, Gallery, Genesis, Oui, Perfect 10*, and *Score*. Ladies and gentlemen, the racist magazine of them all goes to: *Hustler* magazine. To this very day, I remember this one cartoon I laughed at but soon regretted it. It was a cartoon of a watermelon patch with a scarecrow. The scarecrow had a Klansman on it. Did you just laugh or smile? Either way, I wouldn't blame you because I did. Anyways, it was time to leave and come back another day. I did not buy anything then because I didn't know how expensive those adult magazines were. Never mind the fact I didn't have enough money after paying for the bus.

Intermission from the subject:

I'm going to take you to downtown San Diego, where all the adult bookstores were. Besides, I want to explain in detail another reason I was fascinated by White women and where it came from.

My fascination and tolerable nature for White people came from firsthand experiences and various sources. In addition to adult literature, there were: beauty ads, news anchors, nurses, doctors, cashiers, store managers, warehouse managers, bus drivers, principles, and teachers. I repeat, my fascination and tolerable nature for White people also came from, but not limited to, distributed magazines such as: *Seventeen, Cosmopolitan, Vogue, Fashion, Bop, Mademoiselle, Easyriders, Rolling Stone, Life, People, Teen Beat, Us Weekly, Glamour,* and *Harper's Bazaar.* Hey, you the reader, Google all the above-mentioned magazines in the early eighties. Straight up, all you're going to see is White women on the front, center, and back page. If by chance, she has a dark complexion, you'll find her on the back of the magazines. Mixed raced or should I say redbones, are usually with another White woman. It's fucked up, ain't it? You know damn well, Black women come in all shades, so why didn't they show them?

Additionally, there I was, with so many naked White women in front of me, and I wasn't sure which one to pick. After thirty minutes had gone by, I finally chose a magazine and walked towards the cashier. The magazine I ended up paying for was the most racist magazine of them all, *Hustler.* The women they chose to be inside their magazine were all blonde and skinny. I'm saying skinny because when I reflect and compare what's on social media, shit! It makes those magazines look PG rated.

What the hell, March 9th, 1959, we even had a White Ken and Barbie. And it wasn't until 1967 when they rolled out there first Black Barbie named Francie. This doll had White features up until the 1990s. In the eighties, all the superheroes were White men and women such as: Batman, Bionic Woman, Wonder Woman, Incredible Hulk, Masters of the Universe, The Pumaman, The Return of Captain Invincible, Super Fuzz, Supergirl, Flash Gordon, The Incredible Hulk, The Invisible Man, you get the idea.

Majority of the commercials had White people front, back, and center. Another fact, the major television shows starred White people. The television shows listed below were shows I grew up watching religiously. What's even more fucked up, White people dominated radio and television shows and it was so fucking obvious; they weren't trying to disguise it. All the highlighted shows I will elaborate on a bit more. Just so muthafuckas understand why Black men and women over seventy have a "Yassa boss" mentality. Hollywood has played a significant role in that. On that note, buckle up sonsabitches here we go.

All in the Family – One Negro family as neighbors.

Benson – A Negro butler for a bunch of White folks.

The Cosby Show – Negros complained this show wasn't realistic. The father was a doctor and mom a lawyer living in a nice home. The parents were not divorced, arguing, cheating, lying, and crying to get out the hood. Too positive, I guess. Ain't that fucked up? As I mentioned earlier, Hollywood conditioned my mind.

Chico and the Man – Comedy/ At least had two major Negro co-stars in it.

Different Strokes – Comedy/ Two young Negros from Harlem, let's keep it a hundred, shall we, from the ghetto. And adopted by a White wealthy New York businessperson. Keyword: adopted.

Welcome Back, Kotter – Comedy/ OMG! One co-starring Negro among six other actors who were not Black.

What's Happening!! – Comedy/ WHOA! Eight Negros trading starring roles with one non-Black.

Facts of Life – Comedy/ One Negro female actress and twenty-five muthafucking non-Negros.

Flip Wilson Show – Comedy/ Dressed in drag and starred in his own show with special guest who were always White folks.

Good Times – Comedy/ All Negro cast with a positive vibe in the ghetto.

The Jeffersons - Comedy/ Two male Negro actors, four Negro actresses, and three White men in it. A lazy ass Negro as a house cleaner. Stereotypical role yet again. If you were watching this show in another country, we are loud and have lazy Negros as house cleaners. Why hire Negro people, right?

Sanford and Son - Comedy/ Two Negros own a junk yard. Father and son duo.

Room 222 - Comedy/ I'm just going to say there were Negros in starring roles.

That's My Mama - Comedy/ All Negro cast, I'm not saying another word.

Mod Squad - Serious/ Action with one Negro actor.

Now check out all the muthafucking shows listed below. The shows highlighted were either action or non-comedic shows and now compare the number of Negro shows to White shows. When I was growing up all my momma watched were the shows below. With only one television in the home, guess what I was watching? That's right muthafucka, more fucking White people, all damn day. With a sprinkle of Negro shows if she wanted to watch them. As a Negro child, what am I supposed to think of my culture? Additional information: I am using the word "Negro" above because back in the day that's how White folks referred to us.

Here we go with a long fucking list of White shows:

American Girls, The Andy Williams Show, The Bad News Bears, Baretta, Don Knotts, *The Don Rickles Show, Eight Is Enough, The Betty White Show, The Beverly Hillbillies, Bewitched,* **Get Christie Love!,** *Get Smart, Gomer Pyle: USMC, The Gong Show, Green Acres,* **Gunsmoke,** *Happy Days,* **Hawaii Five-O,** *Here's Lucy, Hogan's Heroes, I Dream of Jeannie,* **Ironside, It Takes a Thief, Kojak, Kung Fu, Little House on the Prairie,** *Love, American Style, The Mary Tyler Moore Hour, The Mary Tyler Moore Show, M*A*S*H,* **Mission: Impossible,** *Mork & Mindy, My Three Sons, The New Andy Griffith Show, The Odd Couple, Operation Petticoat, The Partridge Family,* **Quincy M.E., The Rockford Files,** *Rowan & Martin's Laugh-In,* **The Six Million Dollar Man, The Sonny and Cher Comedy Hour, Starsky and Hutch,** *Taxi, The Waltons,* **The Wild Wild West,** *WKRP in Cincinnati,* **Bonanza,** *The Brady Bunch, The Brady Bunch Variety Hour,* **Cannon,** *The Carol Burnett Show,* **Charlie's Angels, Chips, Columbo, Dallas,** *Donny and Marie,* **Dragnet,** *The Dukes of Hazzard,* **20/20, 60 Minutes, Adam-12,** *Alice.*

Fuck it I'll say it, here we are in the twenty-first century, and from my observation, not one fucking thing has changed. Nothing but White people, White movies, and White cartoons shoved down our throats twenty-four hours a day.

Night Four / The Conclusion:

Caught the bus as usual, and this time I had enough money for the bus to the bookstore and the return home. All set to buy my first adult magazine. When I walked in, there was the same cashier again, and it looked like he hadn't changed his clothes. He must have been the owner and slept in the back room somewhere. And just like before, I had a light conversation with the cashier again. Just as he was talking another customer walked up. That's when I walked away, heading towards the black curtain again.

This time it felt different for me. I think because I had been there so many times prior, that it felt natural. I walked to the black curtain and stuck one of my hands through the curtain and walked in. There I was, finally inside the adult magazine room. I had a brain overload malfunction, there were too many choices. Hell, I wasn't sure which one to pick. After about thirty minutes, I had a magazine in my hand walking towards the cashier. The magazine I chose was *Hustler*, more classless women inside. If you were one of the women shown inside of that magazine, I would like to apologize for what I said, okay?

I like the fact that when you bought a magazine the cashier placed it in a brown bag. I felt comfortable knowing no one knew what I had inside of it. When the bus dropped me off at home, I looked to see if moms was home. I could tell she was, so I had to be careful. I opened the door and was surprised that my momma was sleep, so I snuck past her and headed straight for the bedroom. I opened the bag up again and took out my first White woman dirty magazine. It was pussy! Ass and titties on every page I turned. I was so excited that I finally had my adult magazine, that if you had been a fly on my wall watching me, you would have slipped down the wall watching me jack off. I was shooting cum all over the place. One evening I had an idea, why not find one photo of a girl looking up at me. To my surprise, there was one nude centerfold when I opened the magazine. I placed the magazine with the nude White girl face up. Let me give you a visual. My pants and underwear were down by my ankles. I'm centering the dirty magazine knee high. Everything is set and my mom is snoring. I took out my cock and started jacking off as if the White girl was watching me. Damn! I shot a load of hot fresh cum all over the face of the White chick in the magazine.

Mom must have heard me cumming and asked if I was okay, and I responded with a "Yes" and cleaned up myself. I closed the magazine, sat with mom for a while, and had small talk. I wanted to go back and bust another nut all over the face of the White girl waiting for me in my bedroom. Well, that was not going to happen, and you should know why. I didn't clean up the cum from the magazine. It dried and now the pages were stuck together. Fuck! Now that the pages had cum all over them, it was time to go back and buy more magazines from my favorite bookstore. This time the cashier knew my name and wasn't watching me closely like the other times. I needed more than one magazine this time, so I decided to steal three magazines. Yes, I said steal, and I did not stutter.

I made my move and shoved three magazines into my jacket. After I had those magazines hidden inside my jacket, I walked quickly past the cashier. As a result of me walking faster, he stopped me.

While standing on the podium, he looked directly at me and said, "Put those magazines back Cecil." I was shocked and asked myself, *how in the fuck did he know.* Are you asking if I took those magazines back? Yes, I sure and the fuck did. After that situation, I gave up trying to buy and steal dirty magazines. I told the cashier thanks for not calling the police on me. He smiled and said, "I understand why you were trying to steal them." He also said, "I remember my first dirty magazine I stole from a local bookstore. Except I ended up in a juvenile detention center." That's all I needed to hear to make an informed decision. That same evening, I decided to go home and try to salvage the one's I had already bought. Out of the three sticky magazines, none where salvageable. Oh well, Peace!

Doing It In DaPark

I remember this one young slim lady named Tina from fifteen years ago. We dated briefly while she worked at a Publix in the deli department. That's what I'll say for now and hopefully she's reading this book. Let me tell you a little bit about Tina. I was a player when I met her, and she wanted a committed relationship. I had too much going on in life when I met her, but it was fun being with her. One of my memory cells just kicked in, so allow me to take you back fifteen years ago. One day I called her unexpectedly and asked if she wanted to go for a ride with me. Tina responded yes, but like most women, she kept on asking me where she and I were going. It became annoying, and all I had to do was look at her a certain way, and she knew not to ask anymore. I smiled when she finally stopped asking me. She asked what I was smiling about? I said, "Can't tell ya." Telling you, the reader, I said to myself, *good girl*. I like a woman who cares enough to STFU and listen, allowing me to lead. While in my car, I told her we were going to a park in Altamonte Spring. I mentioned this park had a nature walk, and she and I were going to walk along the path. I parked and walked over towards the park. I thought something was odd with the look she kept giving me. She looked over at me and had this "up to no good" look on her face.

I said, "What's up, I see a devilish grin, and you can't hide it either." a few other couples surrounded us also headed to the park as well.

Tina leaned over and whispered into my ear, "I wanna let you know, I'm not wearing any panties underneath this dress."

Time out reader. I don't care whether you are a male or a female reading this part of the chapter, how could you stop yourself from cumming in your draws or panties after hearing someone saying that to you. Here is what I thought, why in the fuck would she say that to a bull?

I said with a devilish grin, "The fuck you ain't." She said it again, "I'm not wearing any panties."

I just shook my head and I tried to not think about it while we were walking across the street headed to the park. If you have not been able to put this book down, thank you. Being honest with you as I have been so far, I couldn't help myself and only had one thought pounding in my head. While we were on our nature walk, I pulled up her dress waist level. As I had her dress in my hand, she took it back from me and spun around like a ballet dancer, I was watching her in slow motion.

As Tina was spinning around holding her dress in her right hand, I could see her nicely shaved pussy. I guess it must have turned me on because as she walked ahead of me, I looked around wondering how I was going to hide my hard cock in my sweatpants. Like I've said a few times throughout this book, as a Black man with a White woman, you never know how well it's received by a racist White person. Once I was certain no one else was around, I told her to bend over and grab the fucking handrails and spread her legs. And just like before, I said to myself, *good girl*. She did exactly what I told her to do. If I had been a police officer, she would have been an easy no resisting suspect. So, fuck it, I might as well treat her like one. I stood behind her and lifted her dress up from behind. As she had her back turned towards me, I told her to take her right hand off the rail and put it behind her. That's when I told her to open the palm of her hand to hold the dress up from sliding down.

It was at that moment, all I could see was her naked bare ass. I had to look around again to make damn sure I could not see or hear anyone one last time. I quickly unzipped my pants, and since my cock was hard any fucking way, I started fucking her from the back. I tell you what, I came quicker than the old lollipop commercial with the owl. I came all up in her pussy, and she didn't clean up. I wish you were able to see me walking around like a dog humping air when I came. Did you just smile? As Tina was walking ahead of me, cum was running down her leg. I'm a sick fucker because that shit turned me on. She said, "Look at my right leg." I could clearly see cum running down her fucking right leg. Let me explain something to you, there is absolutely nothing sexier than a woman not wearing panties and cum running down her legs. I'll never forget that shit and that was my experience when it comes to park sex.

Dominant Submissive Romance

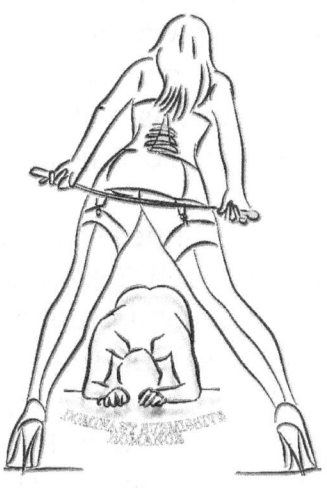

efore I share my personal thoughts and experiences in this chapter, I want to make it clear that I am not nor claim to be an expert on this subject. I'm sure you have your own idea as to what submissive is, and that's okay, I've always known I like submissive women. What I'd like to do is express what submissive means to me. I don't mean the kind of woman that will allow themselves to be treated like a doormat. Unfortunately, some women were raised watching their mothers in abusive relationships at an early age. I would think being raised in a toxic environment would give her the impression that's how men show their love. I'm here to tell you now, a woman should never be a fucking tied up animal in the backyard for anyone. Under no circumstances is it okay, and I don't give a fuck how wealthy he is or his status in society.

On a personal note, ladies you are a unicorn and should be treated as such. Being degraded can be sexy as fuck under the right unique circumstances, in other words, it's a burning desire you have within. In this unique case finding someone who understands your desire's will be exceedingly difficult and rare. So, don't settle to have your desires fulfilled by strangers without an indication your partner understands your desires completely. Respecting the safe word, you both have established should be his or her top priority when the degrading becomes too intense to continue. Bottom line is the following paragraph ...

Motherfuckers who treat women like doormats, think they can do whatever dafuck they want to women and that's not limited to lying, cheating, hitting violently, or treating her less than human, that's NOT an alpha male or a Dom in my book. He is nothing but a cowardly bitch ass muthafucka as far as I'm concerned. So, let's not confuse something as beautiful as the word love with "The Burning Bed."

The right man should appreciate and cherish a woman with old-fashioned southern values, that's now becoming non-existent with this new generation of women. In most cases, women misinterpret being a submissive wife or girlfriend for giving up her independency, when ideally, a submissive woman is just someone who enjoys catering to her man and has a nurturing personality, period

If you are a woman reading this part, I'm writing this for you: I know it's difficult for you to totally submit yourself to a man. But I want to confidently assure you that no matter what he brings to the table financially, emotionally, or physically, you are always in control. And I don't give ah fuck with whom you are involved. That's why it's okay to be selective and submit to the right man who knows your worth and knows how to nurture and appreciate you.

If I am to be the "dominant," then I must be a man with integrity in the relationship. Meaning, I should respect and appreciate my submissive, including, and not limited to, valuing her ideas, opinions, and what she wants out of life. I can show my appreciation with something simple, as saying "thank you." I realized by showing and expressing my appreciation, it allows her to give of herself freely and happily.

A woman should only submit when she's mentally, emotionally, and financially ready and not when she is emotionally insecure, unstable, or physically damaged from the previous relationship. Sometimes, women don't take the fucking time to get to know the man before she submits. Afterwards, she ends up wondering why she's being treated like a doormat. Ladies, before submitting to a man, please evaluate his actions because he needs to earn your trust. Submission doesn't mean a damn thang if the words he speaks, and actions are not aligned. Fucking your partner is different than submitting and you should know the difference no matter how good the sex is.

What I'm about to say next may not sit well with you as an Alpha female reading this, but to me, I feel when the right man comes into your life and truly earns your submission, you should kneel exclusively to him.

When a deep level of connection has been established, kneeling should be thoroughly discussed, and should not be expected. There is a time and place when kneeling should or can be performed. Such as when he walks in from work or just before play time.

Wait, allow me to reminisce, six years before this book was written I remember this White girl preparing dinner for me while I was in her favorite chair watching television. Keep in mind I'm at her home not mine, and it would not have mattered. She kneeled before me while extending her arms with the plate in her hands. Like a good girl, she proceeded to serve me first as it should be, but the difference is, she sat next to me on the floor and ate her dinner. This wasn't forced, but only a position she felt naturally acceptable and normal. Being in Dom/Sub relationship spoiled me, being honest with you. I gave up looking for this type of relationship with anyone afterwards, because she was a special person in my life when I needed it.

Usually, this is associated in BDSM not in vanilla relationships. Kneeling is normally accepted in an environment that understands the dynamics of the relationship. Kneeling can be acceptable when the man walks in the house or when he mentally prepares for a scene he desires. Once again, kneeling is just another way a submissive can show her vulnerability and prove she takes her role seriously in the relationship.

This does not apply to long-distance relationships or online because it's not realistic. I would not encourage this type of relationship because it's unrealistic and should be avoided, this is just my protective personality speaking.

I am sure there's going to be people reading this saying to themselves, I only kneel to the man above. If you honestly believe in this theory, then why kneel at all? Being a Black man kneeling to me means something entirely different in these days and times.

In a vanilla relationship, men are embarrassed when women willingly want to kneel to her dominant. Reiterating what I said earlier, in the right atmosphere and situation, and with the right relationship, I believe it's okay for a woman to kneel to her man. Am I saying you should kneel to your man in public (well, that only depends on the dynamics of the relationship), but in the privacy of your own home, I see no issue with it.

Just before drafting this book, I met a woman walking in a parking lot of a gym I came from. I asked her if she would like to continue our friendly conversation over to the famous coffee shop across the street. It wasn't about sex or past relationships, just talking about life in general, and things were going well. From the intensity of our conversation, I needed to show her how different our personal lives were. So, I showed her a photo of a woman kneeling to me, this is my way of finding out exactly who I'm dealing with. She was disgusted and seemed to believe that no "real" man would ever allow a woman to kneel in front of him. I spoke to myself, you're a closed-minded woman and your entitled to your opinion. It was easy for me to understand why she's been divorced for twenty plus years.

I usually talk about sex within three weeks, it's a fantastic way to ensure two people are on the same page sexually. Just because I mention sex, I never make assumptions it's going to happen. But she made me feel comfortable enough to show her the photo of a girl kneeling, and she was appalled by the photo. I guess you can never judge a book by its cover, and that's where our conversation ended.

It took me years, and three wives, to figure out the type of personality that works best for me when it comes to a long-lasting relationship. I've realized the type of woman I need around me is an open-minded, nonjudgmental woman, with similar life events.

I gravitate towards BDSM because of the type of women I want in my life. I give more of myself in this type of relationship. My ideal place would have a dungeon within my home, full of unique equipment for my partner. That one room in the house no one is allowed unless you have my permission. Where like-minded men and women can be themselves and not be judged. It would include blindfolds, wrist and ankle restraints, floggers, nipple clamps, paddles, canes, vibrators, tape, collars, rope, a padding bench, a jail cell, x-cross, a bed with four iron polls on each corner, and other unmentionable equipment.

I cannot stress this enough, first, establish trust to know when to respect the safe word. If she panics, she should be able to trust her dominant, so don't ever break the trust of your submissive.

A man's priority should be pleasing the woman first. There are men out there who believe, it's all about them getting their cock sucked. If they don't lick the pussy, it's because they don't give a fuck about their partner having an orgasm. Foreplay is not just confined to the bedroom either. Foreplay is every waking moment you are with each other. It can be a look you give each other across the room or the grazing of her ass as you walk by, or a kiss on the neck. Even just saying thank you can be a form of foreplay. I've learned over time, being attentive, telling her thank you for the simplest things she does for me. Most men take a woman's submissiveness for granted and have expectations that are unattainable, and that's where they fail.

I've been to two different BDSM clubs, it really wasn't my thing, but trust is what turns me on the most. Trusting me allows her to be vulnerable knowing I would not break the trust so she can give of herself freely and enjoy the moment.

I only enjoy flogging if the woman is turned on by having it done. There's a method to it, and if the woman can manage intense pain, I'll provide it by flogging their back, thighs, and ass. Usually, it's White women who enjoy this type of scene.

Men would ask me how I am able to flog a woman without any guilt. I tell them, as a Black man, it's like payback for all the times White men did it to our woman during slavery. At least with me, it's done in a controlled trusting environment, whereas during slavery, which was not the case with Black women. Every time I am flogging a White woman and I hear her screaming, it's not because of pain, it's pleasure. I never questioned why White women enjoyed being flogged, especially by a Black man. In their mind, they may feel they deserve it in a twisted beautiful way. Again, it's ALWAYS about trust and making sure the person you're doing ANYTHING with, enjoys it.

There was this one big girl I knew; she's lost weight since the last time I saw her. I'm not going to mention any names unless she wants to come forward. After reading this book, I wanted to tell her that I took a photo of her big ass bending over doggie style (I've since deleted it btw). I was flogging the fuck out of her big white ass with every ounce of power I had, and she just laughed. Her laughing was not directed at me, it was the amount of pain she was feeling which caused her to laugh. She realized it was beyond pleasurable and something she's wanted for a long time. But couldn't find anyone to provide it.

In BDSM, we call this subspace, where she's in a trance-like euphoria while experiencing intense emotions happening at the same time. I flogged her ass until it was purple; she was proud of it and immediately walked into her bathroom to see her bruised ass. No matter how hard I flogged her, she never cried and never used the safe word. After that, I thought I better step my game up, so one day while at work, I discovered a wooden paddle for barbecuing. Sadly, I never got a chance to use it with her, but that's how it goes sometimes.

Another time, I handcuffed a White girl to the frame of her own bed. While handcuffed to the bed frame, I flogged her. I could tell she loved being flogged because her pussy was wet from anticipation. There were specific words I would say to make her comfortable. And like I said earlier, she was always in control. When I am flogging a woman for the first time and she says stop, whatever I am doing at that moment stops, that's where the trust comes in.

There's just something about bondage and submission that I really find fascinating. I've seen the Fifty Shades movies, and I have to say that's not realistic and more like a fantasy. He starts off being a dominant and ends up being submissive in the next movie. That made him a switch. A man that is sometimes dominant and sometimes submissive, they should have kept him dominant throughout both movies. My opinion, they weakened his character, once he submitted himself, she didn't want that type of relationship with him, and the excitement was gone. She liked what they had, and he fucked it up being submissive to her. They had a fascinating topic and ruined it.

Friends How Many of Us Have One

here is something about me that makes people comfortable telling me their most private thoughts. I won't mention this next person's name, but if you are someone that knows me personally, you might easily figure out who I'm referring to. If someone were to suspect who it might be, I wouldn't confirm one way or the other, but what I'm about to relate is a true scenario which has affected me enough to mention here.

As this book reflects, I've always been a freaky individual, something I typically don't share with friends and acquaintances, I don't particularly care to be judged or misunderstood for some of the fucked-up shit I've done in my life. If I happen to share something about myself with you, it's only because I felt comfortable enough to do so. Obviously, I don't give ah fuck anymore at this stage of my life, right? So, keep reading.

One morning, I felt comfortable enough to tell a co-worker named Joel something private. I decided to describe one sexual exploration story from my childhood (**involving a dog). He was the first and only person I had ever relayed this story to in some fifty years. As soon as I was halfway through the story, it became apparent to me that he wasn't who I thought he was.

I expected Joel to say something like, "Wow! Man! How long ago was that?" Which would have given me the opportunity to explain in detail, instead he betrayed me and made me feel uncomfortable. The way he responded, I became embarrassed, and I shut down. I discovered that, some personal information you should not trust your best friend with. I knew things about him, without judgement, and yet he couldn't, or wouldn't, treat me with the same respect. Since then, I have learned, don't call anyone a best friend unless you know, they will not judge you and are willing to take your secret to the grave with them.

To think that this was the same muthafucka who was cheating on his wife. He was boldly flaunting his affair among his co-workers and was blatant about it. Even with a beautiful wife and well-behaved kids at home, he blatantly slung his cock around. As a result, he ended up making a baby by the side piece/co-worker. This man/child has absolutely no conscience whatsoever. Don't get me wrong, he more than likely lied to the side piece for a while, then she finally realized he wasn't leaving his wife for her ass. On the days of picking up his child from the side piece's place, he brought that child, out of wedlock, around his own kids. I'm certain in their confused little minds they wondered who the baby's father was, knowing damn well their mom was not or had not been pregnant, but it's dad's baby? As of when this book was written, we'll just have to wait and see what the long-term effects of his actions will play on his kids' maturity.

I never once made Joel feel bad about his lack of judgement or what he was doing to his family. Yet he judged me for something I did fifty fucking years ago, a complete betrayal in my view, and a valuable lesson. His response made me start to pull away from people even more, I guess you can never know if a friend is real or fake, until you allow yourself to be vulnerable enough to tell them something private. Frank was another guy I worked with at the same location, who said some fucked up shit about me while I was at the lowest point in my life, and I thought he was a friend too. I will explain below, why I said, *I thought he was a friend too.*

I came from California and ended up in Florida and worked for this one company forty-plus years. I thought I was coming into some cash, so I quit my job. Unfortunately, I found out later it was all a sham, I'd been lied to, and it all unfolded. And, once I realized it was a sham, I asked someone from upper management regarding me returning to work. I was fortunate the person I spoke to gave me an opportunity of a lifetime. I was able to return as if I never asked to quit my job of forty years. I want to let that person know, I will be forever grateful, and you have not been forgotten.

So, back to this "so-called friend" of mine, Frank heard I was returning to work, and he couldn't help himself, but to kick me while I was at the lowest point in my life. He was saying fucked up shit about me that had everyone around him laughing about my return. So much that, a manager had to tell him to shut up. People like him attach their claws onto a branch like buzzards and wait to see you or someone fail; it makes them feel better about themselves, I suppose. This same muthafucka told me he used to smoke crack, and even then, I didn't fucking dog him out. He also told me he had fucked around with another woman behind his wife's back. That gave me the impression he would not have a problem meeting this one woman who was a friend of mine. Well, I was wrong. He came over and played with her pussy a little bit with one of his fingers and left. All the shit talking in the aisles with him, all fluff no action.

I have met Frank's wife a few times, and even then, I kept his secrets to myself because it's no one else's business what I tried to set up for him, or what he did with anyone else. It's funny how this muthafucka was the first one kicking me while I was down and out, but at the same time, told me his private fucked-up shit and expected me to never repeat his fucked-up stories. This person has done a few other things to me, but I'm not about to write about it. So, hey if you are reading this chapter asshole, here's a toast to you muthafucka.

When I occasionally see him, I'm always cordial. I'll smile and say to myself, what a piece of shit he is. Even with these thoughts, I've never once repeated any of his private life with anyone until this book. I'm not mentioning Frank or Joel's real names, they know who the fuck they are. Hopefully, Frank's wife will forgive him even after reading this book.

For future reference, be careful what you share with someone, that is, if you have told them something confidential. Bottom line is, only one person can judge another, and that's the almighty man above, besides that man, no one else on this fucking planet has the right to judge another for their discretions. I began to realize most people have their own agenda. You absolutely must follow your own path because there will always be someone around who will disagree and try to derail you. I know writing this memoir, not everyone is going to get it, but that's okay, this is something I'm doing for myself.

At this present moment, I have two close female friends named Sara and Lynn. Sara, I dated, and now we're nonsexual friends, and we both prefer it that way. We talk about our escapades, hers, and mine. When she talks about the men she's fucking, it doesn't faze me. I enjoy listening to her talk about them. It's my way of knowing she'll be okay if anything were to happen unexpectedly. Real friends stay connected and make sure the other is doing okay, always. To me, that's real love. Usually, when I've fucked somebody and it's over, it's over, a closed chapter. But not with this person, it's a cherished rarity that will never be replaced.

** Chapter Must Be The Dog "N" Me

Glory Hole Days

Warning: Go ahead with caution. Here in Florida, there is a place called Fantasyland Adult Theater in Tampa, Florida. From what I can recall, this place had different areas within the building for dirty magazines, X-rated videos, and an area for the title of this chapter: The "Glory Hole" area. Just so you have a visual, it's a large room with black painted walls. In fact, there is no information anywhere on the building once you enter. Only the horny, freaky, devious, kinky, perverse, perverted, twisted, and weird would know of its existence.

There was a website I used to search for couples to party with, and when I say party, it's a code word for fucking or fuck, depending how party is used in a sentence. After being on this site three times, I spoke to a couple that planned on visiting Fantasyland. I was excited because I had never been to this place and had heard so much about it. Yes, I was bold for driving two hours to meet this couple, where the husband planned to allow strangers to fuck his wife, and in some cases, girlfriend. Don't get the wrong idea about all glory holes. In all honesty, if she didn't want to be there, she would not be. I remember when I finally found the place, we drove up around the same time. I was like a kid at an all-you-can-eat buffet. I stood around and waited outside for them to get out the truck. When that didn't happen, I decided to walk inside and wait for them. Finally, they walked in and past me like Donald Trump walking past a journalist from Fox News. I was crushed, they didn't stop to say, "Nice to meet you finally." I mentioned this couple because they are one of the characters in this chapter.

Glory holes are always an interesting topic. It's two strangers walking into separate side-by-side small rooms with closed doors. Except the difference is, there is a three-inch diameter hole in the wall, usually about waist high for an average-sized adult. When I say average sized, I am referring to someone that's between five foot eight to six feet tall. Unless you are a dwarf, this may present a problem.

I'm laughing as I am writing this part of the chapter as a vision popped into my head. I visualized a male little person (I hope I'm being politically correct here) looking through the glory hole instead of pulling down his pants sticking his cock through it. Wait, I need a minute LOL. Okay, I'll say it. I just had another vision, what if there was a little person on both sides, what are they going to be able to do? And that is only assuming they are of the opposite sex. I would pay to see that, seriously. Fuck it, I'm going all in, what if the man is around six feet six inches tall, on one side, and a female little person on the other side. Hopefully, his cock isn't erect, so she can at least suck or fuck him until he is hard. Otherwise, once he becomes hard, there is no way she will be able to suck or fuck it from above her head. Hell, she can't even get on her tippy toes to hang on it. On the other hand, I guess his cock could rest on top of her head. Or better yet, she could wait until he's soft to suck or fuck it again. Let me add a couple of missing sentences to this paragraph. The average-sized man on the other side I mentioned above should warn her to put on goggles before he stuffs his cock through the hole. Otherwise, he will accidentally poke her in the eye from the head of his cock. All right, enough, I'm gonna move on.

Back to The Glory Hole: One time, I was able to be an observer. As an observer, you are among others who are interested in watching from a short distance away only to see. A man put his cock through the hole in the wall and there was someone on the other side. Yes, I was standing on the side three feet away, like everyone else. I was waiting to see what was going to happen next. I just had a thought, remember that song by Grace Jones, "Pull Up to the Bumper"? I guess you can call this, "Pull Up to The Glory Hole Baby," and stick your cock through the hole. Enough! Back to The Glory Hole: Before I tried it myself, I had heard about it, and must admit after a couple of times, I found it interesting. But I could never understand the fascination of going back daily. Do I still have your attention?

As a male, just imagine yourself for a moment trying glory holes for the first time, and the head you received was so damn good you wanted to ask for her hand in marriage. You also wanted to know who was on the other side. Being that was your first time, you were not aware that you can't converse with the person in the joining room. Technically, you're supposed to leave after you busted a nut, but not you, Mr. First Time. You decide to say to your neighbor, what's your name? They don't respond back because they are respecting the rules of that area. You think they are being an asshole, but they're not. You then become angry and wait until you hear their door open. What happened next fucked you up for the rest of your life. It was a man on the other side of your booth. What's a trip, it was your wife's brother?

Fuck! All this time and you didn't know that muthafucka got down like that. Now what do you say or do, huh? I could understand if you were the actor in an X- rated movie and was paid damn good money to star in it. Because you are reading this chapter, you would perform for free, you're a freaky ass muthafucka. There is another reason you would perform for free, it's because you have a copy of this book. Never mind the fact that you are reading this chapter. So, who's the closet freak now? I suppose we would title your movie, "My Brother-In-Law" part one. Because, more than likely, you are hoping your wife's brother is also starring in the sequel. Glory holes can be fun if everyone involved knows one another. Like a group of your freaky ass friends all meet and go together. No vanilla folks here, you muthafucka's stay your ass at home and sit this one out. While the group of y'all finally make it to the place, make sure you book the entire room. That way y'all don't have to worry about strangers trying to get free ass, pussy, or head. If I were there and saw y'all pull up at once, I would friend all of you just before you walked in.

Just saying. Anyway, once you stick your cock through the hole, hopefully you took a damn shower. No woman in her right state of mind would touch your stinky ass cock. Especially, if you don't believe in circumcision. You may have lint all down in there and no telling what else.

Another thing you need to know is, if you are always going to be concerned on who is on the other side of your booth, then maybe just be an observer. Ask to step inside while one of your friends is inside and stay enough distance to masturbate. Just make sure you are not one of those muthafucka's that shoots cum all over the place. That will get you kicked out, and not only that, but you may also get your ass kicked. This type of sexual escape does not just apply to heterosexuals. In fact, if you are sapiosexual, autosexual, demisexual, fluid, heterosexual, monosexual, then at least try this once. If you are lesbian, gay, bisexual, transgender, you may want to part take in the festivities also. I suppose, lesbians would enjoy this sexual activity. I am trying to visualize as I'm writing, and the only vision I have is the woman on the other side of the booth has a big ass fucking clit. LOL! She would pull down her panties and stick her big ass clit through the hole. OMG! I am laughing so hard right now.

I clearly remember saying the hole was only three inches in diameter. I never mentioned width. We can just go head and assume it's two inches at the minimum. Hopefully, that is enough width for ya to stick your transgendered and cross-dressing cocks through to the other side. Wait! I ain't assuming y'all got small cocks either, nor do I personally know or care. Please forgive me, for I have sinned for talking about lesbians. Now, if you have read this far down into this chapter, it's time for me to address the transgender people and cross-dressers again. I guess you mofos are going to have to decide who is fucking who. Or who's cock is long enough to go through the hole. Just make damn sure that decision is made before you muthafuckas enter the booth, okay? If not, You Can Bet Your Bottom Dollar, the two of you will be arguing like a couple of bitches. Peace Muthafucka!!!

In DaSwing of Thangs

 **I** **remember** being on the computer and thinking what it would be like to sign up again on a swinger site. Looking at photos of people having sex and exchanging wives, I wanted in on the action, I was curious about the whole situation.

I've always been direct and honest, so when one of my wives saw me on the computer and asked what I was doing, I told her I was considering signing up on a swinging website, just to check it out. Imagine my excitement when she asked if I was signing up as a single, or as a couple? Oh, hell yes! I signed us up as a couple and thought to myself: Winner, winner ... ding, ding, ding!

I made us a profile, as a couple, and within a month we were getting emails to meet other couples. Of course, it's not as fun as you think. It's not always about fucking, as we must have chemistry with the couple that we're interested in, and they are interested in us. In some cases, the wife is attractive, and the husband is not attractive, or the husband is attractive, and the wife is not attractive.

We went to swing parties in the Tampa area, meeting new people with the same mindset, some who were industrious wealthy people. Yes, there may have been a few racists among the group, but they were polite, if there is such a thing as a polite racist. They would say hello but had absolutely no desire to be with a Black man or an interracial couple. I'm glad I didn't have to witness a lot of that at the parties we attended.

The interesting thing is, the parties that we went to, I never met a Black couple. It even made me wonder to myself, are there any Black swingers out there besides the famous couple we all know? But then again, what the fuck did I care? I'm like a fly among the maggots. White women who were curious about Black men could fuck me! Most White women fantasize about fucking a Black man anyways, if they're not racist, I just said a fact that White men can't do anything about. The bottom line is, if you close your eyes and I'm fucking you, do you really know if it's a White man or a Black man besides the size of the cock? Just kidding!

Most women I played with, I was able to take them out of their comfort zone, they'd squirt and do nasty shit with me that they never thought about doing with their husbands. Whatever they did with me, the husbands benefited from. Some of these wives were not even into anal, until they had anal with me, then they liked it. Husbands would later tell me they had been with their wives for thirty-plus years, and she never liked anal. They always asked what I did to make their wife relax enough to enjoy anal. Before, their wives said no fucking way! Afterwards, the husband could fuck their wives anytime in the ass, and they loved it. I've even had husbands thank me for making their wives squirt. It's always weird when a husband walks up to me and says, "My wife wants to fuck you." Don't laugh at what I am about to say next, but in some of the cases, when the husband asked me to fuck his wife, I wasn't attracted to her. It's impossible to avoid that situation and be polite about it. I'm glad the spouse couldn't read my mind or interpret facial expressions. Because the few times it did happened, I was kicked out of the party. Makes me wonder sometimes if White folks think just because I'm Black I'd fuck any White woman, especially after I've watched White men avoiding her. Fuck dat shit, that's my cue right there not to fuck with that one.

I don't know how it initially started, but if I had to guess, it started when I Googled the word sex, and on the first page something came up regarding swinging, and I asked myself ... what does swinging have to do with sex? This was thirty-plus years ago, and believe me, swinging has a WHOLE lot to do with sex. A few of the swinging sites made me curious, so I had to check it out. I mean, I had to do some further investigation into it. As I looked at these sites, I knew I liked what I was seeing and didn't hesitate to join a few of the websites.

I'm not going to mention which sites they were, but please take caution, not all swinging websites are legitimate. Some have bots responding to your messages. If you want to get into swinging, there are only a few sites worth paying for. If you want to know which sites, I feel are legit, you can always reach out to me.

Anyway, I joined a few sites, and I started looking at some of the profiles and photos that couples were posting. I knew right then and there I had found my alternative home. I said to myself, while looking at one of the profiles, looks like this guy is getting his dick sucked by one woman while eating another woman's pussy. I just assumed he was eating his wife's pussy, while his wife was licking another pussy. I thought, DAMN! To me, this was better than porn, real people were having sex.

I met couples by posting my profile on some of the swinger sites I researched. The next thing I know, I'm talking to a few couples and meeting the husband first, then eventually the wife. Sometimes we'd get together sexually, and sometimes it was a bust because I wouldn't be interested in the wife.

I'm starting to understand why White men despise Black men. Most famous sports figures are Black people, and we have that shit on lock. Guess what else we have on lock? Fucking White women and racist White men can't mind their own business when they see it. Once a White woman fucks a Black man, it's tough for them to consider fucking a White man again. It may also be the reason White racist police officers handcuff Black men first, before they beat the fuck out of them.

If you're a White racist man or woman reading this part and pissed off, keep in mind it's well documented that White racist police officers handcuff Black men before beating them with their batons or shooting them in the back. I can't think of one justifiable reason to handcuff an unarmed nigga and beat the fuck out of them.

Sorry, my ADD got the better of me.

Back to the swinger websites: I joined this one website and really wasn't having any luck, but I did like looking at the pictures. I saw one guy was having a blast. It just looked like everybody was having fun. I finally said, fuck it. To be honest, it's not always about fucking, it's about the relationship and friendships built between people of the same mindset. So, I started going to a place called Trapeze, but I always went alone. It was weird going to something like that by myself.

I've been to a couple nudist resorts in the Tampa area, a place called Caliente and another named Paradise Lakes Resort. On one of these visits, I was approached by a Black man and his girlfriend. He said to me, my girl would like to dance with you. I danced with her, but that was it.

It wasn't until years later I ran into them again, at first, I couldn't figure out why they looked so familiar to me. Then it dawned on me, they were the couple I had met years earlier, at the nightclub on the premises of the resort. Because I had been so new to the lifestyle at that time, I didn't realize that while dancing with this guy's girlfriend, I was supposed to get acquainted and then fuck her. The Black man had arranged it, and I didn't know what to do. Sure, I thought she was cute as hell, but I should have been flirty. Then, if she liked what she saw and heard, we would have been fucking. They lived at Paradise Lakes, so all we had to do was leave the nightclub and go fuck. I had no idea I could have gotten some pussy that night. Although if I had known, I would have been addicted to the lifestyle and would have gone up there a lot more often to see who else I could have fucked. Update: that Black man hung himself after his scandal was exposed.

In the Tampa area, few Black people are in the swinging lifestyle. Of those that are, usually they're Black guys offering themselves to White women and/or White couples, but it is not taboo. I'm telling you, swinging can be fun! If you are two very open-minded (sexual) people AND secure within your relationship AND take your time ... it can be an amazing experience. I say this next part with complete sincerity, if your relationship is secure, try swinging.

If you are a single male, there is a process on what to do, which I've learned over the years. When a couple is interested in you, most single males make assumptions that a couple might be interested in fucking them.

Even if you're a single White or Black male and the husband wants to watch you fuck his wife, there's still a way to go about it. You need to do certain things from the very beginning that will make them comfortable and ensure you'll be a part of their fuck fantasy. As I said before, I'm willing to answer any questions you might have.

After running into that couple from before, I went back a few more times to the nightclub. However, it made me a bit uncomfortable as it reminded me of buzzards hanging around on a tree branch, waiting to fuck and eat something. So, anyway, that's kind of how I got started into swinging. My ads would say: "single Black male available for fun," and that paid off a few times with couples reaching out to me. Update: our country is so divided right now, so as a Black male this is not a good time to put yourself in danger.

Massage Envious

ack in the day, my go-to was asking the woman I'm dating if she wanted a massage. Massages are so sensual, and by not being a professional, there are some boundaries I cross sensually. Usually, when I offer a massage and it's our first time together, nine times out of ten, they're thinking I want to fuck them. Now, I'm going to be straight up with you, and say, yes, I may be thinking about fucking them. But there is more pleasure in trusting me, to relax, knowing I want nothing in exchange. My initial offer to massage, is only to make it all about them. Wait a damn minute, don't get it twisted, if I see an opportunity wezafucking.

I usually start with her lying flat on her stomach, with no towel, and exposing her ass. Of course, in her head, I'm sure she's thinking I'm going to massage her ass cheeks right away. Nope, I skip past the ass and massage her thighs, calves, feet, and then the shoulders. While massaging her back, I lightly use my fingernails against the back, from the neck to above the ass. I do this very slowly and watch her intently. I usually hear clues she likes it harder and if that's the case, I dig in a little deeper. I'm careful of this method because, she may cum, just saying. The butt-cheeks are last because there's nothing like massaging one butt-cheek at a time. Seriously, when I pull the butt-cheeks apart, I see everything the man above gave her. Never mind the fact, it's sexy as fuck to me personally. I am certain she must feel vulnerable in that position and I'm conscious of that. I completely understand, she's trusting me not to suddenly surprise her with something we had never discussed or done.

I massage one hip slowly, then move to the other hip. Next, massage the inner thighs and close to the pussy lips as possible, on both sides. At this point, her legs are slightly open, I'll just graze the pussy, but not touch it. See, I'm already getting her all worked up and wet, I know exactly what the fuck I'm doing muthafucka! Then I tell her to turn over while I massage the front of the thigh and inner thigh. Again, I massage close to the pussy from the front, but never actually touch it. I don't have to do the shoulders as I did that while she was on her back. Next up, her stomach, which some women are insecure about. It's my job to make sure she is comfortable, and there's nothing to be insecure about.

Next, I rub across the lips of her mouth, very slowly, and watch her breathing. It's going to be apparent that she's turned on, so then I move towards her breast and nipples. I'd always warm the oil or lotion in my hands or with my breath.

Massage one breast at a time, slowly. When it's time for the nipples, make a circular motion around the nipple without touching the tip. Why? She is assuming my next move; so, I might as well throw her off my scent. LOL. Besides, the anticipation gets her even more wet. Then, the pussy and clit. And, exactly in that order.

Molested Vs Rape

efore you read this chapter, please be advised, I am not and never have claimed to be a professional therapist or psychologist. I'm a man who has had relationships with women who have either been molested or raped, and in some instances, both. The baby, child, teenager, and adult are traumatized for the rest of their lives. I am an advocate of women having a choice of what they do with their own bodies. Nevertheless, let me get into it.

When a woman has been raped, it's hard for them to ask their partner to duplicate that feeling without embarrassment or being judged. Also, while in their teens, it's hard for them to have an orgasm. How a woman is capable to compartmentalize their feelings is a mystery to me. On the other hand, when a woman has been molested by a family member or the mother's boyfriend, usually the mother knows it's happening or happened. The mother and daughter are usually too afraid to do anything about it, especially if the man is the provider. What's even more fucked up, some moms who know their daughter is being molested, get upset with the daughter! I could never understand why the mother would be angry at her daughter and not the guy. The whole thing reminds me of the movie *Precious,* where the mother treated her daughter like trash instead of kicking out the molesting coward she sleeps with or report him to the authorities.

It's also been my experience, if a woman was molested at an early age, they don't always comprehend what's happening to them. I hope what I am about to say next will be interpreted correctly, so here goes. What if the daughter grew up in a loving family environment, and let's just say the mother is not aware her daughter is being molested. In fact, it's by the husband or boyfriend. Let me explain this the best way I can, I hope it makes sense.

What if the husband or boyfriend experienced being molested and was unaware, they were molested as a child. Additionally, that husband or boyfriend was also loved and cared for by a generational child molester, how do they know what's crossing the line or not? I honestly feel this experience with molestation is hard to detect until the act itself has been carried out on the unsuspecting. And only a trained professional is aware of the signs. Back to what I'm trying to relay to you. What if this generational child molester does it unconsciously the way he grew up by his father or his mom's boyfriend. Nevertheless, he's a grown ass man now and raises his daughter in the same type of environment he was accustomed to. It gets deeper, he does this perversion with his daughter in a sick, fucked-up loving way. In other words, he says he loves her while she's sitting in his lap. Not to mention, he tickles and fondles her inappropriately while his wife is not present. Which means he's aware it's inappropriate because that's exactly what his father did to him as a child. All of this can be confusing once they become an adult.

So, when a woman tells a man they need to be choked and forced against their will, sometimes, they are trying to reenact what's been privately done to them as a child by a family member or someone the family trusted. What are your personal thoughts on what I just said? Something that will make you say, hmmmm.

I've dealt with women who have been raped and molested, so, I'm a little embarrassed to admit those women are freakier. These are the type of women I unconsciously gravitate towards, especially if they overcame the trauma and still like sex. They are normally shy and will ask me in a subtle indirect way to reenact the molestation. I've never looked at a woman as damaged property, and to be honest, I get turned on when they say they've been molested or raped. I've been raped myself in my teens and that's why I'm fucked up even in my sixties. I get more into this in another chapter. To this day, my own dead momma doesn't know anything about this. Yes, this book is therapy for me and hopefully for you as well. Besides, what person hasn't had a rape roleplay fantasy? Anyone who criticizes me for what I just said are the same people who have had the same thought cross their minds.

It wasn't until years later that I became turned on being in a Dom/Sub relationship. And let me tell you, some women don't want to be in a relationship with a sissy, they want that dominated sexually and mentally. This applies to women of all ages, backgrounds, and financial status. That's why when I hear a woman say, do whatever you want to me, that's like waving a red flag in front of a bull!

Again, I repeat, it's important to talk to your partner (or potential partner) about sex, right from the beginning. I have no intention of sticking my cock anywhere, until I have had a mature conversation, and it's clear what our desires are. It makes me crazy when I'm trying to get to know someone, and they don't want to talk about sex right away. They incorrectly assume I want to fuck them right away, that is not the case. Mature adults should have fun discussing the subject. I understand, a lot of women have problems talking about sex, probably because of the way they were raised or if they were raped or molested, but it is extremely important if you genuinely want to get to know this person. And yes, I know there are also immature men out there who don't give a shit about what hole they put their cock in.

Must Be the Dog "N" ME

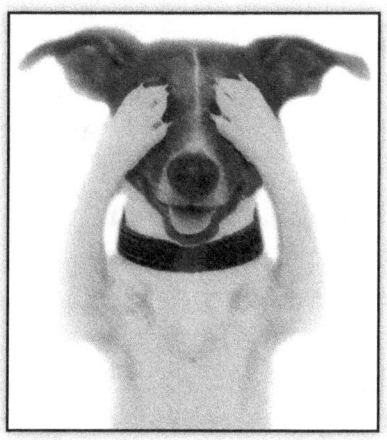

arning, what I'm about to say next is gross as fuck, but keep in mind I was between nine and ten years old, so don't hold it against me, and if you do, fuck you I don't care. This is how mischievous I was, sexually. So, before you continue, you may want to make sure you are reading this on an empty stomach, okay?

Growing up, we had this dachshund, and this dog would walk around the house with his tail all up in the air, and as my dog walked past me, I could see its butthole. One day while my dachshund was walking past me, I had a thought; I picked him up and put him in my lap. I unzipped my pants and then took out my cock and tried to put my cock in my dog's ass. I wanted to see if my cock would just slide into his butt with no lube, it didn't. I wasn't trying to force it or anything. I was afraid I may hurt the head of my cock. My dachshund whipped his head around and looked behind him, I am sure my dog was saying, "What the fuck is the negga trying to do to me?" The look my dog gave me made me feel weird. My cock wasn't going in anyway, so I put him down. I don't know why I did it, except to say, at that stage of my life, I would have been willing to put my cock anywhere if it felt good.

It's a good thing my cock didn't fit or go inside my dog's ass because I could have turned out to be one of those guys who fucks dogs, chickens, pigs, horses, and other animals. You know damn well this sort of sick shit exist, not that there's anything wrong with those who privately do this. There are other things out there people can get into that's far worse, right? I know this story is going to be shared and talked about, a lot. If anyone wants to hold any of this shit against what I did as a horny child, I no longer give a fuck. I'm just keeping it real; this is the kinda shit I did back in the day. I knew nothing about girls at the time. There are people doing far worse than fucking an animal and this is a fact. Let's have fun with this next question I am about to ask, which would you rather have: Your neighbor fucking animals or kidnapping children? Don't you dare say neither one! Pick ... get wit me later.

There is nothing you could tell me that's worse than this chapter, right?

My Gay Azz Cousin

 **know** there is going to be a lot of people out there that will judge me for my indiscretions. So, anyway, I also know what I am risking by putting my life and experiences in this book. In fact, let me set the fucking record straight right now, I don't consider myself pansexual, bisexual, gay, allosexual, androsexual, aromantic, closeted, cupiosexual, Graysexual, Grayromantic, panromantic, Spectrasexual, skoliosexual, sex-repulsed, sex-indifferent, sex-favorable, questioning, queer, Pomosexual, omnisexual, or gynesexual. In all honesty, I may be one or more of the following: straight, sapiosexual, autosexual, demisexual, fluid, heterosexual, monosexual, or plain old sexual. I know after, or while reading this chapter, discussing the interaction I had with my gay azz cousin, you'll either pick or assume several of the above that applies to me.

There's a saying that's been around a while, and if you wanna read it, here it is. If you can't stand the heat then, you better get out of the kitchen. I'm more than ready for all you MOFOs, so here we go.

At fourteen years old, I was living with my mom Beatrice Hicks, we also had a thirty-three-year-old flaming gay cousin living with us named Leon who molested me. To this day, I am foggy how my gay azz cousin ended up living with us. So please forgive me for not having the details of why he was living with my mom and me okay. When I say molested, it wasn't a physical assault against my will, it was the kind of molestation being underage with inappropriate touching and child exploitation. At that age, I thought Leon liked me, and that's how you express it. You would think being fourteen years old, I should've known something wasn't as it seems. Back then, there was no such thing as #METOO or child welfare agencies in predominantly Black neighborhoods. I'm not sure how you learned about sex, but my father died from heart failure right after I graduated from Gompers Junior High School in San Diego, California. As a result of this, I don't remember him teaching me anything about the birds and the bees. As mentioned in another chapter, the only thing I remember about my father was him having affairs and telling me about each one vividly. Nevertheless, the only encounters I've had with men were the one's dating my mom or the muthafuckas who were married and having affairs at my house. Not to mention, my neighbors and the bullies in the neighborhood.

Wait, there was this one kid in San Diego by the name of Dan. While sucking my cock, we were almost busted by his grandmother. Thinking back, neither he or I would be considered gay or bisexual, more so curious than anything.

I know the title of this chapter says, "My Gay Azz Cousin." So, let's get into it, shall we? One evening, when I was fifteen years old, my gay azz cousin Leon, who was thirty-four years old now, walked abruptly into my room and asked if I wanted to fuck him. Me being the curious kid, I said yes. What the fuck was I thinking, right? At that age, I didn't know what to do or where my cock needed to go. I had an idea and that's about the extent of it. I remember watching him unzipping and pulling down his pants while my momma was in the living room watching television. This slick muthafucking child molester knew what he wanted because I sure didn't.

Leon got up on my bed and bent over doggie style. He looked over his shoulder at me and smiled. I asked him, what am I supposed to do and how do I do it?

He said, in these exact words, "Put your hard cock in my azz." He knew I was hard as he saw the bulge in my pants. I unzipped and pulled down my pants. I got on the bed on my knees behind him. Everything I am saying is a bit foggy, so hang in there with me if something seems a bit off, okay? My gay azz cousin must have liked pain because he didn't bring lube or spit in his hand. I'm certain that had a lot to do with why I didn't enjoy fucking him in his azz, I was stretching the skin around the head of my cock, and that shit (no pun intended) was painful as fuck! That's me trying to fuck him, right? Keep reading, it's time for me to pay up.

On a different evening, my gay azz cousin Leon was extremely horny. He barged through my bedroom door and walked right in while I was minding my own business. Like I mentioned above, when his bitch azz opens my door, especially without knocking, his intent is not to talk to me. Being honest with you, I am surprised that my gay azz cousin didn't physically assault and abuse me for his sexual gratification. Anyways, I've always been a person who feels when something is not fair, I want to make it right.

My momma was like that also, so when Leon told me it was his turn to fuck me, I held my head down, looked at the floor, and said okay. It didn't seem like I had a choice in that situation. I unzipped and pulled down my pants, got on the bed, and bent over like he told me to do. And, without warning, that gay azz muthafucka stuck his cock in my azz. In fact, it was painful as fuck! It's not like he had a big cock either, he just didn't use any lube. In fact, that son of a bitch didn't even spit on it before he shoved it in my azz. In fact, once he put the head in, I told him to pull out and get the fuck out of my bedroom.

My momma must have known something was wrong by the volume and tone in my voice when

I yelled at him to get the fuck out of my bedroom, she asked me if I was okay. I wasn't sure what to say. I ended up lying to her, not realizing the effect it would have on me afterwards. Something about that situation didn't seem right. I'm sure this is my reason I like anal sex, as the giver not the taker.

After telling Leon to get the fuck out of my bedroom, there was at least three other times I tried to sneak out of my bedroom while I thought my mom was sleep, I wanted him to suck my cock. My mom must have had superpowers to have heard me sneaking out of my room every night. It didn't matter how slow or quiet I was, every night she asked me, "What are you doing?" I told her I was going into the bathroom, and she said, "Yeah okay." I was in the hallway, pretending to open the bathroom door and close it behind me. I would hurry into my cousin's room where he was waiting for me, already laying near the edge of the bed on his side.

All I had to do was walk up to the edge of the bed, like I am at a cock sucking station, pull up, drop my draws, and get my cock sucked till I came in his mouth. Then, I had to slip back into the bathroom and act like I flushed the toilet. Every time I tried to slip out of my bedroom to have my cock sucked, my mom used her superpowers and asked, what was I doing? I asked myself, why does it matter what was going on? She had an idea, and I was too embarrassed to admit what was happening.

I guess I'm one of those muthafuckas who will try anything once, and if I like it, I'll try it again, that's not the case with being fucked in the azz by my cousin or any man from that point on. Well, that's "My Gay Azz Cousin" story.

Wait muthafuckas, I'm not done talking about my gay azz cousin Leon just yet. Earlier, I didn't mention my cousin could suck a mean cock. As a result, on both sides of the gay parade, fucking men wasn't on my menu. Later, I realized my cousin had other ideas to explore with me and that was asking to suck my cock. Well, since the azz fuck wasn't happening, I gave him one last chance, for some fucked-up reason.

After everything he'd done and tried to do to me sexually, Leon told me sucking my cock would be more pleasurable, and he promised me that I did not have to reciprocate. Now he had my attention because I knew if I did not like that either I could always say no. My gay azz cousin tried again to convince me that I would enjoy what he does with his mouth. He told me, all I had to do was walk in, drop my draws, and watch him suck my cock. There was no way of avoiding him in a nine hundred square-foot, three-bedroom, one bath house. I came every got damn time he did it. And, just so you know, he never swallowed my fresh hot cum because he would spit the cum into a can on the floor next to his bed after I came in his mouth. Man, the noises he would make when he was sucking on my cock was addicting.

With no intentions of leaving anything out of this chapter, here is another memory regarding my flaming gay azz cousin Leon, which leads me to believe, molestation has altered my behavior even as an adult. One day I was at Ocean View Hills Park in Southeast San Diego playing basketball. When my gay azz cousin walked over to the park to say hello. Keep in mind, I knew this muthafucka wanted more than to just say hello. All my gay azz cousin had to do was make that cock- suck slurping sound, and an instant erection like the bottom bunker man I am. At the time, I was embarrassed to be associated to my gay azz cousin, he and I had never been seen together publicly.

I knew damn well I better not display that kind of interaction anywhere I lived, without having my azz kicked or worse. When I was twenty-three years old, it was finally time for me to move from my mom's house into my own apartment. Never having a place of my own, I was excited about it. It was a one bedroom on the third floor. What I also liked about this place is you had to call me on the intercom.

No sooner than a few days after I moved in, my muthafucking flaming gay azz cousin called me unexpectedly. I tried desperately to avoid listening to the sound he was making, and don't act like you don't know what sound I'm talking about either. I ended up telling Leon to come on over to my apartment and suck my cock. Not sure why this time was different, but I came so fucking hard I almost passed out and my knees were weak.

I pushed Leon's head away from my pelvis like he bit me. He stood in front of me as if he wanted to kiss me, and I slapped the cum right out of his mouth. What's fucked up is, he spit my fresh hot cum all over the floor. He cried right after I slapped him in the face and walked out the door and didn't look back. At that moment, I knew it was my last time ever seeing him. The path I was headed, I could have easily ended up like my gay azz cousin. My family and friends would have crucified me. Real example: Why is it, I was able to cum in my cousin's mouth repeatedly, and since then and to this very day, I can't with women. Most of the women I either married or dated have all tried wanting me to cum orally. Trust me, I've had some great BJs over the years, but none were able to duplicate my cousins sucking style. Damn, I hate the memories I have of my cousin. Right at this moment while I am typing, I see him down on his knees making that slurping sound while moving his head back and forth all while using the palm of his hand around the shaft of my cock. The motion of all three I guess can't be duplicated unless you are my gay azz cousin. I'm sad right now, I wished I had been protected from my cousin molesting me. Too late now, he stole my impressionable years and made me who I am today, still confused at times and questioning my own behavior.

There were times when I tried to reenact that experience with my cousin with strange men in my late teens. Nothing came close to what that molesting azz muthafucking Leon did to me. Quick note if you are a woman reading this part of the chapter, most men will not be this open with you with something so fucked up. For him to bare his soul, it's imperative you will not criticize or judge him for something he may not have known was wrong. Wrong in the sense that, he was lied to, and his innocence was stripped from him. Especially if it was a family member or someone he trusted. For him to talk about it, you must make him feel safe from it happening again. It's embarrassing enough, and more than likely, the trauma is buried deep inside him. So, if he does tell you about his molestation, embrace and hug him.

At 9:57 a.m. on July 17, 2022, I woke up with a revelation, and I want to share it with you. It's also why I defend anyone being bullied and understood why Lil Nas X admitted his sexual orientation after he became famous. I understand why so many are afraid to express themselves. I'm shocked that I didn't end up a wrist bent, holding a drink with my pinky finger erect str8 up gay.

Leon was so good at sucking my cock every time I was alone with him, I could have ended up wanting my cock sucked by a bunch of strange men all the time. I would have been a selfish lover if I had been gay. Okay, I'll tell you right now, I'd have to be the top if I were gay. Fuck being a bottom. No pun intended. I am certain somebody is reading this right now saying, why do I like to fuck women in the azz but didn't like it when I fucked my cousin? In the first place, I was underage; secondly, I was curious; and last and most important, my cousin's azz was hairy, seriously! Every time in and out of his hairy azzhole, my shaft rubbed against the hair between his azz. Don't laugh! This ain't funny, it hurt. That's the end of my Gay Azz Cousin Chapter.

UPDATE: I woke up the morning of July 17, 2022 and had a revelation about a male well-known Black actor. And, like most of my revelations throughout this book, I particularly had to write about this one. This actor decided to be the only, I repeat, the only, mammoth-sized Black man to publicly come forward, regarding allegations of cock and balls groping. I feel extremely comfortable writing about this subject, and we are all entitled to our opinions, so here's mine. I feel confident that this male actor gave subtle, and even intentional, signs that it was okay for his agent to grope this actor by the cock and balls (allegedly). How dafuck does a former American soccer player allow another man to grope his cock and balls? Yes, you read that correctly, ALLOWED! There's absolutely no fucking way another man would grab my cock and balls and I wouldn't have said or done something about it, expeditiously.

When my gay azz cousin Leon molested me, I wasn't an adult, I was a damn minor. The actor was a grown azz muthafucking Black man at the time of his groping allegations. Let's analyze his allegations, shall we? He was a big azz soccer player for Pete's sake and surrounded by peers his age and size. I wonder, while showering if he looks over his shoulder and drops the soap? Just saying. Let's follow his career where he convincingly played a manly man until his favorite song came on while sitting in the car in *"Vanilla Girls."* Just before that scene, his manliness was questionable. Hell, if anyone knows questionable behavior, it's me without a doubt, right?

Nevertheless, I am accurate in my damn assessment. Either way, he spoke on the trauma he endured as a child, leading me to believe there's more to the story than what he's shared publicly. As I watch television, his mannerisms are questionable. It's okay, whatever sexual preference he has is between him and the man above. So, don't be surprised when this same actor divorces his current wife to marry a famous LGBT advocate. Yep, you read it right. So, go ahead, criticize me for my criticism. Peace, Love and Hair Grease.

My Shaft, You Damn Right

don't like women with hairy pussies, or hair around, above, or below the pussy lips. I'm not fucking it, licking it, fingering it, or massaging it, but I will shave it if you want me to do one or all of what I just mentioned. When I meet someone on a dating site, I'm patient and will not ask the question within the first couple of conversations. What question, right? You know the one? Are they shaved. If they tell me they have either one of the following: The Full Bush, The Bikini Line, and plan to keep it that way, I don't pursue them. I might be okay with The Landing Strip, that's not something that's going to stop me. As you already know from what I have written so far, I like bald pussies, or the more etiquette word for it, The Brazilian.

So, let's dive right in, why A shaved pussy is my personal preference? After reading this you'll have a clear understanding. There was this one sista I met on a dating site and before we met, we talked on the phone for weeks before meeting each other. I considered myself a gentleman back then and still do. I am not someone who must talk about sex on the first fucking conversation. I only ask about their pussy if they gave me the impression, they are like myself, blunt. If that's not the case, I am extremely patient. Usually, early in the conversation, I like having an adult conversation about shaved pussy. The last thing either one of us wants is to talk for weeks and your preference is a "Hairy Pussy." Oh! A couple of weeks is too soon for ya, is it? Well, then maybe after the third week.

I knew Miss Hairy Pussy for about a month. We only kissed and shit like that and still had not talked about sex. All I can say is, I wished we had discussed sex at the very beginning of our conversations, I could have avoided being in a fucked- up situation that obviously I haven't forgotten. Unlike a famous porch nigga, I have not met him but know of, what's his name that looks like he has an Afghan Hound over his top lip? According to one of his televised shows, if a woman does what that motherfucker suggested, wait two to three months before fucking, and then I realize she ain't shaved too, fuck dat shit!

Here is why it's important for me to discuss hair on the pussy. Before I fucked Miss Hairy Pussy, I didn't ask whether she shaved or not when we first chatted on the phone, but wish I had. One evening while Miss Hairy Pussy's roommate was working, she called and asked me to spend time with her. And of course, I said yes. Even though we talked about sex on the phone, it was our first time together sexually. We didn't waste any time talking once I walked in. She had coco butter skin and a nice body. I watched her take off her clothes, and I wasn't wasting time taking off mine either. Unlike most women I've met, there was no foreplay, kissing, sucking cock, or eating pussy for starters. While she was lying on her back underneath me, the head of my cock entered her pussy.

Immediately, I felt something I had never felt before. She couldn't understand why I wasn't giving it my best. I was trying as hard as I could to have fun, but I couldn't.

Keep reading, it's not for the reason you think it is.

Her pussy was so hairy, I wasn't sure why the shaft of my cock was stinging, and I had to stop. I laid next to her for a little while, and I apologized for going soft while I was inside her. I can honestly admit, I didn't see her anymore after that. She was embarrassed for me, not knowing she was the cause of it. So, I stood up and put my clothes on. In fact, I was bleeding inside of my underwear. Here I am sixty-plus years old and to date, I've not yet felt anything like that since. This was years ago. Here is what happened and the reason I couldn't continue fucking her. As a result of my shaft going in and out of her hairy ass pussy, I didn't realize I was rubbing my cock shaft raw. In fact, I rubbed my shaft so raw, I was bleeding, that's how bad it was. Let me break this down for ya, exactly what happened. The moment I penetrated her, my shaft was rubbing against the hair. To help you with a visual, imagine the hair on her pussy being long enough, that while going inside her, the hair goes too. That's why her hair felt like an abrasive steel wool against my shaft. While I was in the bathroom, I was bleeding when I touched my cock to pee.

All because she had a hairy pussy. At the beginning, if she and I had that adult conversation about her preference, what happened to me would not have happened. There go those weeks of conversation, and our first fuck date is all gone to hell now. I'm certain there's guys out there that like hairy pussies, and this may not have happened to them. Nowadays, when I find out a woman has a hairy pussy, to this very day, I don't fuck with them.

If you are a man reading this chapter and like hairy pussies, make sure they shower before eating the pussy.

Think about it for a second you nasty MOFO, there is sweat and urine in that hairy mixed drink. A woman without hair is the way to go, plus, if they have any pimples or anything else wrong with their pussy you can see it beneath the hair. You can't see the pimples and whatever else is going on underneath their hairy pussy.

Well, you may not like my opinion, but that's my take on hairy pussies, and guess what? IDGAF! I'm sure there are men out there that like hair all down there, I'm just not one of them. Oh, and one last thing, spitting hair out of my mouth while I'm eating the pussy is annoying and a deal breaker.

One Shitty Situation After Anotha

s the reader, you are going to have to gauge if this is the sickest thing you've heard of someone doing, okay? So here goes, since shit does not bother me, there was another woman who I was fucking in the ass and ... Wait a minute, let me start from the beginning on how I met her. Back in the day and even now, most of the women I have met are online. Which brings me to when I lived in San Diego, I met this one White woman named Susanne from Germany. She told me she only dated Black men. I asked her why and she told me, Black men treat her better than White men.

I thought Susanne was being vague, so I asked her if she could be more specific. She hesitated and smiled at me. I said, "I'm curious why you feel that way about White men when you're White your damn self." She looked me dead in my eyes; I was not expecting this answer.

She said, "They fuck me better." I had a look of shock on my face. She asked me what was wrong.

All I could say was, "Don't be shy now, continue."

Susanne said, "Okay Cecil, it's like this, Black men fuck me more passionately than White men. I like rough sex with some passion mixed with it."

I said, "Stop beating around the fucking bush and explain why you like rough sex."

Susanne said, "I liked to be choked, held down and slapped on the ass while being fucked." At that point, my ears went up like a dog that heard something in the grass, in other words, she had my complete attention. "I don't want the man I'm fucking asking me what I like. I want him in total control and take what hole he wants without giving a fuck what I want. I'm uncomfortable when men ask me what I want and that's what White men do."

Susanne continued, "I like a confident man that knows exactly what he wants and takes it from me. When I say take me, I don't mean rape me, I mean just do as he pleases. But the difference is, with Black men, I know my role right away by the way they treat me." What she said next blew me away. "Besides, Black men make me feel submissive because I don't like being in control in the bedroom." Well, I'll be damned, I have another fuck buddy in addition to the stable of bitches I already had.

One day Susanne called me to come over to fuck her as usual. She had called at the perfect time because I was already in my car. I turned around and headed over to her place. This time was different, she had already had a few drinks, and it was only two p.m. eastern time. I could tell the difference with her slurring her words while she said come on in. Okay, I'll admit, I like women who have had a few drinks before I fuck them. Drinking takes away all their inhibitions, and they are ready to fuck without a lot of talking. That was the case this time when I walked in, she was naked and ready.

I guided her towards the bedroom and pushed her down on the bed. I was not about to waste any time and hurried taking off my clothes. Once I had my clothes off, I climbed up on the bed with her. I did not feel like kissing because all I had on my mind was fucking her.

While having my cock sucked, I was playing with her pussy, and then I turned her over, so she was face down and ass up. Susanne always had lube inside the nightstand, and I opened it and put some on my cock. She knew I was about to fuck her in her ass, and she didn't say one fucking word. I lined up my cock and slid it in her ass. It felt so good, but I didn't want to cum right away. I kept taking my cock in and out of her ass. While looking down at her asshole, I realized there was shit on my cock, fingers, hands, and sheets. You would think that would have stopped me, right? Like the song by Bishop Bullwinkle, "Hell 2 Dah Naww Naww Naww."

Regardless of the shit, I was having so much fun fucking her in her ass, I did not want to leave the bedroom. An idea popped into my head, *why not use her sheets and blankets to clean off my cock*, I'm one nasty muthafucka. I grabbed a hand full of her sheets and kept cleaning my cock off with it. Every time I pulled my cock out Susanne's ass, I had shit. I hope you are not eating anything right now, are you? There was shit all over the damn place other than where I was fucking her. When I finally came in her ass, I was wondering why she was still the entire time.

I'll be damned, Susanne fell asleep at some point, and I did not even notice. Now I was ready to go into her bathroom and clean up. It's a good thing I decided to take my clothes into the bathroom and put them on. You would never guess who was sitting in the living room. Her fifteen-year-old daughter had walked in from high school while I was in the bathroom and was sitting on the couch. The look on her face when I walked past her made me look away embarrassed. The bedroom door was wide open, her mom still sleeping, face down ass up, with shit all over her and the sheets. Well, that's how I am going to end this one shitty situation after anotha.

Peep Show Booths

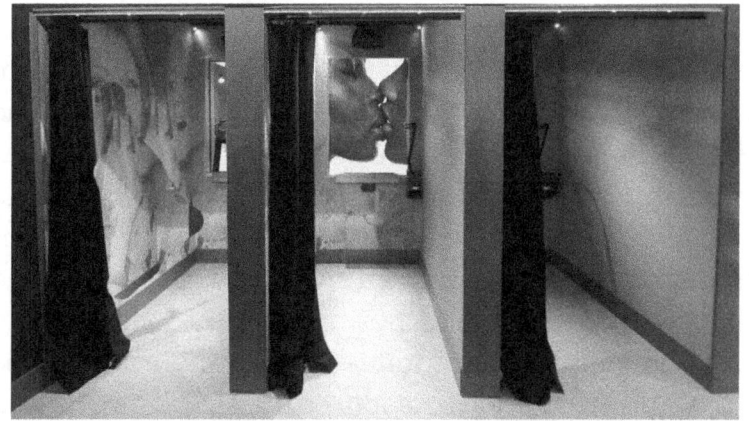

ey there millennials, have y'all ever been inside of a peep show booth? Depending on your age, I bet the answer was no. The only conceivable way you could know about peep shows is your daddy told ya, or you googled it. If you are fifty plus years and above, then you may know from curiosity. I am going to take you back into time" down memory lane with me. Like a (Cave Man)," The JCB (1972). Are you ready?

FIRST TIME:

Around two a.m., I got in my car determined to walk into my first peep show booth. The main room is dirty magazines, exclusively. And just like the bookstore I mentioned in another chapter, this one also had an area for eighteen and over. As I was walking around inside of the dirty magazine room, I was trying to get enough courage to go into the X-rated video area. I could partly see inside that room and noticed there were other men walking around like zombies. What I mean by that is, when you give a man too many choices, they become disoriented. Well, you know me, I want to know why they had that blank zombie look on their face. Once I walked in the video room, all I saw was X-rated videos on the wall behind a glass case. There was an assigned number, one to fifty for each X-rated video as a reference. This would allow me to choose which video I wanted to watch. While checking out the videos on the wall, I noticed a Mexican man walking around with a mop bucket. I watched him for a while and couldn't understand why this man needed a mop bucket. After time had passed, I figured out why. Then I became disgusted they hired a Mexican to clean up cum from muthafuckas jacking off on the floors inside the peep booths. It made since, every time I walked in that place it smelled like Pine-Sol.

SECOND TIME:

The first time, I wouldn't go in because the peep booths would allow anyone to walk in on the person that's inside. And as soon as you put your quarter in the slot, a light would warn the person trying to enter that someone is already inside. That wasn't enough of a deterrent for my privacy. I can say that honestly because someone walked in on me even though the light was on, asshole! On my second time back, they had added a chain to place across the door opening after you walked in. There was a law, I suppose, in San Diego, which would not allow doors closed. And that's why people were able to walk in the booth without concerns of invading someone's privacy. Never mind the fact the person inside the booth may be masturbating. LOL. They also redesigned each peep booth like a maze. In fact, when you walked in, you couldn't immediately see who was inside. I felt better and safer walking in after they made the changes. With those changes, I went back on a regular basis. This place knew I was spending money at their location on peep show booths. They must have been watching me from the moment I placed my first quarter in the slot.

I would never go inside a peep booth after someone just walked out, I could see cum on the floor. I could slip and fall in someone's fresh, hot, still steaming cum. I only walked in a booth after it's mopped and cleaned up by the Mexican man. Once inside the booth, I made sure the chain was across the door and the warning light worked. Do you remember the numbers under each video behind the glass case I mentioned? I realized, you put your quarter in the slot to watch one of the videos from the wall you were interested in. What a money maker that was back in the day. One quarter only bought you thirty seconds of that video. Hell, it would have been cheaper to have bought the video and watched it at home, for less.

You wouldn't have to deal with a bunch of strange, perverted men like myself, walking around watching me while I'm watching them. Did I jack off while inside of the peep booth? I damn sure did but was always afraid someone wouldn't give a fuck and walk in on me.

It happened once, a man walked in on me, even though the chain was up, and the light was on. I remember walking in one booth I thought was clean, and there was cum splashed all over the screen still. Obviously, I walked out of that one, SMH. I tried another booth and there was a motherfucker waiting inside. He intentionally did not put up the chain, and I saw him jacking off. That man acted like I was supposed to join him in a circle jerk. I became angry because he violated my eyes, reminding me of my cousin all over again. I turned around and walked away, seconds later, that man walked out. And like the cum on the floor clockwork, the Mexican man came again with his mop bucket.

THIRD TIME:

Another time I went back and watched movies and jacked off as usual. But this time, guess who was waiting for me when I walked out of the booth? That's right you guessed it, the Mexican man with his mop bucket ready to walk-in after me. I walked past him embarrassed and humiliated. Well, think about it, you heard the saying; young dumb and full of cum, right? That's why the Mexican man was waiting for me to come out. The owners and the Mexican man both knew my name after a while, ain't that fucked up. Eventually, they were giving me free tokens. Damn!

FORTH TIME:

The fourth time going back to watch more X-rated peep show videos, I saw someone I worked with, and we both looked at each other and started laughing. We both knew neither one of us were ever going to say anything. From then on when we saw each other at work we just smiled, and we knew what that meant. It meant neither one of us can pull a girl and that was our secret cum release place.

FIFTH TIME:

Oh, and I forgot to mention this earlier. There was one other time and my last time when I walked in one of the booths, and I sat in someone else's cum and now had cum stains on my pants. I know if I had seen someone come out of a peep show booth with a wet spot on his pants, I would wait for another guy to walk out afterwards with a smile on his face. Or he had cum in his ass prior to going on the booth. Either way, it wouldn't be a good look. I immediately went home took a shower and never went back. Anyways, that's my peep booth story and I'm sticking to it.

Pimpin' Ain't Easy

**arning,** read with caution and an open mind because the language you are about to read in this chapter is all related to my past experiences. The way I was raised by my parents, altered my personality to who I am today. For all you so called saints, I'm hoping you don't take this chapter personally. I will also share my opinions, and I'm anticipating reading or hearing yours, all relating to this book or chapter.

Pimpin' Black people can be easily disguised by non-Black production companies in many ways, solely from my perspective. In fact, BET has been pimping us for decades and it's not going to change anytime soon. Fact 1. All the writers and producers of blaxploitation movies were White or Jewish men, as far back as I can remember. Fact 2. Those mofos made a truckload of money from exploiting Black entertainers. Fact 3. They only produced and distributed blaxploitation movies stereotypical of Black men and women.

And positive role models starring Richard Roundtree as John Shaft in 1971, a dark-skinned man who portrayed a Black alpha male, pistol packing, take no prisoners ass-kicker, while busting down doors and beating down White man. *Foxy Brown* starring Pamela Suzette Grier as Pam Grier in the seventies, portrayed a Black sista as a no ass kissing, sexy ass-kicker with big breast. Wait, growing up those were the two big reasons I watched all her movies. And *Cleopatra Jones* starring Tamara Dobson portrayed an attractive, dark-skinned, intelligent, multitalented sista as an undercover agent. Side note, she died from complications of pneumonia and multiple sclerosis, she was fifty-nine.

Fact 4. Here we are in the twenty-first century and still portrayed negatively in movies, television, non-Black owned news stations, and now on social media. Fact 5. As a matter of fact, anyone who looks like me are typecasted as drug dealers, pimps, gullible, ignorant, dumb, fatherless, drug addicts, fake ministers, beggars, hung, maids, servants, no sir, yes sir, no mam, yes mam, can I, may I, subservient, coons, co-stars, clowns, cheaters, liars, slave catchers, breeders, slow, illegal gun carriers, gang bangers, illiterate, gold teeth wearing, thieves, lazy, hoes, prostitutes, pickaninnies, jigaboos, sambos, mammies, savages, Jezebels, ass twerking, Americoons, BDN (big dumb nigger) used in the movie *The Green Mile*, criminals, bucks, democrats, Mandingos, Swamp-Runners, and crows.

Fact 6. One thing for certain, we ain't no muthafuckn' mass murderers, and DATS DAH THE FACT, JACK.

There's a famous rapper who calls himself 50 Cent; he produces and directs stereotypical entertainment for profit, like a Black twenty-first century Pied Piper. I would like to elaborate further on the success of 50 Cent producing and directing blaxploitation television shows. May I continue? Consequently, all decisions relating to his ideas are contingent upon his SLAVE MASTERS approval such as:

- *Power* – "Ghost," a drug kingpin reports to his overseer, A WHITE MAN for business purposes, named Simon Stern. In other words, Ghost is not the HNIC (head nigga in charge).

- *BMF* – Glorified drug dealers as brothers, selling drugs and killing niggas, yet again.
- *Power Book II: Ghost* – A teenage son of "Ghost," another drug dealer with a portion of the above with collard greens, with a slightly, white cast as the side dish.
- *Power Book III: Raising Kanan* – Nothing short of left-over potato salad from the above sentences, with raisins in it, with a teaspoon of sour cream.
- *For Life* – Just anotha so-called innocent nigga locked up in prison trying to get out.

Fact 7. After 2 seasons, poof, done. In other words, his masters decided it wasn't showing us negatively enough. You would think after a classic movie called *The Shawshank Redemption*, he wouldn't follow up a classic with another nigga trying to get out of prison. Just saying! I'm just sharing my opinions and you can agree or disagree.

Fact 8. There is no way you can deny that all the above television shows are stereotypical of Black men and women. Do you wanna know what the fuck I grew up watching?

Your bitch ass needs examples of blaxploitation movies. The movies below were all funded by White men controlling the narrative. Let's start with one of my all- time classics in the blaxploitation era. And right out the 1975 Caddy we have:

- *Super Fly* (1972) – Niggas as pimps and street hustlers, directed by Gordon Parks Jr., a Black man funded by a White entertainment company.
- *Petey Wheatstraw* (1977) – Cliff Roquemore, Black director and funded by a White entertainment company.
- *That Man Bolt* (1973) – Henry Levin, David Lowell Rich, let's assume two White men.
- *Friday Foster* (1975) – Arthur Marks, White producer, who thought of the title of this movie, *The Legend of Nigger Charley* (1972) – Martin Goldman (let's just assume he's White).
- *Black Caesar* (1973) – Larry Cohen, White producer.
- *Willie Dynamite* (1974) – Gilbert Moses, Black director, funded by a White entertainment company.
- *Coffy* (1973) and *Foxy Brown* (1974) – Jack Hill, White producer.
- *Dolemite* (1973) – D'Urville Martin, Black director.
- *Across 110th Street* (1972) – Barry Shear, White producer.
- *Sweet Sweetback's Baadasssss Song* (1971) – Directed by Melvin Van Peebles but funded by a White entertainment company.
- *The Mack* (1973) – Michael Campus, White producer.

If you are of any other ethnicity than Black, what muthafucking movies, actors and actresses did you grow up idolizing and mimicking? These exploitive, White producers and directors knew the long-term effects of producing these types of movies, exclusively for Black communities.

Here we are in the twenty-first century, and I can see what's happening with leading, Black, strong masculine male actors and their plan is working to perfection. Just keep reading, it will be obvious why there is less roles available for positive Black male actors. Lately, more Black men are appearing on television dressed up as women, and it must be confusing for a young Black male these days and times, just ask me. In my opinion, *P-Valley* is just another blaxploitation series approved by a non-Black production company. In fact, it's the same entertainment company of 50 Cent. Honestly, P-Valley reminds me of To *Wong Foo, Thanks for Everything! Julie Newmar* starring Wesley Snipes. So, if you are open minded then pick one and watch it. Thank you, Dave Chappelle, for turning down the producers for not dressing up as a woman. Even though there was another popular Black male actor that said he would never dress as a woman, and I googled his name and I be damn he was dressed up as a woman. Fame seems to make people do some fucked up shit.

Btw, have you seen the movie *Day Shift* directed by J. J. Perry and starring Jamie Foxx with a cameo role with Snoop Dogg? I researched the director and I ain't sure what ethnicity he is exactly, but I am damn certain he ain't Black. While watching the movie, I am also paying attention to how many Black actors are in it and what their roles are. I also take notes as to how much time the White producers are giving the Black actors in comparison to the White actors. This movie gets two thumbs down and a soft cock. Google what the fuck I am about to tell ya, I counted fourteen non-Black actors and five Black actors in this stanky ass movie. And out of those five Black actors, besides Snoop, you might as well have three runners-up at a potato sack race.

In most cases, when writers and producers have written a part for a Black actor, I take notes as to the characters they are portraying in big, budgeted movies. Especially, if they are using their name as the headliner. This movie didn't disappoint my expectations of being just another subtle form of blaxploitation. Why in the fuck am I using this word again? Because non-White writers, producers and entertainment companies still pimp out Black actors for capital gain. Final approval is by a White man by the name of Master Reed Hastings. Let me break it down for you, because I am certain most of you are used to being bamboozled. One Black actor in a starring role played by Jamie Foxx, and a cameo role with Snoop, and Snoop's part was just to bring in the Black viewers. There is no fucking way you can give a RAP ICON like Snoop fifteen minutes unless it was about the money to help the sale of that crappy ass movie. Now for what fucking pissed me off. In fact, I had to walk away and come back later to watch the rest of it, after I cooled down.

So here goes what pissed me off about this movie, besides, it being poorly written. Why the fuck did Jamie and Snoop have to bow down and report to the White man, Troy played by Peter Stormare. When Jamie walked through the door of the office, I predicted his boss was going to be a White man. And I'll be damned if I was right again. Then to make matters worse, Jamie had to beg the White man to get back on the force, and I was sick to my fucking stomach.

In fact, he made me forget he starred in *Django*. Jamie if this review gets in front of your eyes, why in the fuck would you allow yourself to literally beg a White man for anything? You might as well had sucked his cock under the desk he was sitting behind. You muthafuckas think y'all slick yet again. How come we always must play in subordinate roles.

Well anyways, that's my informal review, and opinion of the shows above. Earlier, when I mentioned men dressing up as women, my middle finger wasn't towards a well-known, land-owning producer in Southwest Georgia, who also dresses up as a woman. The difference is not from necessity, but from a positive, studio, Blacks in positive roles, land-owning perspective.

Fact 8. Keep in mind, just because there were Black movie directors back in dah day, doesn't necessarily mean the funds came from a Black entertainment company. In other words, White production companies can also control the narrative. Get my drift? So, what has changed? You guessed it, not one damn thang! Just a moment, if you are of any other ethnicity other than Black, and you are reading this book, Thank You. I am sure this book has been difficult to swallow, right? (No pun intended.)

Fact 9. I purposely said that to say this, while a handful of well-paid Black entertainers are starring in big, budgeted films. The rest of the well-known Black entertainers become co-stars to their White counterpart. Especially, if it's a positive and impactful series or movie. Next time you're scrolling through your entertainment source, look for diversity in your favorite movies or series with White men and women in leading roles, then do a comparison with Black men and women in leading roles. Pay attention to what's available. Email me your opinion if you feel the need to prove me wrong.

I'm sorry, I drifted off the topic slightly and now I am back. I grew up idolizing those muthafuckas that had leading roles in blaxploitation movies. In fact, I wanted to imitate their lifestyle and swagger.

When I finally met a pimp, he was a cool guy. He asked if I wanted to fuck one of his hoes, but I wasn't into that sort of thing. Besides, I had enough bitches without having to fuck one of his. Around that same time, I met this Black girl and started hanging out with her. During the day she had a part-time job as a cashier at a placed called, Thrifty Drug Store, in San Diego. One day she decided to come clean and told me she was a prostitute at night. In other words, she was a hoe, and it didn't bother me. In fact, I made no attempt to stop her. Besides, I was cool with it, because in my mind, whatever she felt she had to do for money was her business not mine. Anyways, who was I to judge her, right?

She tripped out because I was more open-minded than her previous boyfriends. The next thing I knew, she asked me to hang out with her. Okay enough of the bullshit and let me tell you about my Pimpin Ain't Easy days.

As I reflect, it was more about taking her out to do hoe business and having her back if anything were to happen. I will never forget this one time I had a knife, because there was a man threatening to harm my bottom bitch, all because he wanted free pussy. As you already know now, I was there to make sure she was safe. In certain instances, I drove alongside her watching, while she was walking on the hoe stroll in National City. She would give me the money, but I spent only a fraction of it on myself. By the way, the paragraph you just read, my editor felt I should not have included this information. She was concerned I would be ripped to shreds for having this in here. As you know, my pimping days was while I was in my early twenties. So, what do you think as the reader, was this a good or bad decision?

I just found it interesting as fuck to be around somebody who was a hoe. In fact, it's not a coincidence that blaxploitation movies made this subconsciously acceptable behavior. As time went on, I now have my bottom bitch established, plus a girlfriend at the same time. I made sure they met each other, and come to find out, my girlfriend wanted to be in my stable. Now, I have two girls to watch and make sure they were always safe throughout the evening.

There was this one evening while driving down Market Street in San Diego. I watched her check in with me just before fucking a John. Once she was done, all she had to do was wave and that was her way of letting me know she was okay. After fucking the John, she went back to work on the hoe stroll. After months into my double life, I started talking to another girl who tricked a couple times for money occasionally. I let her meet my bottom bitch and they became friends right away.

Of course, a basic car while pimping just wouldn't cut it. Just like those white produced and funded blaxploitation movies, I bought myself a stereotypical 1976 Cadillac Seville. I put a couple thousand dollars into it, got a big chrome grill with the Bentley girl on top and a fifth wheel in the back and the chrome "S" bars on the sides with the fake fur on the steering wheel. Everything the white blaxploitation and media made us believe a nigga needed while pimping in the hood. Damn, I'm the typical dumb ass muthafucka nigga, with a car that told every police officer within a hundred-mile radius, I was pimping. OMG! I just had a thought as I am writing this part of the chapter. Police were known to arrest pimps back in the day. So, with all the years I had been pimping, why wasn't the police after me? I am damn sure it was because I was pimping Black women only. I am certain if I were pimping White women or even one White woman, they would have beaten me with their batons, or arrested me saying they smell weed in my car. Oh wait! Imagine pimping in the streets without police officers harassing, imagine going to court with no trial.

Nothing about pimping (or me) was low-key back then. I was blatant with my pimpism, and it seems stupid now as I clearly reminisce, oh my god. Here I am driving around the neighborhood in my Caddy with three to four girls in it. All the neighbors knew I was pimping, but not one neighbor had anything negative to say to me. They knew I was a good kid and didn't say anything because it wasn't any of their business. Driving around in the neighborhood was interesting because all the neighbors knew

I was a fucking pimp. No one ever said anything to me or my mom about it. While driving, my girls were walking looking for Johns in downtown San Diego. I picked up this big Mexican girl that called herself Babies, who my girls met the night before. As I was driving around with the Mexican girl in my car, the police stopped them and gave them a citation for 647b, which was for prostitution.

There was a kid in my neighborhood who I attended Abraham Lincoln High School with, in San Diego. Every time I pulled up to talk with him, he called me the tennis shoe pimp. I never wore dress shoes, only sneakers. I was not the typical dressed pimp I had seen in Black exploitation movies.

At this point I had been pimping for a couple of years. Staying between my mom's house and at a hotel with my hoes. I had about $10,000 stashed away at my mom's house in a can, so I thought. One day after work, I walked in, and my momma was sitting in her favorite chair as usual. I said hi momma as I always did, but this time it was different because in her hand was the money I stashed away. She found it and was curious why I had so much in a can on the top shelf. What the fuck could I say? It's her fucking house, and I'm busted. It became obvious, it's time for me to come clean about where that money came from. In other words, I had a lame ass reason I hoped she believed. She asked me how I earned that money, and where it came from? She knew my day job wasn't paying that much and she knew my spending habits. And, since all she heard were crickets, she asked, why was all that money in a can and not my bank? I made up a quick lie which she accepted, but she still had this look of disbelief on her face. She knew I'd been out all hours of the night and hanging with at least two girls, and she wasn't stupid.

She never called me a pimp to my face, but she was suspicious. She just said, "Boy, something is gonna happen to you, you need to stop whatever it is you're doing."

Prophecy. There was this one evening while on Sunset Boulevard in Los Angeles, California, the police stopped me and harassed me and my girls over something they "thought" was happening. No matter how the police officers interrogated the girls and me, neither one of us lied on each other. The police station had no choice but to release me after being in jail for forty-eight hours. Never mind the fact, on court day, no one showed up to testify against me.

Oh man, that could have changed my life differently than it is now, because I would have gone to jail or prison for that shit, if found guilty. About that time, I had been contemplating getting out of the pimp game for a while anyway. Especially, knowing the police officers were watching me very closely, and because my mom didn't raise me to be a pimp. It was time for me to make a decision that felt right.

The Prophecy is in effect: One evening, my bottom bitch came in from a long night out. She didn't want to wake me because I was sleeping. The hotel we stayed at was in National City, California. While I was sleeping, she left me $900 on the nightstand on my side of the bed, before she fell asleep. I remember waking up and counting the money, and I could have put it in my pocket and drove away, but I didn't. Instead, I just looked at her lying there in the bed, all knocked out sleep, from being out all night. I left the money on the nightstand and never looked back. I also knew it wouldn't be right to leave my bottom bitch stranded, just because I didn't want to pimp anymore.

The only reason I left while she was sleeping, it's because I did not want her to talk me out of my decision. I am certain if she had awakened, she would have asked me not to leave. And as much as I cared for her, I would have stayed. Plus, I wasn't happy, and I had already decided what was best for me. I got into my car and looked up at the room she was in, then drove off not looking back. I went back to my mom's house while she was sitting in her favorite chair. Judging by the big ass smile on my momma's face, she was happy to see me once I walked in the door. Dammit, just as I walked in, I received a call from my bottom bitch, she asked me why I left her while she was sleeping. I told her why, but she couldn't comprehend why I didn't take the money on the nightstand. She was accustomed to me pocketing the money after the end of the night.

I told her I left the money for her, and I also didn't want her to be without a place to stay. I wanted to be sure she had enough money to survive on. I told her from this point on, the money you make is yours, I'm done and don't want to be associated with any of it, anymore. I walked away on my own terms, and I never looked back. I felt better about myself once I stopped pimping, but it never stopped me from turning into a hoe and fucking a bunch of fine ass bitches after that. Pimping kept me practically handcuffed to those hoes, and I wanted to spread my seeds around more than I had been.

Before I knew it, I had Black women, White women, Mexican women, Old women, Fat women, Skinny women, Rich women, Bad breath women, Stuck up women, Married women, Divorced women, No shame in their game women, Big titty bitches, Small titty women, Foul mouth women, Wanna B White women, Red head women, blonde hair women, Bald head women, Can I have a dollar woman, One legged women, No teeth women, Bad breath women, Unemployed women, Welfare women, Homeless women, and Stank Ass drunk women, all in my thick black book. I was making up for lost times for damn sure, I guess. Well anyways that's my "Pimpin Ain't Easy" story. Prophecy fulfilled. Peace.

Pulling Dat Hair

mall *Chapter: Before I get into hair pulling, please make sure it's her real hair from the skull. With a certain ethnicity, it's not real depending on hair color and length. If her hair is past her fucking ass, then it's fake as a muthafucka. You will also know it's not her real hair if she keeps patting her head. I'm laughing as I wrote the last thing I just said. All other ethnicities with long hair may also be wearing a weave or extensions, but at least, it's close to the actual length and color, so it's hard to tell.*

We all know some women like their hair pulled, while acting like you own dat pussy. But there's a right and wrong way to pull a woman by the hair. There are some stupid muthafuckas out there that think just grabbing women by the hair and pulling on it will turn them on. That's so far from the truth, it's ridiculous. Note: If you are a man reading this chapter, I wrote this with you in mind. As a man, you should never pull a woman's hair until you have talked about what pleases her. Whatever turns the both of you on and off should be a mutual conversation, so there's no misunderstandings. That #metoo movement is real.

Never pull near her forehead. The closer you are to her forehead, you're pulling her neck up and back, dangerously. Grab the hair as close to the skull as possible, then slightly pull hard enough to make her feel you are in control. And pay close attention to her body language and the sounds she's making. Do this wrong, and she'll not only be turned off, but we can naturally assume, she ain't horny either.

Selfish Muthafuckas

lot of guys that I've talked to over the years have given me the impression they are some selfish minded fuckers. It's all about them when it comes to sex.

If you are a woman reading this chapter, I don't blame guys for being selfish lovers, I blame the women they fucked in the past. I'm just going to be straight up and say this, when you are with a man for the first time sexually, and he doesn't take his time with you, then that's on you. In fact, if that muthafucka is selfish the very first time you fuck him, that will tell you everything you need to know. Honestly, you should tell that muthafucka to get the fuck out and go home immediately (of course with some tact). I completely understand some women are uncomfortable expressing themselves openly to their partner. Find a way to make yourself comfortable talking about sex to your potential partner. I promise you if you do this, you won't make yourself feel used, unless you like that sort of thang LOL.

And when a guy is extremely attractive (in your eyes) and takes care of himself physically, this type of man is used to women giving up their cookies on the first date. Some women are insecure and will say some shit like this to themselves: "Oh, this guy is attracted to me, he likes me, me?" They say this as they don't know their own worth, and therefore, think little of themselves.

When an attractive man sniffs for a woman who thinks this way, he already knows she is willing to put up with his bullshit. Some women finally get it after years of neglect and leave him, no matter the sex and how attractive he is. Don't play stupid now while reading this, knowing good cock and tongue will fuck your head up.

Ladies, here are some of the signs that you're dealing with a selfish man: he wants his dick sucked every time he stops by to see you, and you get nothing in return; he cums and then rolls over and goes to sleep and doesn't give a fuck if you nutted. If you are paying attention, there are some signs to pay attention to before fucking him. More examples: no foreplay, he thinks his cock is enough to please you, sending you pictures of his cock, does not bathe before fucking you, his underarm smell and when he notices it, he doesn't apologize, he will not let you play wit yourself while fucking you, he gets jealous when another man looks at you, never prepares dinner, licks your pussy just a couple of times before sticking his cock in, does not use lube, does not play with your breast while eating the pussy. My list is longer than I am willing to share in this chapter. But you get my drift. There are a lot of guys out there with this mentality. Especially if you're a woman over the age of forty, I'm certain you've dealt with at least one selfish lover in your life, right? How did you feel afterwards? Did you speak up and tell him you weren't satisfied, or did you wait until he wasn't around and masturbated? Know your worth, ladies!

Shave It Lick It

s I've said, you meet all kinds of people at swinging parties. It always surprises me how many husbands have not shaved their wife's pussy. With one of my wives, I never had to shave her pussy because she was damn good at it herself.

One couple in Florida, who I stayed in touch with after my divorce, invited me to their home. While there, my friend's wife, Sue, decided to take a shower. My mind immediately thought of shaving her pussy. Keep in mind, they were good friends of mine during swinging, and afterwards. In fact, she and I had fucked prior to asking if she wanted me to shave her pussy.

And being the good Samaritan I am, I offered to shave her pussy. To date, I've been the only man that offered to shave her pussy. I found it ironic that her husband of thirty-plus fucking years had never shaved his wife's pussy. I often think to myself, as many years as they have been married, why not shave it, and eat it? Go figure!

I can only imagine how difficult it is for a woman to shave between her booty cheeks. If I had a business, my clients would be women who need their pussy shaved exclusively by me.

Anyways, Sue's husband looked shocked and puzzled that I even offered. After she stepped out from the shower she said, "I have everything ready." She had a towel underneath her ass, shaving cream, and her favorite shaver. When I walked into the room, I acted as if I'd shaved his wife's pussy before. I did not want to show too much excitement, not knowing how her husband was going to react. First, I dipped my fingertips into the warm water and held my fingers above her pussy, this method allows water to drop from my fingertips onto her pussy. Of course, I did this a few times until her pussy was nice and wet from the water I applied. Then, I reached over for the can of shaving cream and added some into the palm of my hand. Confidence and trust will allow her to enjoy being shaved.

In other words, place the palm of your hand over the opening of her pussy either on the right or left side. By doing this exactly, it will keep you from cutting the lips of her pussy and stop shaving cream from going inside of her. Here comes the trust again, once both sides of the pussy have been shaved, it's time to shave just inside the lips of her pussy. Pull back the right or left side of the lips to shave visible hair. Once this is all done there is one more area that needs shaving, and that's between her ass cheeks. Tell her in a firm voice to bend over doggie style and pull her cheeks back. This will allow you to shave between her ass for any visible hair as well.

To anyone trying this in the privacy of your home, make sure it's nice and quiet. The one thing you don't want to happen while shaving is sudden noises, and suddenly, she's in the ER if you know what I mean. There is nothing sexier than a woman laying on her back at the edge of the bed with her legs back, trusting me to shave her pussy. It immediately reminds me of that old lollipop commercial on TV, where the kid would ask the owl how many licks does it take to reach the center of the lollipop? Some of y'all may be too young to remember that commercial, when the owl takes the lollipop from the kid, licks it twice and bites it and says, "One." That's exactly what happens to me after a couple of strokes with the shaver, I want to lick the pussy.

Shit Just Keeps Happening

I'm not trying to destroy people's families and shit. So, there was this married lady I knew named Lisa I was also married at the time. I used to go to her home and fuck her in her bed a lot while her husband was away. I worked the morning shift during the week which made it easy to meet her. She was a teacher and lived forty-five minutes away from where I lived.

Anyway, what I discovered about Lisa, while fucking her, she would accidentally shit on the bed. I excused the first couple of times it happened because it only happened if she was cumming. She would always apologize and feel embarrassed about it when it happened. But see, I always accepted, shit happens sometimes (no pun intended). It only meant that whatever I was doing, it felt so damn good she couldn't control it from happening. Well, after the first time it happened, she was self-conscious, I had to reassure her that it was no big deal. It took a while for her to relax after shitting when she was cumming. Shit never did bother me, as you know if you have read "Shitty Shitty Bang Bang."

There was another time Lisa shitted in the bed after an orgasm, but this time I didn't say anything about it. I saw it on the bed while she was blindfolded at the time.

Pardon me for what I'm about to say next: I am certainly glad I found it before I passed out from fucking her, if you know what I mean. Could you imagine tossing and turning while sleeping, and wake up with shit all over you? So, when I found it, I immediately picked it up with my fingers (ewww!) and quickly placed it inside some writing paper that was on the nightstand.

Then I got out and put it underneath the bed, hoping Lisa wouldn't see it. When she took off the blindfolds, she walked into the bathroom and suddenly turned around and asked, "What was that on the floor under the bed?" I must have looked stunned and wasn't sure what to say. I know she knew it wasn't there earlier, I had to come clean about it. I forgot to put it far enough under the bed so she wouldn't see it. But didn't want to put it too far under the bed, then wouldn't be able to reach it. Lisa said, "Cecil please tell me what's that under the bed."

I hesitated, I said, "Well it happened again." She was apologetic again and said she was sorry. I was trying to hide the fucking shit, so she wouldn't apologize again. I said, "Look, shut up with all that, I told you, when 'Shit Just Keep Happening,' I take it as a badge of honor that you had a good orgasm." Lisa became comfortable enough to have an orgasm knowing she can't stop the inevitable, we laughed about it.

Btw, ladies if this ever happens to you, hopefully the person you are with is understanding. Especially, when it happens over the age of fifty years old

Shitty Shitty Bang Bang

If you have a weak stomach please skip this chapter,
YOU HAVE BEEN WARNED:

or *some fucked-up, twisted reason, I like women who have been raped or molested. Wait! Do you have a shocked look on your face, then please continue reading this chapter. My reason is simple, they were able to overcome the trauma, and it made them who they are today, stronger, and self-sufficient. Especially, those allowing themselves to be involved with another man sexually. Being with a man could easily remind them of their trauma all over again. When a woman can confidently share her experience being raped or molested, it does not give anyone the right to manipulate or traumatize them all over again. That's why it's so important, to ask a lot of questions wanting to understand their past sexual experiences, before having sex.*

There was another White woman named Sunshine in Florida, (are you a Black woman reading this chapter and shaking your head? And, just said to yourself; this muthafucka likes White women it seems? Draw your own conclusions if you like).

Continuing: Sunshine had a horrific experience with a boy she trusted growing up. Later in this chapter, I will give you more details relating to her horrific experience.

Her horrifying experience stripped Sunshine of her innocence and is now buried deep within her mind. That experienced may have a lot to do with why she can be downright nasty minded, and you wouldn't know it by looking at her. I was lucky enough to experience that freaky side of herself. Sometimes I would take Cialis two hours before her arrival, seriously! You want me to elaborate on why I needed Cialis, don't you? Okay well, here goes: She likes pinching and playing with her own nipples while I am eating her pussy. That only means she's enjoying what I am doing down there. I would know she's enjoying herself because I would look up and over the mound above her pussy to see what she was doing.

While licking Sunshine's clit, I like to stick my fingers all up inside her like I'm a gynecologist. *Do not ask me why I like doing that either, I don't have a clue where that idea came from.*

Playing with Sunshine's pussy with my fingers, wait, you may be asking yourself, how many fingers, right? Her pussy hole could handle three lubed fingers at a time, for starters. Of course, while playing with her pussy, her eyes were closed, and I like that. Why? Because it allows me to make that, OMG face like Wendell Pierce, in *Waiting to Exhale* while in the meantime, Lela Rochon was staring up at him.

At this point, I'm reaching for the lube to start playing with her ass, still eating her pussy. Sunshine's head goes from right to left like she's possessed and mentally in a good place, I try to keep her there.

I now have two fingers inside Sunshine's ass and before you know it, four fingers up to my first joint on my hand. Now, depending on my mood, I would take my other hand and use four fingers in her ass and pussy at the same time. Usually, I'm all excited at this point and I'll shove a pillow under her ass. With this freaky bitch, as she is tilted, I am using four well-lubed fingers in her ass and pussy up to my knuckles. Don't laugh, but sometimes I wish I had a mining hat on so I could look up in her ass. That's fucked up, ain't it? Only like-minded muthafuckas will be able to relate to what I just said. Hello by the way ...

By fingering Sunshine's ass, I would know if she had to use the bathroom or not. Sometimes there's some shit hanging around up in there, and I would use my fingers and pull whatever amount of shit is in there out.

Gross huh? I am very aware I must have been dropped when I was a baby. Who else out there does fucked-up shit like that besides me? I am not talking about people on the Internet either. Some of the porn I watch makes my story PG rated. But again, those are the same people who will be able to relate to my story.

I know what you are thinking, you just asked yourself, what happened to the shit I pulled out of Sunshine's ass, right? Well, I made sure I had a roll of toilet paper nearby, to place the shit inside of it. In fact, I had enough toilet paper to clean my fingers and between her ass cheeks, if needed. Besides, why should I gross her out while she's possessed, and her eyes are rolling around in the back of her head. I thought to myself, just keep going and worry about the shit later (no pun intended). Later that evening, I finally told her what I did, and she was grossed out but that didn't stop her from coming back for more with her nasty self. Trust came into play again when I experimented with nipple clamps and flogging her. Btw, I am not about to explain what flogging is right now. For all you vanilla folks, google it and in the search bar type in "flogging BDSM" and that should satisfy your curiosity. I appreciated Sunshine's trust in me, and that's especially important for us to have fun with one another. Throughout this book, I'll repeat, trust is the key.

Sunshine's Horrific Experiences:

I hope you are still reading this chapter; there's something I want to share with you about Sunshine. I had known her for a while and realized she wasn't able to achieve an orgasm. This wasn't something I discovered right away, but over time. Don't you dare say the size of my cock had something to do with that either, asshole.

Keep in mind, it didn't matter how long I fucked or ate her pussy, she wasn't going to have an orgasm from it. The fun I had with her was making her squirt all over my pillows and sheets. But, yet again no orgasm.

Sometimes with my left hand I would use four fingers up to my second knuckles in the pussy and with my right hand up to my second knuckles I would use four fingers in her in her ass simultaneously, when I stop after she would become lightheaded, and that's about it. As a woman reading this, was that her way of having an orgasm, by being lightheaded? Can you relate to her in some ways? Ladles, what is it like never having an orgasm with a man? What is it like masturbating and it only feels good but can't have an orgasm? What is like being married to your husband more than ten plus years and never had an orgasm? Do you lie when asked if you cam when a man ask? Have you faked all your orgasms with your husband, and how did it make you feel afterwards? Do you go from one relationship to another searching to have an orgasm with strange men? Do you feel less than a woman for not experiencing an orgasm? Does not having an orgasm make you feel there is something wrong with you?

To be straight up with you, I feel like when Sunshine was raped, she compartmentalized the trauma and didn't want to retrieve it. Hold on a moment before I continue, I woke up on July 8, 2022, around four a.m. to add this revelation, she may be unintentionally and unconsciously not wanting to experience an orgasm, in fear she's giving up the one last thing she has control over. But, if I were going to use my gift for assessing her, I would say, she's scared to allow herself to be completely pleasured by any man, because of the rape she endured. In either case, I am not, or claim to be, a psychologist or therapist with a degree in assessing a woman's state of mind. What has been your personal experience after being raped or molested? How did you overcome feeling you had something to do with it? Did you ever tell anyone? If you did, how was it received?

These are questions I have always wanted answers to and hope one day a woman will come forward and tell me her story. Besides the ones on television, I have not met personally.

My opinion only, I've noticed when a woman has been raped, they tend to categorize themselves as defeated, ashamed, and not worthy of love. Some turn to drugs and alcohol to numb their memories. And the cycle continues until they seek help. After talking to this woman for a while, her story became fascinating because she began to realize what wasn't working and made some major changes in her life.

UPDATE: it's been six years since she's taken a drink and I am proud of her accomplishments.

Should've Known Betta

here was anotha White woman named Tori, who was ready to fuck me, more so than me wanting to fuck her. Keep reading, I'll explain why I say this. We had a couple of conversations on our cell phones, after which this bitch threw caution to the wind and was ready to meet up at my house within days of our conversation. I was like, "Damn, I like this shit." Sometimes I just want to fuck, to see if we have anything in common. I am being a hypocrite when I said, "bitch threw caution into the wind." I was also taking a risk inviting her to my home, right?

By fucking on the first meeting, it's easier getting to know one another, and hopefully no one is disappointed, and that's just my opinion. The last thing I want to do is talk to someone for weeks, and in some cases months, only to find out we are not on the same page sexually. Life is too fucking short to waste time and energy on someone you are not compatible with in and out of bed.

And look, I read what someone (S.H.) wrote in his book, that, women should wait at least six months, before giving up the cookies bullshit. I said to myself, who is this mofo giving advice and why are women listening. There's not one pill for all situations. But who am I to judge, I am sure he made a shit load of money from saying what women wanted to hear. It's what ole school players and pimps do.

Back to Tori: Fucking her was fun, she liked being slapped on the ass, hair pulled and nasty talk. She would cum easily if you're fucking her the right way and with a decent size cock. This woman didn't like anyone eating her pussy, only because she has vaginal orgasms and clit stimulation did nothing for her.

Of course, now that I'm drafting this book, a thought just came to mind. Not licking Tori's pussy meant less for me to do to get her in the mood. All I had to do was let her suck my cock, pull her hair a little, and the next thing you know, she's ready to fuck. Besides, since she was multi-orgasmic, a decent-sized hard cock could satisfy her easily. I thank the Universe all the time for giving me a decent- sized cock to please some women.

Tori was a little on the heavy side, but I still liked being with her. *Wait! Before you continue reading this part, I am going to need you to visualize what took place between her and me, while fucking her in the ass. Hopefully, you will find it funny. Okay, let's continue.*

One time I was fucking Tori in the ass and pulling on her hair, and she was blindfolded. Not to mention, she was slightly bent over with one leg up on the bed and the other on the floor. So, while I'm fucking her in the ass, I started slipping in this big ass puddle that was underneath my feet. Not being in this situation before, I was a bit confused where the puddle came from. Of course, I am now distracted, because of the puddle on the floor. I didn't want to stop fucking her either.

Now, I am forced to decide what should I do. Eventually I pulled my cock out of her ass. I looked down at the floor one last time, and said what the late great Rudy Ray Moore would have said, "BIIATCH, do you realize that you're squirting all over my floor, while I'm fucking you in the ass?"

Tori responded, "No way, are you kidding me!" I told her not to move, so I could put on some tennis shoes to keep from slipping in it. We both laughed when I told her my tennis shoes weren't keeping me from slipping in her squirt puddle. I mopped it up off the floor so I could continue, but I kept on my tennis shoes for safety measures. I was so turned on with her squirting all over the floor, it wasn't long before I released my cum in her ass. Of course, that was only after I cleaned up another massive puddle of squirt off the floor. She also loved to be dominated and slightly disrespected, which made it fun seeing her.

I would say shit like: "Bitch, get on your knees,"
and she would do it. Keep in mind, I know the type
of woman I can get away with calling them a bitch,
and they're the ones that turn me on the most.

I had to stop fucking Tori; she was a female version of how I used to be some years ago. She was fucking a lot of other guys while fucking me. I didn't have an issue with that, but she's too quick wanting an exclusive relationship. If a guy were to fuck her and afterwards say he wanted her all to himself exclusively, she was willing to jump into that situation after only a date or two. In my opinion, to be in an exclusive relationship with someone takes time. Depending on how she was raised by her parents and the men she's dealt with before, I don't necessarily blame her for this. Abandonment issues or not knowing your worth can make anyone needy and desperate.

Even though I spoke to her that way, at any time Tori could have told me not to. In all honesty, she's always in charge and no means no. Straight up, she's just making me think that I'm in charge, because she likes it too. She could have just as easily got up and put her clothes back on and left. Just because I told her to "Get on your fucking knees and suck my cock bitch!" It doesn't mean a damn thing unless she's into it. Bottom line, a woman is always in charge. Any man who thinks telling a woman what to do without her concerns for safety, is nothing but a punk ass bitch himself.

The only way I can see a self-respecting woman submitting herself to that shit without consent, would be with a gun pointed at her head, or if she were trying to avoid getting the shit beat out of her. That muthafucka needs to go to prison and get his ass fucked every single night the entire time he's there. And don't even stitch his ass up, just make sure he heals naturally.

Back to Tori: As I was saying, this bitch was just fucking too many guys, in a brief period. I decided it was better if she and I remained friends. But of course, sometimes things don't go as planned, and she reached out to me several months later. She caught me during a moment of weakness, when I was tired of masturbating a couple of times a day. This bitch was reaching out to me to see if I'd invite her to stop by, and I said, "Okay, fuck it, come on by." But wait, that was only after calling me as she was leaving Daytona Beach, after fucking another man. I should've known betta.

A couple of weeks later, Tori had some concerns relating to symptoms she was having. You would think being a teacher she would be intelligent enough to see a doctor first, right? Nope! The bitch decided to google her symptoms instead and misdiagnosed herself having AIDS.

Tori then made a conscious decision to get in her car and was going to drive back to Daytona to address it with the man she had fucked before me that day. This bitch had the audacity to think that he was the one that had given her AIDS. Never mind the fact, she fucks a new guy after a couple of conversations, and in some cases, the same day ... and more importantly, she didn't even have this diagnosis confirmed with an actual doctor!

I just want to let you know; I'm not judging Tori for her decisions, I'm glad she called me while driving to meet up with this guy to deliver some shocking news. She had no way of knowing his reaction to her allegations without her even having all the facts. That muthafucka could have beaten the fuck out of her and made her disappear. As far as I'm concerned, I saved that bitch's life by talking her out of driving to see him again. I know the Universe intervenes when it absolutely must do so, and it intervened that day, by her calling me before she drove to meet him again.

And yes, I had myself evaluated just in case you're wondering, and of course the test was negative. Meaning, I didn't and don't have AIDS, and I plan to keep it that way. I did however learn a valuable lesson, and I said to myself, I'm never putting myself in that kind of predicament again with anyone. I remain AIDS free. I am certain you are saying to yourself, I am bold for sharing this, right? I'm an open book (no pun intended) and have nothing to hide.

Slap Dat Ass

It wasn't until I was in my late fifties, I discovered some women love being slapped on their asses, and not in a playful way either. The first woman that asked me to slap her on her ass scared dafuck out of me. I seriously thought dat bitch had a few screws loose. My mom raised a respectable young man and slapping of any kind was punishable with a belt. So, yes, I was confused and hesitant to provide what she asked of me. Close your eyes for a second, and imagine the look I had on my face, while she was ass up doggie style. Were you able to see the "what the fuck" expression on my face?

And of course, I aim to please, not disappoint. So, my first slap on her ass was done with some hesitancy. I am laughing as I write this part because she looked over her shoulder and said: nigga please! It was at that moment I knew there was no turning back now. I proceeded to slap her ass until my hand was pulsating. She turned slowly and faced me with tears in her eyes just to say, "Thank you daddy." She looked embarrassed for saying *thank you daddy*, and I reassured her that it was okay.

With some experimenting, I found out the harder you slap dat ass the better and will make them cum, easily. From what I was told, a woman who likes being spanked says it's indescribable and takes them to a place within their mind. Most women can't explain what ass slapping does for them, and that always puzzled me personally. There has only been a handful of women I fucked, who honestly understand why they love it while being fucked. What's fucked up, most of the time it hurts me more than it hurts them, afterwards, I use ice for the palm of my hands. And for some fucked up reason, looking at a nice fresh slapped ass is a turn on for me. If we ever meet, please don't ask me why either. Because the only answer I'm going to give you is...I don't know.

Small Cock No Homo

ome of you may ask, have I ever been jealous of another man fucking my girlfriend or one of my ex-wives, while in the swinging lifestyle. Well, there was only one time that I may have been jealous. It was after one of my wives fucked two guys at the same time, she came out of the bedroom and said her knees were weak and she was shaking. I knew both men she fucked and knew they were good at what they did. She could have picked either one of the guys alone, that would have been fun enough, but she had them both at the same time. Damn!

I can't imagine what that must have felt like for her, but I could easily tell it was a good one. One guy was in her pussy and the other was fucking her ass. She loved anal sex anyways, so the only way I could duplicate that would be if I reached around her back with a dildo and put it in her ass and my cock in her pussy. So going back to what I said about being jealous, I stopped being jealous and told myself it's just sex and she loves me, I was never jealous again after that.

Even if another man were able to make her squirt, I would say to them, damn you are good and would high-five them. Once you overcome the idea it's just sex, it can be rewarding for both of you, and a lot of men do not understand that. Guys where I used to work would ask me these questions, how can you watch somebody fucking your partner?

My answer is usually, my partner was fucking before I met her. And if we ever divorce, she will be fucking somebody else at some point. So, why not fuck while I am watching her, and I am right there making sure she is okay. And sometimes I do not even have to be in the same room. Anyone she chooses to be with I know will not hurt her and I am okay with that. I normally walk away so that she can have a fun time and have an after-sex conversation or whatever. It's just sex and friendship in most cases. So, that is why it's never been a problem watching my partner with another person because I am open-minded enough to let her enjoy herself. I don't care if another man has a bigger cock than mine. Why should I give a fuck because I have her heart and again, I say, it's just sex.

Back in the day, my co-workers would ask me, aren't you afraid that your wife might leave you for another man who fucks her better?

Sometimes, people don't recognize they're insulting me because of their own inadequacies in the bedroom.

If one of my wives were to leave me for another man because her sexual experience was different, then our relationship already had problems. I have watched one of my wives having a fun time with somebody and it doesn't even phase me. Matter of fact, I like hearing about it while on the drive home sometimes.

There was this one guy that had a small cock, half the size of mine, and in fact, I'm seven and one-fourth inches (yes, I am claiming every inch) ain't no shame in my game. One of my ex-wives said to me that it was the best time she had with someone who knew how to use it. Plus, he licked her pussy the way she liked and did all kinds of other positions she enjoyed. I remember being curious about his small cock satisfying her, and she reassured me whatever he was doing with his small cock, she came more than once, and as Kevin Hart would say, "NO HOMO." A lot of guys think it's all about the size of their cock and that's not the case whatsoever. If you happen to watch porn, only half the cock is inside the pussy anyway.

Also, depending on the size of the cock, he can't even go pelvis to pelvis. Watch porn and when the guy pulls out his cock from her pussy, only half the cock has pussy juice on it, the other half is dry. If the man is not careful, he could easily damage the woman because there is only so much cock that can go inside of a woman's pussy.

There is only five to seven inches from pussy lips to the back wall of the pussy anyway. I completely understand some women want or need a big cock guy because they want their walls pounded and all up in their stomach. They want to feel the pain afterwards. I understand that shit, but hey, it's not going to be from me. I will put a fist up in there or long ass dildo up in that pussy if she wants her wall pounded.

I know some guys are intimidated by adding toys, massage oils, vibrators into the bedroom. Hell no, not me. I love that shit, because see, this is my understanding. If you bring toys into the bedroom and she likes it, you are going to fuck and eat her pussy. So, I do not understand why guys are intimidated by toys. To me, it just adds to the fun.

Squirt In My Mouth

had a polyamorous relationship with an attractive, thick Black woman, with big fucking titties, named Jazmin. OMG! This woman's titties were massive. We met on Tinder, and then after a few conversations, we exchanged cell numbers. I enjoyed talking to her; she was laid back, fun, and interesting. Considering we were getting to know one another, she caught me off guard by sending me pictures of her pussy, she must have thought I'd be turned on by them. In all honesty, it had totally the opposite effect, I was completely turned off. As I was looking at the photos, I said to myself, *WTF?* Oh, is that her pussy?

First, she was a plus-size woman and had taken photos of her pussy with hair on it. I personally don't find that attractive especially short nappy hair. Wait muthafucka before you criticize me for saying nappy, keep in mind, I don't like hair on, around, or near the pussy, okay? Besides, don't we all have a preference?

Back to "Squirt in My Mouth."

Even though I never asked for those unattractive pussy photos, it didn't stop me from wanting to get to know her. And I'm sure she was confused, I didn't respond the way most men would have after pussy photos appear on their phone. Eventually, she trusted her instincts and came over to my place. We sat down and I didn't waste any time and said, "Look, I'm going to tell you something you should never do again," it wasn't those exact words, but close. "I wish you had not sent photos of your pussy to me." She had a shocked look on her face, then she asked me why. "There is one simple reason and it's because those photos did absolutely nothing for me. In all honesty, if you knew how many pussies I've fucked and licked over the past sixty-plus years, you would have known betta. In fact, what's more important to me, is who the pussy belongs to and what's in your heart." I went on to say, "Please, never send photos of your naked body to any man unless they are someone you have met and trust. It makes you look desperate, and you are degrading yourself, unnecessarily." She managed listening to my advice well, and that made me even more interested in her. It was constructive criticism anyways, would you agree?

When guys take photos of their cock and send them to strangers, it means they're insecure. Besides, ladies don't assume sex with someone like this will be reciprocal either. And yes, I'll admit *right here and now, in my early twenties I did that shit, then I grew the fuck up. Immature men send photos of their cock to strangers, it's like they think women have never seen a cock before. They have forgotten that natural childbirth has been around for ages.*

In other words, if your cock isn't the size of a baby's entire body, then don't send cock photos! Besides, most women over forty have seen all shapes, sizes, and colors anyway. I've always felt women should report men who send uninvited cock photos of themselves, to the authorities. Eventually, they would get it and cut that shit out.

Back to Miss Big Titties Jazmin:

She was hardworking, sexy as fuck, and fucking her was fun as a muthafucka. Oh, and she could squirt like a water fountain. She also loved being fucked in the ass while playing with her big titties. I regret telling this story, she allowed me to be Cecil and wanted to submit herself to me. This one time we went to an event in the Tampa area, and people kept saying how good we looked together. I had on my favorite goth clothes with a top hat and biker boots, all black of course. Jazmin wore a black dress with a black corset. The fact she is five feet nine in height made is stand out big time. It took all the attention away from me and I was happy about that. Being six foot six, most people notice me right away and confuse me with being a basketball player. I am going to confess and say, that's mostly White muthafucka's who ask that question. Black people don't go around asking other White, Asians or Latino's how tall they are. We ain't nosy like that and usually we M.O.B (mind our business) anyway.

Jazmin was the most open-minded Black woman I had ever met. Before her, I assumed only White women were freaky and open-minded, especially when they knew I was fucking other women while we were together. And DAMN, when I'd lick her pussy, she's the only woman I've ever known that squirted in my mouth while I was licking all up inside her pussy. I'm talking about all up my nose, and all over my face. Her pussy would get so sloppy, silky wet. I'd never had a woman do that before. Usually, a woman's cum leaks from her pussy and drips down towards her asshole while I'm eating her pussy. I'd always pay attention to when she was ready to cum. When she's ready she would squirt just a little bit into my mouth. And, when that happened, I knew she was getting ready to cum, while rubbing against my face. There was so much squirt coming from her pussy, there were a few times I had to stop. I was afraid she would soak up my bed to a point of needing another one. Sometimes, while her eyes were closed, I would rub her squirt all over my bald head.

I know, nasty muthafucka, right?

I had that Jazmin on lock, then I fucked it up. As I've said before, most Black women would never even consider submitting herself to a man. I'm sure most of you are thinking she must have been abused to even consider kneeling to me, right? If you're a Black man reading this part and feel that it would have been wrong for Jazmin to kneel to me, then so be it.

And, if you're a Black woman, I know you're thinking the exact same thing. And I'm sure you're also saying that a Black woman shouldn't kneel to anyone, unless it's God, right? Whatever! If it's in the privacy of our own home, why in dafuck should you care? Besides, it was her that wanted to submit to me. However, at that point in time, I wasn't in the right frame of mind for her to be submitting herself to me. Believe me, kneeling to me is not something I take lightly. It's the purest form of respect a woman can give to a man that's proven he's worthy of her submission. She was opening the car and restaurant doors for me. There is absolutely nothing wrong with a man being taken care of, and I don't mean financially. I'm certain if she were to tell anyone in her family what type of relationship we had, they would think that I was pimping her or she was my sugar momma. At that time in my life, I wanted to be treated a certain way, like this other White girl I was also seeing at the time.

Let me explain what fucked this all up and caused things between us to unravel. I knew

Jazmin was going to a school reunion, and I wanted her to have a fun time. I had told her that if there was some guy, she knew from back then that she wanted to fuck, or he had wanted to fuck her, then go for it. We had an open relationship, and hell, I was with her to enhance her life, not suppress it. I don't have any insecurities or jealousies. She went to the reunion and there was this man there that had liked her back then, so they finally decided to fuck each other. She told me all about the encounter, in detail. She said that being with him was as if she was fucking me, that she almost fucked up and called him my name in the middle of it. That's how good this guy was. I was laughing my ass off and wanted more details.

I told Jazmin I wanted to meet this guy so we could fuck her together. I was hoping he would come to Florida to visit her, and she'd set it up for him to call me. She tried to set it up, but the bitch ass muthafucka couldn't handle it. According to her, he and I had the same size dick, and like me, he also liked bringing toys into the situation to enhance playing with her. He and I could have had so much fun with her. Think about it, she would have had a dick in all her holes before it was over with. She and I were both disappointed, as she had never fucked two guys that were so similar at one time.

Then one day, I happen to be on Facebook and see that she had posted photos with this guy having breakfast or lunch. This is when everything ended between us and let me explain the reason. I had gone with her to visit her family and friends and these were down-to-earth people, we had a fun time. Her family and friends knew of me, and then here she is posting photos with this other guy, it made me look like an SAP (Urban Dictionary: foolish, gullible). This is where I drew the line.

Since Jazmin's family and friends didn't know we were in an open relationship, they weren't going to understand and would think she was fucking around. I told her, unless they knew the kind of relationship we had, you absolutely cannot take photos with another guy and post them on social media. I'm sure her family and friends saw her social media post and were wondering who's that guy. If I were to ever go back and visit her family again, they'd be thinking to themselves, "I wonder, does he know about that guy she was taking photos with?" And I'm sure they'd also be thinking I'm some limp ass muthafucka, she's out fucking someone else, as they would not have known what we agreed on. I was so angry, and that ended our relationship. I wasn't the same after that, and she knows who she is. Most women are attention whores who *put all your damn business on social media, Like: what you ate, drank, and who you slept with. Why?*

The Alpha Female Mentality

hen most women hear the word submissive, they immediately become defiant. And I concluded the reason the word submissive is so misunderstood, is from previous abusive relationships. I'll say this one last time so the woman in the back of the room can hear me: being submissive does not make you a doormat. The only way you can be treated like one is by allowing it to happen, and not speaking up for yourself.

Earlier in the year, I added myself to a dating website and I added, I am dominant. Most of the women who contacted me asked, does that mean you have to be in total control, and the woman has no say so in the relationship? And some wouldn't ask and just assumed I'm an asshole. Only a small handful knew the true meaning of the word sub or submissive. Most alpha females could not help themselves commenting on my profile instead of ignoring it. I would laugh to myself and shake my head for saying stupid shit.

Calm down alpha females, *it's not that serious.*

Then I realized it's not a woman's fault for having that mentality, I personally blame the men in her previous relationships prior to not knowing anything about me. I can't imagine a little girl growing up watching her mother being abused verbally and physically. I do know it affects their adult life, and the decisions they make choosing the men in their lives. As I mentioned in one of my chapters called "My Gay Ass Cousin," I know what it's like growing up in an unhealthy atmosphere. Examples of that would be, hearing mom talking about her father with another woman. A man having an affair, I honestly don't know the effects it has on his children. What could be even more devastating is growing up with a dishonest father and realizing once you become an adult. I am certain that has long-term effects on the daughter that cannot be reversed.

One of my best friends is an example of that, she needs to feel in control of every aspect of the relationship she's in. Oh, and by the way if you are ever driving anywhere with her while in the passenger seat, expect to be told when to stop, turn, and speed up. I am certain something happened in her prior relationships to make her feel that way. Read this completely because I am going somewhere with this story so hang in there. Below is one example I can remember explicitly. After visiting her apartment several times, I noticed she had two different Internet companies for which she was paying. I could have noticed it and not gave a fuck, right? Never mind the fact, it's not my apartment, or money. You would think I would mine my own business. But that's not who I am, if I care about someone. So, one day I decided to ask how long she had been paying for two Internet companies.

With no hesitation, she told me a little over a year or so, and I thought to myself, why? (Btw, that's not all I said to myself.) Of course, I wanted to say something when I brought it to her attention but chose not to say anything at that time. After several weeks had past, I asked how much she was paying for the two Internet companies, and she didn't know the amount exactly. I asked myself, *who's paying the bills then, if she doesn't know the amount?*

I also told myself, either she is loaded with money or just doesn't care. When she told me the amount, I scratched my damn head on how much she could be saving by getting rid of one of the Internet companies. She had already been paying a little over a year for both companies. To give you a general idea how much she was paying, it was approximately $185 a month. So, me being the observant man I am, I asked her to shut off one of the Internet companies. Her response was when she had time. Several weeks had gone by and I asked again if she turned off one of the Internet companies. Immediately, she became irritated, and I never asked her again. I knew her walls were up and there was no way I could penetrate that wall to convince her to think differently. Her past experiences with men made her defensive as if I were trying to force her, when in all actuality, I was looking out for her best interest.

I was right in my assessment of her situation, but her own insecurities would not allow me to help her. UPDATE: three months later she finally turned off one of the Internet companies and saved about half of the $185 a month. It doesn't matter when she decided to do it, it only matters that she did it. To the men reading this chapter: if you care about who you are involved with and realize they are defensive. Usually, it's from a previous relationship, so thread carefully and have patience and find your way in without her noticing. Additionally, it requires an old- fashioned woman who understands a man's role in the relationship.

The AOL Days

his chapter is dedicated to those over fifty years old. Remember back in the AOL days when Internet was slow as fuck, compared to cable Internet now. Your computer would make that sound and you couldn't wait to get online. Back then, there were not as many dating and kink sites as there are now. Of course, anything and everything I was into could not be found on AOL. That's why chat rooms were so convenient for me. In the privacy of your own home, just search for an interesting subject, choose a chat room with people in it, then introduce yourself. Most of the time when searching for chat rooms, I was unaware there were people that lived in the same city, and in some instances, some were my neighbors. That's why exchanging photos wasn't a good idea, just for that reason. In fact, if you discovered your neighbor, it's something you wouldn't admit to. There was this one time me and the neighbor discovered one another. It was awkward for a while because we both knew each other's secret, especially his.

Before realizing we were neighbors, he said something profound such as, he wanted to meet

Black bulls and suck their cocks. And considering at the time I did not realize he was my neighbor; the plan was to provide that Black cock. How my neighbor discovered me, was the title of my chat room "Black Cock" or "Black Man Available" and horny for a White boy to suck my cock. Any chat room title with Black in it would draw in the flies like fresh shit out the butthole. If you are a White Christian or White Nationalist, don't get your panties all tied up in knots for what I just said. In fact, I'm exposing what White men secretly want to do with Black men. The trip is, most White men who have thoughts of sucking a Black man's cock are usually your neighbor, best friend, your father, uncles, your brother, your coach, and in fact, priest have been caught sucking cock in general. This is well documented and can be researched, so don't hold me accountable for unveiling this fact.

I just had an ADD moment, back to the subject:

After leaving my chat room titled "Black Cock for White Boys," I would then read the messages I had received. Every message was from married, White gay and bisexual men, or muthafuckn' cock suckers on the downlow, wanting to hook up. I started chat rooms because it was boring sitting around in front of the computer waiting for someone to join in. So, one evening I made sure my computer and chat room was always available to join, even though I was nowhere near the computer.

When I woke up the next morning, I was always able to see the screen names of whoever entered my chat room. For some reason, no matter if you left a message or not, I was still able to see who entered.

I would copy and paste their names in the search bar and searched for their profile. Once I found the profile, I would leave a message. If they responded I would say: I noticed your screen name in my chat room last night and is there anything I can help you with. Sometimes they would respond back saying, they would like to suck my black cock. And some changed their screen names by the time I responded. After a while of doing that, I started finding men that loved servicing Black men. Servicing means, sucking. Do you as the reader, honestly think I'm going to say no to a hot wet mouth in exchange for the palm of my hand? Fuck dat shit! Like the game show, Bob: I'll take a hot wet mouth behind curtain number two please!

In all my teen experiences with men, I was the top and that was made clear while talking to them. Wait, are you still judging me? I don't care if you are a male or female reading this, just imagine being horny as a muthafucka and someone is willing to lick your clit or suck your cock with no reciprocation, after a few conversations online. You must exchange cell numbers because most muthafuckas on AOL were usually men in high profile or corporate positions that have this fantasy.

Their desire to be humiliated and be told
how to lick and suck a black cock and balls,
turns them on beyond anything they have
ever experienced. Ain't that ah bitch?

The Black Bull and Cockold

This *was twenty years ago, so it would be interesting if both are still alive and remember me. Yes, I know, I was a freak then and still a freak, muthafucka! Also keep in mind, the couples I played with were all White, wait, hold on a minute; should I be politically correct and say Caucasian, instead? I have met two interracial couples over the years, and when I did, the man was White, and the woman was Black. I already mentioned in another chapter how I feel about that. So, I am not about to address it again here in this chapter. Therefore, when it comes to meeting Black couples, I've not met any at the places I was partying at, and not a single Black female to be found.*

There was this cockold couple, Mr., and Mrs. Collins, who lived in Melbourne, Florida. We met online, and after five conversations on our cell phones, just like clockwork, Roy the husband decided to send me photos of his wife Jackie. I thought she was attractive and responded with two thumbs up, and that's how it usually starts. When searching for couples online like Mr. and Mrs. Collins, I must be careful because usually its single men jacking off and posing as couples. I know how to weed through them with a series of questions. The questions were: How old I was? Where did I live? How long had I been on the website? Have I played with couples before? Was I married or single? I responded I was married, and he responded with two thumbs up. He knew me being married I would not become attached to his wife. He also knew a married man would be discreet and mature enough to manage their lifestyle. This muthafucka was bold enough to ask what the size of my cock was. Of course, I told him because I had nothing to hide (no pun intended). Believe me, if our conversations were not genuine, I would have just not responded and blocked him from further contacting me. Besides, I knew his reason for asking, and it's because you don't bring a Vienna sausage to a party when the host already has one.

Anyway, Roy the husband invited me to their home after feeling comfortable with our communication on our cell phones. I am not used to meeting couples living in gated communities. One of the main reasons, there is documentation of your arrival. After giving the guard my name, I proceeded to their home. I will admit, this was nicer than anywhere I ever lived in my life. I almost became insecure because of the Ferrari and Harley in the garage. It was time to leave my insecurities in the car when I arrived and parked.

I got out of my car and walked towards the front door and rang the doorbell. Once I rang the doorbell, Jackie opened it with a big smile, wearing a white mini skirt and no panties. Fuck it I'll say it, that mini skirt was just below her ass cheeks.

No fucking way she could bend over and pick up anything without exposing her pussy. She must have known I like that kinda shit, I sure in the hell didn't mention it before my arrival.

After the door closed, Jackie turned around and walked ahead of me. Just like dogs, I wanted to sniff her ass, but instead I stared at it thinking, *I'm tapping dat ass later.* The whole time I was there, his wife was checking me out with a big smile on her face, like she was about to devour three hundred pounds of pure unsweetened chocolate. Of course, I was checking her out also, the moment she opened the door. So, Jackie and I proceeded to walk towards the living room, and it almost look like she was walking in slow motion. We both sat on the couch directly across from Roy. Since this was our first-time meeting face to face, Roy wanted to talk to me before properly introducing me to Jackie. Roy told me he made sure his wife Jackie was wearing something nice, just for me. Additionally, she had on heels that matched her dress. While she was sitting down, I asked her to stand up and model for me. That was my way of getting us all in the mood, the reason I was there. In most cases I know when to take it to the next level. I try to pay attention to the couples' body language and subtle eye contact between them. After talking to Roy and Jackie for a little while, I saw an opportunity to proceed to the next level.

I looked directly at Roy, and then said, "OKAY, enough of this fucking talking, I need you to sit in your favorite chair and don't you fucking move until I say so." Roy sat down in the chair like a good boy, and he didn't even ask why. Then, I told Jackie to stand up and directly face Roy. Like the sexy White bitch, she was, she did exactly what she was told. Then I said to Jackie, "Look into your husband's eyes, and don't say one fucking word, unless I give you permission." I told Roy, "I'm going to tell her to do something, that I'm sure you will enjoy watching." While Jackie was standing in front of her husband, neither one said anything. Next, I stood up slowly, walked behind her, and unzipped her short dress. While unzipping her dress, I whispered for her to reach out to hold her husband's hand for balance, then take off her shoes. Of course, she did not have on stockings because she wasn't wearing panties. Guess what? In her asshole, that bitch had a stainless-steel butt plug with a cosplay fox tail the entire time I was there. Damn, if I had known, that would have been my cue the moment she opened the door. No wonder she was leaning to the side while she was sitting down LOL.

If you are asking yourself, how did I know she had a stainless-steel butt plug with a cosplay fox tail up her ass? While she was standing in front of her husband balancing herself, she bent over to remove her shoes, and I saw it. As I was standing directly behind Jackie, she was in front of her husband looking down, shaking from excitement. I could also tell Roy was turned on because he was feeling on his cock on the outside of his pants.

It was at this point that I decided to really turn the heat up full blast. So, while she was standing in front of her husband, I told her to lift her arms up so that I could remove her dress. I threw her dress on the couch so that she was naked in front of me and her husband. I took a step back for a moment, turned the tables, and looked at Jackie like ah White slave owner. I was impressed with her body, and I liked the cellulite on her legs and stomach. In my eyes, this made her naturally attractive. I then slowly walked behind her again, with my hands reaching around from behind her, and I lightly pinched her nipples.

Occasionally, I would stop playing with Jackie's nipples so that my fingers could slowly run down her stomach to her clit. I would play with her clit slowly, in a circular motion. Holy shit! Each time I touched her clit, she squirted on the floor, and it ran down her legs. Damn that was sexy as fuck, watching it gush out of her like that. When I sensed she was about to cum, I stopped. Normally, we call that cum denial, but you vanilla folks may wanna call that being a teaser. I am not only teasing the wife, but I'm also fucking with Roy's head, who's still sitting in his chair, watching me playing with his wife's clit, titties, and thighs. Putting my fingers inside of her pussy is one option while other women are stimulated from touching everywhere else.

I whispered into Jackie's ear, "You're my bitch now," as I thrusted two fingers inside her pussy repeatedly. I could tell she was wet, her cum was thick and milky when I pulled out my fingers. I then told her to turn around and face me so that I could stick my wet cummie fingers inside both of our mouths. I made her lick each finger slowly, until I was completely satisfied every drop of cum was gone. That was so fucking sexy, and only in America, can an old ass nigga like me, do what I just did to another man's wife. Right afterwards, I said to myself, this White man allowed me into his home and watched a nigga, stand directly behind his wife, playing with his wife's pussy. At this point, her pussy was wet and cum was running down both of her inner thighs and down unto the floor. I said aloud, "Oh shit! This bitch just made a puddle of squirt on the fucking floor!"

The husband thought she was done cumming, but she came again, from excitement. And, just like before, I reached down and gathered up the cum running down her thighs. Then turned her around to face me, so that her and I could lick my fingers together and kissed each other passionately. After two hours had gone by, I was hungry, and the husband asked if I wanted anything to eat. I said, "That's not a question you should ask me. Tell Jackie to ask me that same question."

Roy told his wife, "Honey, ask him what he wants to eat."

Jackie said, "Is there anything else besides eating my pussy and fucking my pussy ass that I can prepare for you Sir?"

I said, "Not at this very moment, maybe after I make your husband watch me fuck you and after I pull out, he can clean you up with his tongue."

And here we are yet again, another White couple that desires his wife servicing a Black man. Check out "Under The Cover" if you have not already read it.

Another time, she called her husband while he was at work, I overheard her saying, "Guess who's with me."

Roy said, "I know who you are with. You are with Cecil, right?"

She said, "Yep and we are going to the beach for a little while."

This sort of thing doesn't usually happen unless trust has been established. Otherwise, I would have had to wait until Roy came home from work, to go to the beach with her alone. Unexpectedly, Roy wanted to talk to me on the cell phone for a second. He wanted the details of what my plans were for Jackie at the beach. I said, it's not about what my plans are for Jackie, but how you will benefit from what I do to her. I told him to imagine me playing with his wife's pussy while he was hard at work. I said it in a way that would turn him on, and my tone wasn't polite about it. Right after I said it, he knew to hang up the phone and wait till he came home to hear all the details about it later. So, while I was playing with Jackie's pussy in the car, she was squirting all over my hands and the leather seats inside the car. Damn it! I was having so much fun playing with her pussy and making her squirt, I forgot to look up and around occasionally. When I finally did look up, dammit! I saw a parked police car just on the right side of us at a distance. I became scared immediately, I thought the officer was using binoculars to see what Jackie and I were doing. Just go ahead and imagine a White woman with her back against the door, parked in a parking lot and a nigger in the car playing with her pussy. She would have to do all the explaining, saying it was okay, and we knew each other. It's a damn shame I had to think that way in the first fucking place, right?

In fact, at any given moment, that officer could have easily driven over and asked what we were doing in an empty parking lot. Also, imagine if that officer decided to make some assumptions and called for back-up. Luckily, the police never came over and I kept playing with her pussy. Man, they were a nice couple, and I'm not sure why we lost touch with one another. Role-playing can be fun when there is trust between all parties involved.

A lifestyle that comes with its share of criticism from ignorant people.

Ending Note: Cockold lifestyle has always been interesting because people from different financial and ethnic backgrounds can be secretly involved without being detected. They don't share their private life with anyone or participate in public events. I can promise you, cockold couples can be your best friends or family members and no one would know. The cockold lifestyle is not openly discussed for fear of being misunderstood by their peers. My opinion, there is absolutely nothing wrong with this lifestyle. It's three consenting adults fulfilling their fantasies together. No one is under coercion, and all involved has knowingly made choice to fulfill a burning desire with someone who understands the lifestyle.

The Black Fluffer

ust venting my frustration: There was a person I used to work with, I am not going to mention his position within the company, he's not worth the dog shit you stepped on under your knock off brand named tennis shoes. All I will say is, I always thought lil Bent Wrist was gay from the moment he opened his mouth. And when I say gay, I mean sugar britches, bent wrist, and talked with a lisp gay.

Let me state this for the record, I have never had a problem with gay people, just this muthafucka I'm talking about here in this chapter.

I am certain while reading this, you may even think I'm gay or bisexual. At this stage of my life, I don't give a fuck what you think or say about me. I consider myself as sexual, meaning, I am game for anything that involves women and sometimes men if they like sucking and swallowing my baby makers. Putting it bluntly, I do not mind a man sucking my cock as a fluffer, if I was starring in an adult movie. And, if you do not know what a fluffer is, or never heard that term, it's a man that sucks on another man's cock and gets him erect for a scene in an adult film.

So, for me, a typical situation would involve the husband or boyfriend wanting to suck my cock until I am erect, so that I can fuck his wife or girlfriend. I am all for that because his partner will be excited while watching us. I never had a problem with a guy sucking on my cock if I am the top and about to fuck his wife or girlfriend.

Remember, I have ADD (attention deficit disorder) so, sometimes I go off the topic.

Back to this guy I used to work with lil Bent Wrist. I will admit in this book, there were times while working with him, I imagined dat muthafucka on his knees, sucking my Cialis-taken Black cock. And while lil Bent Wrist is on his knees, I would tell him to open his fucking mouth and make sure his tongue was at the bottom. I would then slap the side of his face and place a mini spider gag over his mouth. How much more degrading could I be towards this muthafucka, keep reading.

Not only would I slap the side of his face and shove his face against my pelvis, but I'd also make damn sure his lips were against my hairy muthafucking balls.

Because that would be payback from his lies against me. He is the reason I am distrusting today, after some fucked up shit that happened at work. I still crave for him to be on his knees and sucking my cock every time I see lil Bent Wrist.

After a few minutes of him sucking and licking my hairy ass balls, I would release some hot, fresh, cum in his mouth. As I am standing above him, I would slap his face, and say, you're a good little bitch, now swallow. Afterwards, I pull up my zipper and walk away, while leaving him on his knees pissed off. Of course, after he calms down, he'll text me later to ask, when can he come by, to do it all over again. Damn it! Then I woke up angry, like I said earlier, I imagined it.

The Drunk Neighbor

My mom, who I talk about in the chapter called "Dear Momma, Beatrice Hicks," usually went to a sewing class in the neighborhood every Tuesday. My momma had nothing else going on in her life, so sewing replaced men. After momma went to three of those sewing classes, I realized I could be alone and do as I please. I don't mean drugs or girls, it just means I could watch whatever I wanted on TV, and that's about the extent of it. For two months, every Tuesday, momma was picked up and taken to class.

I'm briefing you on her consistency for a reason because it's odd how the universe works, let me now explain. One Tuesday, momma decided not to go, and I found that strange. She wasn't feeling sick, she wasn't mad at anyone, and she wasn't even being lazy. She picked up the phone and told the person who normally picked her up she wasn't going. I asked if she was okay, and she reassured me she was feeling good. I was really looking forward to spending time alone while she was at her sewing class.

You as the reader know how I am wired, hopefully what I'm about to tell ya next, you'll understand.

The universe knew how perverted and devious I was. Therefore, the universe knew ahead of time to prevent something perverted and devious from happening. So, when I heard her on the phone telling her friend not to pick her up, I went back into my bedroom. And no more than twenty minutes of hearing my mom say she wasn't going and me closing my bedroom door, I heard the doorbell. I immediately assumed my mom changed her mind and decided to go after all. In fact, I opened my bedroom door again and walked back into the living room. When I walked back into the living room, my momma wasn't wearing her usual clothes for sewing. I was really confused and waited to see who was ringing our doorbell. Remember me mentioning the universe? This is when it kicked in ...

Of all the nights my mom decided to stay home, our neighbor Shameka rang the doorbell. She was drunker than a White boy at an all you can drink beer festival. Shameka was so drunk, my mom had to help her get back home. She was slurring her words and thought she was knocking on her own home, that's how intoxicated this bitch was. I wish you could have seen her stumbling around our house and holding herself up on our chairs. I thank the universe that our neighbor weighed about 110 pounds soaking wet. Otherwise, I would have had to help her home by myself instead of my mom. This is my first time telling this story.

Coming up, I'm about to admit something embarrassing. Please keep in mind I was around seventeen years old when this happened.

I will honestly admit, if I had been home alone when our neighbor knocked on our door, I absolutely would have wanted to see her naked. That same evening while stumbling around in our home, she looked directly at me and said, she wasn't wearing panties or bra. Not sure why she blurred that out but, imagine being a seventeen-year-old boy and an intoxicated MILF tells you something like that? I acted like the neighbors in a well-known movie, "Hey Miss Shameka."

I told you at the beginning of this chapter the universe knew a head of time. But then again, with all the fucked-up shit I've seen going on in my mom's house, beyond any doubt, I would have tongued kissed her, and more than likely she would have vomited in my mouth because she was so intoxicated. I would have sent that intoxicated woman home with saliva running down her face like a big ass great Dane licked her all over her. Without considering what if she became pregnant, then what? From what I was told, you can get a woman pregnant by kissing, at least that's what the adults in my family told me.

And if the police would have been involved, they would have had evidence. All the investigators would have had to do was cotton swab her face and put her under a black light. They would have seen saliva all over my clothes, hair, and eye lashes. I most certainly would have gone to jail if my mom weren't home. Like I've said in a different chapter, I know there's an Angel watching over me, especially in this situation and since then.

The Perfect Man

he one thing that trips me out about women, they are looking for the perfect man in their life, and there's no such thing. I have dealt with women that were hard working, honest, nurturing, loving, attractive, business-minded, strong, smart, diligent, and sexy as hell, in every single imaginable way. And when they give of themselves to somebody, they are exclusive and will give a man all the attention that he needs and deserve. This type of woman is selective, you would think right?

The women I described above usually ends up falling in love with the following personality or behavior:

His shit doesn't stink muthafucka, the wife beater t-shirt muthafucka, the pant sagging muthafucka, the thirty-inch gold rims on his car while living with his momma muthafucka, renting rims muthafucka, loud ass music muthafucka, always saying I'll pay you back next week muthafucka, the flashing money muthafucka, the too many baby mommas muthafucka, doesn't pay child support muthafucka, the always asking where the fuck are you muthafucka, the why haven't you texted me back muthafucka, always smelling like smoke muthafucka, the looking at his text messages muthafucka, the one who looks at Pornhub muthafucka, never cooks muthafucka, never tips the waitress muthafucka, always wants his cock sucked muthafucka, has already lied to you twice muthafucka, the won't lick your pussy muthafucka, he cums then sleeps muthafucka, the speaking in slang muthafucka, the selfish muthafucka, quit five jobs in a year muthafucka, all day playing video games muthafucka, expect you to pay for everything muthafucka, ain't trying to find a job muthafucka, insecure muthafucka, soft cock muthafucka, drug dealing muthafucka, always high muthafucka, alcoholic muthafucka, niggas say convasate instead of converse muthafucka, bitch ass muthafucka, fake gold chain muthafucka, never positive muthafucka, always blaming the White man for his failures muthafucka, never owns up to his mistakes muthafucka, jealous muthafucka, immature muthafucka, fake gold teeth muthafucka, and texting other bitches muthafucka, sex addict muthafucka, and last and most important of them all, doesn't love and respect his own momma muthafucka.

And we all know that, if a man disrespects his own momma that gave him life, then why should he treat any woman that comes into his life any differently?

I'm confused AF, as I'm writing this chapter. The women I described above usually end up NOT falling in love or gets bored AF with the following personality or behavior below:

You know the type of guy I am talking about, right? The geeky looking muthafucka, the respectful muthafucka, always complimenting you muthafucka, always asking how you are doing muthafucka, doesn't try to fuck you the first date muthafucka, kisses you on the forehead muthafucka, says hope to see you again muthafucka, can I see you tomorrow muthafucka, may I call you tomorrow muthafucka, says I miss you muthafucka, doesn't assume his fucking ya muthafucka, doesn't slap you on the ass muthafucka, asking to come over to see you muthafucka, always courteous muthafucka, understands you have a life muthafucka, never checks your phone muthafucka, asks can he spend the night muthafucka, doesn't assume his spending the night muthafucka, not always up in your business muthafucka, ask how your mom is doing muthafucka, not looking at your little sister muthafucka, not looking at your mom muthafucka, does not have wondering eyes muthafucka, respects your privacy muthafucka, respects your ideas muthafucka, listens to you muthafucka, does not lie muthafucka, inspired to improve his situation muthafucka, always positive muthafucka, can keep a job muthafucka, has a car muthafucka, and of course, loves and respects his mother muthafucka.

Ladies: Everything you want to know about a man will reveal itself by watching and listening to how he treats his momma, sisters, or other women in general.

I was talking to a friend Sue; I've known for years from where I worked as a cashier. Every time she shopped at my location, she made sure to come through my checkout. We always flirted with each other. There was this one time she was shopping and didn't know I was watching her from one isle over. My co-workers came over to me and said, "Damn bruh! Did you see the chick in the soup aisle." I acted like I didn't know her. It was always funny watching men's reaction every time Sue walked in the warehouse. Her Asian husband at the time knew of me and was cool with us flirting with each other. Even though they divorced, she and I remained good friends.

Since it was a nonsexual friendship, Sue was comfortable telling me that she decided to step outside of her comfort zone from flirting and fucking niggas. Nevertheless, she knew they were not relationship material and decided to switch it up. Because she was tired of the niggas she had in her stable, she decided to date a nerdy looking White man exclusively, even though she had an attraction for well- built niggas. Btw, she never said the word nigga to my face, and I will have to assume that's not her mentality. On the other hand,

I don't know her every thought either. One never knows until it's time to choose sides.

If the character in this part of the chapter is familiar to the person reading it, then I want to apologize in advance for what I am about to say next: I'm glad my White female friend couldn't read my mind, because when she mentioned her preference in the men she liked fucking (niggas), but also said, they were not relationship material, it made me think back to the days of slavery. Oh! So, you can fuck niggas from the plantation, but they're not good enough to be in a committed relationship with. Read on because this gets better.

Back to the story: One day I stopped by Sue's place of business just to have a conversation like good friends do. She told me that after her divorce, she became a wildflower and made up for lost times, if you know what I mean. Afterwards, she decided to switch it up and go out with this one nerdy White boy. She said, he was as square as they come, like totally the opposite of what she's used to. He acted in a way that made her question why she was even giving him an opportunity. She was not attracted to him right away, she told me. But she was on a mission to leave her past behind her and she ended up falling head over hills with the nerdy muthafucka.

Now, here goes the fucked-up part, that nerdy asshole ended up breaking her heart. Unlike all the niggas she's fucked, none of them broke her heart. This spineless POS, decided to go back to his ex-wife and abandoned her without notice and that shit fucked her up emotionally. I mean, I could just tell the way she was talking about him. It took Sue a while to trust anyone else. So, the moral of this story is most people do not pay attention to the details, and I am sure there were obvious signals she wasn't paying attention to. All you must do is allow the person to be themselves for approximately three months, to determine what life would be like in and out of the bedroom. How does he or she treat you around their friends having dinner. Most people do not take the time to do that anymore. What trips me out about guys over fifty-five years of age, you would think they know better right? I was told that men tend to ask to be there man right out the gate? Like what the fuck is that all about? Like what about, uh, talking on the phone, texting, hanging out for a while, find out if you have the same things in common such as watching TV shows or working out and music.

It takes time to get to know all the above, before becoming exclusive. people go into an exclusive relationship too damn soon and do not allow themselves time to know the other person. Now, the one thing I must add, it's hard finding someone who wants to fuck on the first date. If we don't have the same mindset, then let's have an adult conversation about sex to see what we have in common. Because the last thing we need is to talk for months, then come to find out we are not even on the same page sexually.

The ultimate relationship for me would be polygamy before I get too fucking old, and when I say old, I mean in my eighties. I'm living in a nice pad with two women that are bisexual. We all live in the same pad and go places together, cook, eat, sleep together, and have sex in my purple dungeon. In this dungeon, there is a throne, so I can chill and watch my girls eat each other's ass and pussy. My dungeon would also have cameras inside for those who are curious on OnlyFans. And I'll tell you what, with just two women in my life, I would not even consider adding another female unless she's famous and wanted to become part of our family. If she is not famous, fuck that, that's straight up greedy. I had someone in my life in a comparable situation, before this book was written.

She knew I had someone else in my life, but our bond was different, and I fucked that up. So, if I'm ever in that situation again, I would make sure I love them equally.

The Sexy Moaner

used to love going to this one place in Altamonte Springs, Florida called the Why Not Lounge before it closed. I should have seen it coming because it was a hole in the wall kinda place. Even with bad service and cleanliness issues, I loved going there. I can't count how much pussy I pulled from there. Being honest, it wasn't a lot because I was too damn shy, in other words, I lacked confidence back then. I recently checked the rating on google, even though it's closed, and they had a lot of one-to-three-star ratings LOL. Now that I have taking you down memory lane with me, back to why I called this chapter "The Sexy Moaner."

One evening, I was in Why Not Lounge with my girlfriend Rachel at the time, and there was a White woman on the other side of the bar boldly staring at me while I was on the dancefloor. I mean, like, staring at me intently, so I stared right back. Three weeks later, I decided to head out to a club called the Backstage Billiards International Drive, which was located inside a hotel. That evening Rachel was at work. As I'm sitting at the bar glancing around the room, I saw the same woman who had been staring at me at the Why Not Lounge. I couldn't believe she was here alone like myself. When I finally realized that it was her, I looked back in her direction, and she was gone. I thought I missed my opportunity, or it was someone who looked like her. The next thing I knew she was tapping me on my shoulder and wanted to sit next to me. She boldly introduced herself to me, and usually I don't like aggressive women. I offered her a seat next to me and we spent the rest of the evening getting to know one another, then left to have breakfast. After breakfast, Lillia followed me back to my car to chill a bit longer. Women always have an idea if they want to fuck a man or not. It's us men who are not sure if we are fucking or not. So, while sitting in my car with Lillia, I was breaking all the rules and asked her to spend the night with me. She stood firm to her first date rule of not fucking on the first date. See what I just said? First date, which was not our first date, which was our first-time meeting without Rachel with me.

We met a few more times after that, and the next thing you know, we're having incredible sex together. However, there was something I found distracting when I was with her; it was the sound she made while cumming. I mean, the way she would moan, it was a little distracting. Of course, I learned to adjust to her moaning, I knew she must be having a fun time, and I must be doing something right.

From that point on, whenever I've been with someone that expresses pleasure their own certain way (i.e., moan, scream, giggle, laugh) when they cum, I've learned to adjust my reaction. It's not fair of me to tell these women to stop or shut up, or even ask why they make a particular sound. And any guy that does, is messing it up for the next time they get together. In fact, they should allow her to be herself. Also, if he mentions how she cums, she'll shy away from cumming like that in the future.

She will also be afraid to relax and enjoy herself completely. I would never make a woman feel that she can't be herself, no matter how she cums. Now, of course, some are so fucking loud I'd have to slap some fucking duct tape over their fucking mouth. Honestly, there have been times I had to do just that, because they were so fucking loud (no pun intended). That's what happens when you live in cheaply made apartments or condominiums. Sometimes IDGAF and would allow them to scream if needed, I knew the neighbors knew the difference between cumming and someone needing the police.

No one wants the police, you know, on a wellness check. Me explaining to the police, I'm just over here fucking and eating her pussy, and she was screaming and cumming. You know, I can't always keep my hand over their mouth, I have other things to do with my hands and fingers that they'll enjoy far more, so out comes the tape. A small piece works like a charm, they can cum and scream all they want. And all I hear is mmm or MMM, it works damn well. They can still be themselves and enjoy everything to the fullest, knowing how loud they are.

My relationship with the loud moaner Lillia went on for a couple of years. When we first fucked, she wasn't into anal, but over time she trusted me. I had made her comfortable enough and she had really started to enjoy it. She really was good for me as a person, but as usual I fucked that relationship up because I had so many women I was trying to juggle at the same time, it really was ridiculous. I had like six I was seeing, and there are only so many days in a week. I was maintaining that many at once because I would space them out, I'd see three or four a week, and slip in one more depending on what was going on, even though, I was dating Rachel. I'll say this again, read my "My Gay Ass Cousin" and "Dear Momma" to understand why I was cheating on Rachel.

After my divorce from one of my wives, I didn't quite have my shit together. At one point, Lillia said something to me on the phone that set me off, and I retaliated by making her feel like shit. Of course, after that episode, I thought it over and was out of line. I was angry and took it out on her, I really fucked it up. By then it was too fucking late to take it all back, way too late.

Years later and I still miss her as a person. She was tall too. I'm six foot six, and she was around five foot eleven, a subtle change to the type of women I usually fuck. And damn, she'd let me do anything to her. I still love her and wish I hadn't said all those things I said, I'm not perfect. I had a lot of things I was going through at the time, my own problems with which I was dealing. She had been there once before when I hit rock bottom, so I really should have treated her with more respect. If I had, we could have remained friends, even nonsexual friends, I would have been okay with that.

If by chance she reads this, I'd like her to know that I think of her often, and I'm so deeply sorry for the outcome of our friendship.

Unfaithful Muthafucka Part One & Two

Part One

efore you read this chapter, read "Dear Momma, Beatrice Hicks," it explains in detail why I am the way I am. And by no means am I trying to downplay my behavior.

One of my ex-wives was not freaky at all. Having sex with her was just okay, in fact, the best sex I have ever had was with only one of my ex-wives that I am not mentioning in this chapter. Vaguely put right?

Out of the three ex-wives, I had an affair on Mya while she was at work, and this will be her first time finding this out by reading this chapter. So, if Mya becomes angry with me after reading this, I'm not apologizing, but acknowledging my unfaithfulness. While she was at work, I fucked Mary, a White girl, I found in an AOL chat room. She didn't live too far away and was also married. After we talked for a while, she trusted me enough to pick her up. In the neighborhood I lived in, all the houses were approximately ten feet apart. I needed to figure out a way to bring her into my home because I had nosy neighbors always looking out of their windows.

So, when I pulled into my neighborhood, I made sure Mary was leaning over as close to the floor as possible. Then I opened my garage door and drove in. Once the garage door had closed completely, I wasted no time telling her to get the fuck out of my car. Since we already spoke on the phone for a few weeks, I had a good idea what she liked. I invited her inside my home, then I told her to turn around as I took off her clothes. I started with her shoes, pants, blouse, panties, and left the best for last, her big ass bra. Once I unsnapped the last clip of her bra, her titties dropped and bounced around for a couple of minutes, like two big ass water balloons tied together. I remember telling her to face me, so that I could visually see her big ass titties. And, while she was naked and vulnerable, I inspected her big ass titties like I bought and paid for her at a slave auction. Besides, White slave owners treated Black women the exact same way during slavery.

After inspecting Mary from head to toe, I commanded her to drop to her knees like a command from a White police officer when approaching an unarmed nigger, with his hands in the air. My cock was hard and ready for her mouth, but she couldn't see it because she was blindfolded. She must have known I was close by because before I could say open your mouth bitch, she opened it. I said to myself, damn she's good or this bitch can see through the blindfold. With the head of my cock, I decided to tease her lips and tongue.

I rubbed it around her outer lips ever so lightly and she tried to reach for it. That's when I backed up and said, "Bitch did I tell you that it was okay to use your hands to suck my fucking cock?" She bowed her head as if she knew she fucked up. That turned me on talking to her like that. Then, I leaned over her and placed one of my fingers inside Mary's pussy. I could feel and taste she was enjoying being told what, when, and how to do it. Then I demanded her to lay face down while I applied my favorite lube on the shaft of my cock, then I fucked her in the ass till I came.

She did not want me to make love or fuck her like I cared about her, she could easily get that from her husband. So, I decided to make her walk naked and blindfolded into my garage. I then told her to put her arms out in front while I tied rope around her wrist. Then I said, put your fucking arms above your head so I can tie them up to the garage door brackets. Of course, she was nervous and excited because there was cum running down from her pussy unto her thighs.

I flogged Mary a few times in places where her husband wouldn't notice. She told me they only fucked once a month, and that would give her plenty of time to heal from the bruises from being flogged. Besides, it was time to take her home. And just like we came into the garage, it was time to pull out, (no pun intended). So, I told her to lean down again, while I opened the garage door and drove out of my neighborhood, so my nosy ass neighbors wouldn't notice. I dropped her off near a bus stop just in case someone she knew saw her. We never saw each other again, after that one time together.

Part Two

Before I get into this "Unfaithful Muthafucka Part Two" story, if you are a woman reading this chapter, why would you get involved with a man you can't trust? You women have an intuition unlike anyone on this planet. Y'all continuously put up with unnecessary bullshit from lying ass muthafuckas on a daily and it amazes me. I don't blame men lying because I blame the woman for dealing with unnecessary liars. What do I mean by unnecessary liars? It's my way of saying he lies about petty shit. In other words, over something that he should not have lied about because it may not have been important to you. So, on that note. Let's get into the reason I called this chapter "Unfaithful Muthafucka Part Two."

I used to work with a guy named JoJo at a warehouse in Florida. One day I asked him if he wanted to work for me on some deliveries, I was behind on. At the time, I had a delivery business of picking up and delivering furniture from stores.

While out making deliveries, his girlfriend at the time kept blowing up his fucking cell phone every couple of minutes. The entire time all I kept hearing him say was, "I am with Cecil, and we are making some deliveries." It's not like he only said it once, it was at least five times. And this bullshit went on for an hour are so. This spineless muthafucka wanted me to tell her he was working for me.

I was driving and JoJo was in the passenger seat, so I could hear the conversation. Even with his cell phone close to his ears, I could hear every word she was saying to him. I was irritated at his behavior. He was acting like a little bitch instead of manning the fuck up and telling her he'll talk to her when he gets home. After some years had passed, I realized that he was submissive and must like being spoken to that way. And that is based on how he dealt with his girlfriend at the time.

No male should allow anyone to speak to him any ol' kinda way. Especially a crazy ass bitch blowing up your cell phone every few minutes. There was a reason she treated him like that. When they first met, he cheated on his girlfriend with her. It all makes sense now why she was blowing up his cell phone every few seconds, doesn't it? She was concerned he would do to her what he did to the girl before her. I saved that information for last. Why am I telling you this story? It's because men are quick to call a bitch crazy and not tell you the whole story.

Who Would Have Thought

I don't drop names so let's just call her Maria, because this woman has family and just recently moved. I don't wanna do or say anything that would jeopardize her security. Now that I made that clear, let's go. There was this one thick Black woman I knew in her sixties, and she knows who she is from what I write in this chapter. Initially, I was not attracted to Maria's dating profile at first. Even though she was around five feet nine in height, she was larger than most women I've fucked. I liked her personality and the way we communicated through our messages online. Eventually, we exchanged cell numbers, and she sent me some G-rated photos. I said to myself, she's a nice-looking woman and I liked her hairstyle. She and I talked about everything from being in the swinging lifestyle to what we both enjoyed sexually. Being straight up with you as the reader, I enjoyed talking to her so much on the phone I forgot about Maria's size. That judgmental attitude went out the window with her personality.

As we continued talking, it was my responsibility to be honest before continuing our conversation and before we met. I liked our conversations and wouldn't mind continuing with no expectations leading to anything else. I also told her why there shouldn't be expectations. I wanted to be honest about her weight or should I say size. Do you feel what I told her was offensive? She didn't and thanked me for my honesty. I also didn't want to lead her on, thinking there would be a relationship or anything sexual at the beginning. *Off the chapter for a few sentences, I have never been a man that slept with someone unless there is a connection.* In her case, it was our conversation, her smile, her honesty, similarities sexually, and last, just the way she spoke to me on the phone was unexplainable.

At some point, I decided to put my differences aside, it's not like either one of us is talking about marriage. We both decided to take one day at a time and that made her comfortable continuing to talk to me. After some weeks had gone by, it was time to meet. She drove here to Orlando and visited me instead. When Maria arrived, I watched her slowly get out of her car, and she looked in my direction where I was standing waiting for her. While I was watching her walk towards me, I had all sorts of ideas running through my head. When she walked up to me, I gave her a big hug and was glad she made it. As I opened the door and she walked past me, she had on some kinda snake charming perfume that made my dick hard immediately. Once she was completely inside my apartment, I locked the door. Fuck it, I wasn't about to waste any time talking to her. While I was walking up behind her, I looked at her as if I had on a pair of those x-ray glasses they advertised in the sixties.

Honestly, I was not attracted to the clothes she had on, and since it was a long drive, we can assume she needed to be comfortable. As I mentioned earlier, I wasn't turned on by her size but liked her submissive and nurturing personality.

In fact, our similar paths being in the swinging lifestyle also helped. The more we talked, her weight didn't make any difference to me, she turned me on in every other way imaginable.

Now that I gave you some boring insight about her, "Let's Get Crackin'" by Shock. I blindfolded her and placed both of her hands on the counter. I then said, "Spread your fucking legs wide open," and I started playing with her pussy and breasts. I whispered in her ear, "You better not take your hands off my countertop, and they are to remain in place until I say you can remove them."

If Maria had disobeyed me, I would have told her to go home, it's just that simple. I guess she didn't want to take the chance of me sending her home. Like a good girl, she submitted herself and kept her hands on the counter. While she stood there, I watched her spread her legs apart. The dress she had on stopped just above her feet, so I lifted the dress just past her ass. I held one end of the dress in my hand as I stood there behind her. She didn't have on panties and all I could see is this big, juicy caramel colored ass.

Please keep in mind that this woman totally trusted me while being blindfolded. Never mind the fact that was our first-time meeting.

While Maria was standing there naked, she didn't know what was about to happen next. I knew it was turning her on because while she was blindfolded other senses kicked in, like touching and hearing. When her senses kicked in, I barely touched the middle of her back with one finger, and she jumped. I caught her off guard because she wasn't expecting it. Another reason I knew I was turning her on, she was shaking with excitement. I love taking my time, that's why it's all about the woman as it should be. Personally, penetration is the last thing on my mind when I'm with someone I care about. Sticking my cock in her pussy, mouth, or ass, that's easy, but getting her to be aroused is more gratifying. So, while her hands are still on the countertop, I slowly rub her nipples in a circular motion. I'd do one nipple and then the other as I whispered naughty shit in her ear. I don't say the same fucking thing to every woman that places her hands on my countertop.

I say whatever the vibe I'm feeling when I'm around that person or what I see, every woman is unique. As I touch certain parts of her body, I also watch her breathing and her legs; when they are shaking, that means she is so turned on and can't stand up straight. That's when I use my hands between her thighs, and I don't touch the pussy. I liked running my hands up and down inside her thick thighs and keeping her guessing on what I'm about to do next. I just graze the pussy before I rub on her beautiful large caramel stomach. Then I rubbed on her breast again and I kissed her on the back of her neck. I reached around and I played with both of her nipples, this time very softly. I could tell if she wanted her nipples pinched a little harder. I sensed that's what she wanted, and I pinched a little harder and a little harder. Her breathing increased, meaning she was enjoying her nipples pinched harder. I watch her body language to know when to back off from how hard I'm pinching her nipples. The reason I know when to back off a bit is because I give a fuck about her and I'm paying attention to all the signs. I barely touch the clit with just a little pressure on it.

Okay, it's time to step it up so I put my hand slightly around her neck like I owned her. I already knew I could lightly choke her because we talked about it, and most importantly, she trusted me. My suggestion is do not perform the choke move unless you've already discussed it.

Make sure trust has been clearly established before you put your hands around her throat. I can guarantee if she doesn't have trust in you, she will tense up and not enjoy herself. This message is to all you guys, don't play with a pussy with dirty hands. Wash your hands thoroughly before putting your fingers inside the woman's pussy, otherwise she can develop an infection. I say this because I knew this one nasty muthafucka who didn't care about hygiene. Best example I can give is this one. At a swinger's party, I watched a man play with a friend's dog outside. At that time, it didn't matter to me because he had been out there for a while. He finally walked in and asked my friend to play/party with him and I'll be damned, she developed an infection the very next day. Are you asking me in your mind, why I didn't warn my friend? I assumed he gave a fuck and would have washed his hands. I asked her later, what happened after you said yes. She said they went straight into a bedroom, and he ate her pussy and then played with her with his hands. Damn! That nasty muthafucka, If I had known I would have stood up for my friend and told her not to touch that asshole. Anyway, wash your fucking hands and clean under your nails.

Important:

Role-Play Choking: Watch her breathing and body language, it'll tell you everything you need to know, only if you give a fuck that is. And, if you don't give a fuck, keep your fucking hands away from her neck, you are a selfish muthafucker. I bet you don't even lick the pussy and if you do it's only going to be a couple times before you stick your cock in. Selfish motherfuckers are the reason I drafted this book in the first place. I've talked to enough women and heard a good majority of men don't take the time or don't give a fuck about a woman's feelings. And some, make no attempt to get her ready, only to hurry up and stick their cock in without got damn lubrication

Enough, back to "Who Would Have Thought." Maria still had both hands on the counter, legs spread, obeying my commands. I rubbed her clit slowly with my hands around her throat. She had an orgasm like she had never had before. In fact, her legs almost buckled from doing that. I stood back and watched her legs shaking. Just to think, I was doing this to a big beautiful Black woman, and I must admit, sex with her was incredible. I honestly think our lives being parallel to one another made all the difference fucking her. She's the only Black woman to this day I've met and was in the swinging lifestyle. What I also like is she had a subservient mentality, but at the same time, she was respected by her co-workers, they didn't need to know her personal business. Back to the caramel-colored Black woman.

One evening I had her in my room blindfolded, of course. I told the bitch to get up on the bed and spread her legs, I just stood there and watched. I told her to spread her legs as far as she could, so I could stand on the side of the bed. I used my right hand and played with her pussy, that girl squirted all over my bed. In fact, I had to squirt proof my bed because of her. She apologized for wetting up my damn bed and said she's never had that happen in her entire life. I'm thinking to myself, here she is in her sixties and she's telling me she's never had anyone play with her like I did. I also thought to myself, all the fucking this woman has done and as many guys as she's fucked at the parties, I am the person that understood her thoroughly. What the fuck is up with these guys not even taking the time to do half the things I've done with her. I would play with her so much she always fell asleep, and her pussy was so sloppy wet when I was done. There was this one Saturday afternoon, she squirted so much that I took my hand filled with her juices and I showered her own orgasm all over her pussy. Another time I made her squirt, there was so much of it that I made it drop through my fingers and all over her body, face, and breasts. Eventually that ended, but she knows who she is by what I said, and I thought I'd mention her in this book. I completely understand if this reads like another chapter in this book. With all the women my cock has entered, it's always possible to have repeated some acts on different women.

I want to be straight up with you, this book may have typos. It was more important to get my story out of my head and computer, than to become discouraged. I also wanted to make sure this memoir was genuinely from the heart. Authenticity is missing these days, and I am bringing back the only way I know how, raw without a condom. (that's just me though). So, you have a choice, either suit up and go raw when you read this memoir. Or, send it to someone you may know, period.

Who the hell am I, right? I am just a Black sixty-four-year-old man who's not afraid to share his thoughts, risky predicaments, scandalous sexual experiences, and questionable decisions. Don't you dare act like you don't admire someone like myself. **If you were easily offended by foul language and my personal opinions, then I am going to highly suggest you let me know about it.** I am going to share an example with you …

Don't take me around your family or friends, because you can't predict what I am going to say or do. With the mentality I have, there's one foot over an open grave, and one foot firmly on the ground beside the grave. This gives me the freedom to be obnoxious and unpredictable, so I've been told. As a child, I was exposed to lies and manipulations from my father and throughout my entire family. Being around my cousin, who was a disgraceful womanizer and who constantly lied to my mom and his wife, taught me how to manipulate my girlfriends to my advantage. Watching someone I loved and respected being lied to when I knew the truth really bothered me.

I knew not to tell my mom, and my reason is in one of my chapters where I go into more detail. I realize now, everything I talked about in this memoir, has to do with my mentality towards women today. By no means, am I giving me or anyone else a pass for their behavior, what I am saying is, most of the f'd-up shit that happened in our childhood is subconsciously buried and can resurface unknowingly and unexpectedly and at any time. (**I am not a licensed therapist or psychologist.**) I am just a man who's willing to allow you to see me raw. In this memoir, I also share my unfiltered opinions in a way I am sure some of you will understand and appreciate. I ain't releasing this book for my own personal pleasure, I am releasing it because I know I am not alone. I also know I am that old ass MOFO (look it up) who's not afraid anymore. I honestly feel like I should walk around with a warning sticker on my forehead that clearly reads "Maintain A Safe Distance."

- AF (as fuck)
- ain't – don't have
- BDSM (bondage and discipline, dominance and submission, sadism, and masochism)
- betta (better)
- Btw (by the way)
- Dafuck – the fuck
- FYI (for your information)
- HNIC (head nigga in charge)
- IDGAF (I don't give a fuck)
- LOL (laugh out loud)
- M.O.B (mind our business)
- M.Y.O.B (mind your own business)
- OMG (oh my god)
- POS (piece of shit)
- SMH (shaking my head)
- STFU (shut the fuck up)
- SYH (shaking your head?)
- WTF (what the fuck)

谢谢你 – ありがとうございました – धवाद - Gracias

THANK YOU
SERIOUSLY

** I would really appreciate it if you would share your thoughts by leaving me a review regarding this memoir. By the way, Thanks Again for you time.

*Ksu_slobodaniuk – Artwork front & back of book. Thank you for patience with all the changes I wanted. Plus, your ongoing support and input can't be thanked enough. I hope to meet you. - Дякую тобі

*Alerrandre – Book Cover Layout and Design / Thank you for your patience also, with the subtle changes I needed.

*AL – Proofreading services, professionalism, and accuracy thank you for. Plus, it was hard finding someone who was willing to put their differences and judgment aside.

*Transcriber136 – Transcriber / I was horrible when this all started, you took my cell phone audio and translated the best you could, given the circumstances.

*Imaginboxstudio – For me holding the Letters B&W art on each new chapter.

*Mosesistheone – Transcriber / It was only a few chapters, but you also did a good job and I appreciate your services.